Forged Steel

H. A. Titus

Forged Steel by H. A. Titus
Published by Magical Ink Media

Cover Designer: LoriAnn Weldon
Creative Team: Mary Schlegel, LoriAnn Weldon, Andrea Graham, Cindy Koepp, and Ralene Burke

Printed in the United States of America
ISBN: 978-0-9965256-0-2

To Justin
To the stars and back, my love

chapter 1

If downtown at two AM was a mathematical equation, the answer would be 'creepy times ten.' I took a gulp of room-temperature coffee.

Outside our booth window sat a table full of Goths who clutched their coffee mugs like weapons and glared at anyone who got too close. An apparent dress code of mile-high spiked hair, ten pounds of facial piercings, and exposed boxers made the sidewalks an even bigger freak show.

Across the table, my roommate, Marc Gillam, stretched his arms above his head. The metal bracelet on his wrist clanked on the back of the booth. His mouth gaped in a silent yawn.

"Ready to go back yet?" I asked.

"Nope. Are you?"

"Oh, no. I love sitting here with my contacts getting all grainy and my chin dragging in my latte. I'm good." I took another gulp. "Just surprised you want to stay out this late with finals coming up."

"Josh, please, like you care about finals." Marc stared out into the café, drumming two fingers on the lip of his coffee cup.

I shrugged and turned back to the window. Rather than watch the passersby on the sidewalk, this time I watched the ghostly reflection of the café interior. It reduced the café to a wash of warm browns and bright splotches of clothing, the faces of everyone around me blurred beyond recognition. Even my own long face, spiked hair, and brown eyes looked vague.

Twenty-three years old, five ditched bachelor degrees, and just a few points away from getting kicked out of our military-strict college. Marc was right. Who cared about tests anyway? I yawned.

Marc ran his hand through his dark blond hair. "Heard you had a meeting with your school counselor this afternoon."

Small talk? From my best friend? I looked at him and raised one eyebrow. "Yeah. Turns out that my trig professor didn't appreciate me hacking the school BlackBoard and changing the class schedules." That'd been the least I'd done, but apparently it was the proverbial straw, which made Professor Blackaby a camel. The mental picture made me snicker.

Marc rolled his eyes. "Genius Josh strikes again."

"If I hear that nickname one more time, I'll kick your butt so hard it'll be your new belly."

He grinned. "C'mon. All you need is a pocket protector, and…"

I kicked his leg under the table.

"Ow! What're we now, in grade school?"

I crossed my arms on the table and rested my face on them. "Dude, why are we really here?"

"Do we need a reason?"

"Mister Perfect decides to sneak out of his dorm on a weekend, when he should be studying for finals. No, I don't need any—" I rolled my eyes and immediately regretted it when my contact stuck in the corner of my left eye. "Gah, that burns!" I pawed at it. The contact came loose and dropped into my palm.

The doorbell jingled over the coffee shop entrance. I glanced toward it. One of the aforementioned guys with mile-high hair ducked into the café's main room, his eyes running over the crowd as if he was looking for someone specific. Even with only one eye functional, I recognized the squirmy scar on his neck and the Mohawk hairdo. Blake Davis, a guy I'd gone to high school with. The gigantic linebacker's hair was purple now, and he had a few more facial piercings than when I'd known him, but the scar was too unique to be anyone else.

I started to wave.

Marc hissed.

"What?" I glanced at him.

Marc slumped down in his seat, his face turned toward the window. "I don't especially care to talk to him right now."

I lowered my hand, but Blake had already seen me. He waved back, but instead of coming across the room, he just stood by the door, staring at us. At Marc, specifically. Another guy with a spiky blue Mohawk came in the door and stopped beside Blake. They exchanged a few words, and then the blue-haired kid ducked back out. Blake never took his eyes off us the entire exchange.

"Creep," I muttered.

Marc shifted in his seat and finally looked at Blake. His eyes narrowed.

Blake grinned, the silver stud in his lip twinkling, and pointed at Marc in an "I'm watching you" sign, first two fingers in an accusing V. He turned and pushed out the café door. For a split second, as he crossed the threshold, his skin seemed to waver, a chunk ghosting away to reveal a flash of green scales clinging to his forearm.

I blinked hard.

The door slapped shut behind Blake, and he disappeared from my sight.

"Dude, did you just see that?"

Marc flicked a wadded up napkin at me. "What?"

Okay, fine. I shook my head. "Never mind. I still have one contact out. That's got to be messing with my vision."

"Probably."

Still, though, that had been weird. Scales? I shook my

head, stretched my eyelids apart and stuck the contact back in. It felt like it was full of sand. "Geez, if I'd known you were going to make me stay out this long, I would've brought my glasses."

I fished a small bottle of contact solution from my pocket and dropped some into my eye. Something rustled across the table. What was Marc up to? I blinked, feeling the solution dripping down my cheek like a tear, and glanced at him.

Or, where he should've been sitting. The seat was vacant, his coffee mug sitting to the side where he'd left it. I glanced at the door in time to see Marc step outside.

Blake came up to his side outside and draped his arm oh-so-casually over Marc's shoulders. Marc's steps were slow and draggy as they headed out into the parking lot.

I frowned. Marc had a phobia about people's hands or arms getting anywhere near his neck. Even Sarah, his one-and-only girlfriend during high school, hadn't been allowed to put her arm around him like that.

I stood up and wove my way around the tables, mindlessly calculating the numbers I saw on random tables' checkout slips as I tried to figure out what business Blake had with Marc. *Three hundred seventeen bucks and sixty-one cents.* This place was making a killing.

I slid out the door and glanced around. Marc and Blake had disappeared. A few dozen cars crowded the small parking lot, which was overshadowed by the taller office buildings and warehouses the café was squeezed between. One light sat in the middle of the lot, flickering as if it were ready to die. Between the parking lot and the alleys that opened on either side, there were too many places to hide.

I stepped into the lot and cocked my head. Since the traffic in front of the coffee shop was mostly on foot, the occasional car buzzing by wouldn't bother my listening that much.

As I neared the middle of the lot, I heard a clatter from the alleyway on the right. I spun around and squinted into the shadows. The alley shot between a warehouse with broken windows and a defunct grain elevator. The brick walls were swirled with colorful graffiti, though I couldn't see more than a few feet in. The shadows lurking in the back of the alley were perfect for people who didn't want to be disturbed.

Maybe that was the point, but it was hard to believe that Marc would have even known Blake. I'd only known the guy because his family had, briefly, lived across the street from my family. The guy had been suspended from high school once or twice for drugs and fighting. Marc wouldn't have involved himself in something like that.

Would he?

As I neared the alley, I heard voices. One was definitely Blake's—low and growly, like he was gargling a mouthful of gravel. The other was Marc's panicked voice, cracking and pitching like he was going through puberty again. Or like he was freaking out, like when his dad had died earlier this spring.

I slipped closer, hugging the back of the grain elevator.

"...don't know how many times I have to say it!" Marc sounded mad, despite the girly pitch. "My dad destroyed his key. I've never seen a cipher like this. It's not like I can Google the numbers."

"Blodheyr thinks you're stalling," Blake said. "If you're so stuck, why don't you ask your genius roommate for some help?"

"There's no way I'm involving Josh. He wouldn't—"

Thud.

Marc yelped.

I slid around the corner and crouched, hoping Blake wouldn't notice me. He had my friend pinned against the brick side of the grain elevator. Marc's sneakers dangled close to three feet off the ground.

Wait a sec—

As I watched, the human Blake turned into a ghostly image and faded, similar to what happened if I looked at something while crossing and uncrossing my eyes. A huge monster appeared in his place. His skin was the mottled greenish-gray I'd glimpsed in the coffee shop. His purple Mohawk became a series of dark, bony knobs that started on the crown of his head, continued down his neck, and disappeared under his 2XL shirt that bulged to the point of popping seams.

He still hadn't noticed me.

Blake's clawed hand tightened around Marc's throat. Marc dug his fingers into the monster's arm, jaw clenched.

I scanned the alley, trying to find something—anything—I could use as a weapon. *What am I thinking? There's nothing short of a nuke that's even gonna make this thing blink!*

"Your father's neck was easy to snap, Marc Eothan Gillam. Yours will be easier, I think. You're more cowardly than him, running away from the Underworld. As if it isn't in your blood."

What the...

Something big slammed into the small of my back, snapping my head back. I tumbled forward, pavement scraping along the length of one forearm, and made a personal acquaintance with the alley's overflowing dumpster. The smell of old coffee laced with rotting banana peel jammed up my nostrils.

Before I could recover from the whiplash, a hand gripped the back of my shirt and hoisted me into the air. I flailed my arms as I twisted around, coming face-to-face with Blake's blue-haired friend, who was now as tall and ugly as Blake. I pawed at the guy's arm, but couldn't get a good grip on the slick scales.

"You idiot!" Marc yelled.

For once, I had no comeback.

"What should we do with this one, Scyrril?" The blue monster gave me a brain-rattling shake. "You wanted him, right?"

Blake—Scyrril—grinned at me, revealing brown-stained teeth filed into sharp points. My hands shook as my heart worked overtime. Brilliant, Josh. Stupid, stupid, stupid. *We're so screwed.*

"If we take him—" Scyrril's words cut off with a deep bellow. He jerked away from Marc.

Marc hit the ground with his shoulder and rolled to his feet. In one fist, he clutched a dagger, the blade glistening with blood. He grabbed a long, thin case from the ground.

A sheathed sword.

Marc drew the katana and ran at the monster holding me. The blue monster dropped me. I scrambled backward until I ran into the grain elevator.

The monster sank into a crouch, his clawed hands held in front of his body like a boxer. Marc gripped the katana's hilt with both hands. Behind him, Scyrril was struggling to rise, one hand clamped over the gash in his side.

The blue monster struck, claws going straight for Marc's face. Marc ducked and came up inside the monster's guard. He swung, but the sword was at an awkward angle, and the monster easily deflected the swing downward. The point of the sword dug into the pavement. Marc stumbled forward, and the monster grabbed the back of his shirt, forcing him to stay in a crouch.

Marc still had the dagger in his other hand. He reached around the guy's leg and slashed at the back of his knee. The monster roared as it pitched forward, nearly knocking over Scyrril as he scrambled to his feet.

Marc grabbed my shirt and hauled me up. I stumbled, my brain numb, not ready to communicate with my feet.

"What just—"

"Move!"

Marc dragged me behind him for several yards. Finally I jerked free and ran a few feet behind him. He dashed past the coffee shop and onto the street. I dodged one of the few cars coming through the intersection. The horn blared in my ears. We ran down the street, passing several closed boutique shops and one open bar before hitting another intersection. Rather than wait for the light to turn, Marc turned left on the sidewalk.

I glanced behind me. I couldn't see the monsters behind

us, but somehow, I doubted that meant we'd lost them.

Marc grabbed my arm and pulled me into another alley, then shoved me. I lost my balance, tumbled into a pile of full garbage bags overflowing from a Dumpster. They squelched as Marc jumped in beside me.

"Are you—what—" I started to stand.

Marc pushed me back down and dragged a long piece of cardboard over our heads. "Stay still," he hissed. "Too much rotting junk here for them to smell us. It'll throw them off."

I pulled my feet up under the cardboard. The smell of rotting vegetables and who knew what else seeped through the bags and soaked into my clothes. I took a short breath through my mouth and nearly gagged.

Marc elbowed me.

I pulled my jacket sleeves over my hands and pressed them to my face. Marc lifted one corner of the cardboard and watched the alley entrance.

A minute ticked by…two…three…

Blake and the other monster walked into view, back in human form. The blue-haired dude limped heavily on his right leg. They paused in front of the alley, and their human forms flickered once, twice, before sliding away and revealing their monstrous forms. Blake drew in a deep, phlegmy breath.

"Ugh. Humans," he growled, pressing his hand to his side. "I can't smell them anywhere, thanks to this dung heap."

"Marc will be trying to hide now," the blue-haired one said. "Let's go check Angel's garage. He'll probably be heading there."

The two jogged off.

When their footsteps had faded, Marc flung the cardboard off our heads. "Crows take them! Just a few more weeks! Almighty, wouldn't that have been enough? *Siabhra diabhal…*"

He stood and started down the alley, muttering under his breath.

I trotted after him, brushing away the flies that buzzed

around my head. "Marc? Care to explain what's going on?"

He glanced at me, his lips tight. I stepped back, staring at his eyes, unable to look away.

His eyes were flashing through different shades of blue. Each flickering color came, spiked as it filled his entire iris, and faded away to be replaced by another color, reminding me of the Northern Lights

I'd once seen as a kid.

Forget what those monsters were.

What was my friend?

chapter 2

Marc eased away from me, the colors in his eyes calming to their normal blue. "You saw that?" He pointed to his eyes.

When I didn't answer, he groaned and ran his hands through his hair. I watched him cautiously, trying to process what had just happened.

This is a dream. It has to be. I would wake up tomorrow in my bunk bed at school. Marc would already be up, studying or doing his daily one hundred sit-ups and fifty push-ups. I'd tell him about my dream, and we'd both laugh at the absurdity of it, and then we'd go to class. Or maybe I'd skip class, and he'd gripe at me for it.

This is a dream.

Maybe that would work on most people, but my brain wasn't easy to fool. I rubbed my forehead. My forearm burned with the movement, and I twisted it around. Ragged edges of skin clung to a bloody scrape, bits of black tar sticking in the wound. I never felt real, aching pain like this in my dreams.

This is real. I clutched the back of my head with both hands, dug my fingers into my hair until it hurt. My gut felt tense and cold.

"That's the only injury you have?" Marc asked.

I snapped my eyes up to him. Marc still stood several feet away from me, his arms folded over his chest. His eyes still looked like normal human eyes.

"Care to explain?" I asked again.

Marc scratched the scruff on his chin. "It depends."

"On what?"

"On what you saw."

I stared at him. "What I saw? Dude, I don't know what you're on, but I saw two really creepy shape-shifting monsters who probably wouldn't mind taking off our limbs." My breath caught in my lungs. "That just made me sound certifiable."

"Depending on who you talk to." Marc started walking up the alley, heading for the intersection.

I jogged after him, brushing my fingers on the brick wall beside me, hoping it would ground me in reality. The rough, grainy texture of mortar and old brick pulled at my fingers. We passed another Dumpster, and the sour smell made me gag. Again.

Yeah, definitely not a dream.

Marc paused at the end of the alley. He looked up and down the street. It looked deserted, and the shop windows were all dark. A stoplight stood right in front of us, the light just changing from green to yellow.

Marc hurried across the deserted street and turned, hugging the curb as he walked.

"Marc?" I caught up and fell in step on his right.

"It's pretty complicated, but—" he shrugged. "I should've known that this would happen. Stupid of me to think I could escape the Underworld."

"Huh? What, you're involved in some kind of Mob stuff?"

Marc snorted. "If only."

Oh-kay. What was he into, that he acted like the Mob was a bunch of pansies?

He tugged at the hem of his hoodie, then tucked his hands into the pocket. "Underworld, with a capital U. Anyone who used that for the criminal world stole it from us."

"Sure. And who's 'us'?"

He glanced at me, and I got the feeling that he was judging me. Like I was back in grade-school doing a science fair. I'd won a lot of those easily. My throat tightened. *Don't think I'll win whatever he's judging me on.*

"The fae," he said finally, turning around to face the sidewalk ahead of us. We turned again at another intersection, coming into a busier part of town. Cars zipped by us on the street. A tattoo parlor advertised its rates in neon colors across the street, and the windows of bars were all shining brightly. A gas station, free-standing at the corner, illuminated the night shadows around it with harsh white light.

"Fae," I said skeptically, easing closer to him to let a group of drunk guys stumble past. "Sounds like you're part of a LARP group."

He barked a laugh. "Yeah, again, if only." Marc jabbed his thumb at a couple walking across the street from us. "What do they look like, Josh?"

I glanced at the man and woman. They were both blond and wearing clothes that weren't exactly high-end but decent. They weren't supermodels, but they weren't off-the-deep-end ugly either. Just ordinary, average folks. I blinked again, and a ghostly image of the man and woman hovered in front of them, covering something I couldn't quite see. I concentrated, looking past the glossy veneer, and it floated away, dissipating in the chilly night air like smoke.

The woman now had platinum blond hair and piercingly green eyes, and the ears that poked through her hair curved to a graceful point. The guy's skin was ink-black, his short-cropped hair a silvery white. His blue eyes were doing that same weird Northern Lights thing Marc's had done.

The woman glanced at me, raised a finely-shaped eyebrow, and nodded, like she was acknowledging I could see her true self.

I gulped and looked away. "Fae. You mean like elves."

"*Sidhé*," he corrected.

"She…what?"

"*Shee*, Josh. The Fair Folk from Gaelic legends."

"Sidhé. Whatever."

"'Elves' works too, but I'm one of the few who won't deck you if you call us that."

I looked at him. Marc looked perfectly human right now. I sputtered out a laugh.

"What?" Marc asked, looking genuinely surprised.

My laughter was on the edge of hysterical. I staggered to the front window of a darkened shop and leaned against it, wheezing. My brain was going to short-circuit. *Elves and monsters. Ha. Nice one, buddy.* "Okay, I got it. This is a joke, right? To get me back for making your laptop look like it was broken?"

Please let it be a joke. It would be so much easier as a joke. A remote part of my mind realized that I was grasping at straws, at any chance for an out, but I pushed the knowledge away.

Marc grabbed my arm and jerked me upright. "Get a hold on yourself. This isn't funny."

I shook free. "You think I'm just going to accept the whole 'elves' explanation?"

"Fae." Marc shoved his hands in his jacket pockets and walked away.

"Whatever." I shook my head. "Just because I'm a fantasy nut doesn't mean I wish I lived in Narnia or Middle Earth. I'm perfectly content to *not* be chased around by trolls and orcs all day, thank you."

Marc whirled. His eyes spiked with unnaturally bright color again. The look sent a shock through my gut and kicked the residue of hysteria out of my system.

He shoved his finger in my face. "Then you'd better figure out how to protect yourself. Now that you can see past the glamour, you're in for all sorts of surprises." He stomped away.

I stood still, blinking at his retreating back. If this really was a joke, how were his eyes doing that? How had that couple changed the way they looked as I'd watched? How had Blake and his blue-haired buddy turned into monsters? There were no special effects that could produce those kinds of results in real time.

How stupid could hysteria really make me?

I ran after Marc, who had disappeared down another alley. When I caught up with him in the parking lot of a music store, I realized where he was heading.

Saint Bartholomew's College.

"Why are we going back?" I asked.

"Glad you decided to join the party," Marc muttered.

My brain was still struggling to wrap around the whole thing. *Elves—no, fae. Sidhé. Fair Folk. Irish legends. I know next to nothing about those. Ugh. Need caffeine—now.* "So. Fae. You're fae."

"Half-fae," he said.

"What did you say I could see through?"

"Glamour. That couple I pointed out to you? They were using glamour to make themselves look like ordinary humans. It's how Sidhé hide themselves from the world. Only other Sidhé and humans who have spent a great deal of time around anyone with Sidhé blood can see through glamour."

"But you—"

"Half-fae don't have glamour. I really do look human, except for that stupid *d'anam fuinneog*."

I tried to replicate the words. "Fwi, fwin—what?"

We dodged around a group of gangbangers carrying beer bottles. One of the guys glanced at us. I didn't make eye contact, focusing instead on Marc's pinched expression.

He brought his right hand to the bracelet on his left wrist and rubbed his thumb along the smooth metal. "*Danuhm fwin-ngog*. Soul window. When my soul is troubled, my eyes are troubled. It's a general proverb about eyes that got started because of the fae. Most of us try to control it because it's not something glamour masks. Humans generally freak out when they see someone's eyes acting like the laser show in a rave club."

"That's…weird."

"It's said the Almighty created us in that way so we would be totally honest with each other." Marc snorted. "A lot of good that did. Being honest can get you killed in the Underworld. Even the Seelie know that."

"Seelie..."

Marc grimaced. "Okay, there's really no simple answer to that. The easiest way to explain it..." He gnawed on his lower lip. "Seelie are friendly—or, I should say, *friendlier*—to humans. They'll still screw over a human if they can, but at least they won't skin you alive like an Unseelie would."

He was quiet for a moment, and I let my brain chew on all the information he'd given me. Seelie, good guys, sort of. Unseelie, definitely bad guys. "You're Seelie?"

"Lucky you, I guess."

"So Blake is an Unseelie?"

"No, *Scyrril* is a troll." Marc spat and grumbled something under his breath that sounded like more gibberish Gaelic. "Technically classified under monsters, though still Sidhé. Anything that comes from our world is Sidhé. Seelie and Unseelie only apply to the 'elvish' race of Sidhé."

I followed him over a business office's neatly trimmed hedge and through their small stretch of grass. A four-lane street, McCullen, was to our right. We were close to the college. We ran across the road and jumped another hedge, approaching the college from the back.

"And why were they after you?" I whispered.

Marc shook his head and motioned for me to be quiet. We ran across a small park and paused at the side of the street, next to a clump of bushes. Marc crouched down on one knee. I leaned over to catch my breath as he studied the area in front of us.

Across the street was a hedge and a metal fence. The dorms of the small college campus poked above the hedge, most of the windows dark, even this close to finals. Our dorm was the closest to the street—easy to access after sneaking out, but whatever was easy for us would likely be easier for Marc's enemies.

After a few moments, Marc leaned over to whisper in my ear. "I don't see anything out of the ordinary, but I go first. You keep quiet. Got it?"

I nodded.

Marc stood up and touched his hip, drawing my attention to the long, elegant katana hanging from his belt. Right. I'd totally forgotten he had a sword.

"What—"

Marc hissed and flicked his fingers, like he was flicking water droplets at me. He stood up and dodged across the street, his hand on the sword's hilt. I ran after him. By the time I reached the street, Marc was on the other side of the fence. I wriggled through the hedge and the warped section of the fence. When I stood up, Marc was using the drainpipe on the side of the building to climb up to our second story window.

He stepped onto the wide ledge outside the window and motioned for me to stay on the ground.

Hey, no argument here, dude.

I fidgeted, glancing from side to side as Marc disappeared inside our room. It would be just my luck to have one of the security guards amble down this side of the dorms. That would get me kicked out for sure—it would be my third offense in the last two months, something they couldn't ignore.

A yelp came from our room, and Marc dove out of the window. He hit the ground and fell forward in a roll, his shoulder absorbing some impact from the drop. I glanced up. A scaly, blue-tinged hand was disappearing from the window.

I drew in a sharp breath and scrambled for the fence.

"No, this way!" Marc snapped.

I changed course and ran after him. What was he—why were we heading for the parking garage?

Glass crashed behind me. I glanced over my shoulder. A blue shoulder protruded from the lounge floor facing the green. Alarms blared into the night.

Marc hurdled the wooden security gate. I ducked under it and ran into the concrete one-story parking garage. The lights were off, even in the security office at the back of the garage. Marc skidded to a halt by his car, a drab Ford Taurus in the middle of a bunch of sports cars.

I braced my arms against the car's trunk, gulping in deep breaths. "That's no good! What about the keys, you idiot?"

Marc dropped to the ground and scooted his head and shoulders under the car's rear bumper. He emerged a split second later with a grimy key dangling from one finger. "You really expect weekend lock-up to slow me down?"

He unlocked the car. I scrambled into the passenger side. He twisted the key and slammed the car into reverse just as the monster—another troll—crashed into the garage. Marc barreled through the exit gate.

I ducked and clutched my arms over my head as the wooden boards splintered against the front of the vehicle.

Marc swerved out onto the college road. Another crunch—that would be the street-side gate at the security booth—and my body jerked to the side as we hit the city street, tires squealing.

I twisted my head around and looked out the back window. The troll stood at the entrance to Saint Bart's, clutching his shoulder as blood trickled between his fingers.

I chuckled. "Way to go, Andretti."

Marc didn't answer.

I looked over at him. The light from the dashboard washed his face in pale green. One hand held the steering wheel in a white-knuckled grip, the other hand fisted over the gearshift like he was hanging on for dear life.

"They shouldn't have found me," he ground out between his teeth. "They shouldn't have known where I was going to college."

"Why not?"

"Do you think I went to a super-strict college by choice, Josh?" He smirked. "C'mon, admit it. I'm not Saint Bart's material."

I raised my eyebrows. "And I am?"

"You have your issues, dude, you know that."

"Gee thanks." But he was right. Mr. Perfect didn't belong on an exclusive college campus with kids who caused trouble if they were given an inch. "So you transferred to Saint Bart's from MSU because you thought whoever is chasing you wouldn't be able to find you there."

"Just like I did by moving from Evangel to MSU, and before that, SBU to Evangel. Saint Bart's is safer anyway. It's not like anyone can just pop in off the streets, thanks to their security." He relaxed his grip on the gearshift and rubbed his forehead.

I looked outside, watching the darkened buildings and streets flash past. Marc skirted around downtown and got on the main highway through town. From there, he pulled onto the interstate heading southwest.

I frowned. "Why are we heading toward Republic?"

"Dropping you off at your folks' first. Then I'm getting out of here."

"What? Hang on!" I whirled around to face him. "What did you get yourself *into*, Marc? No way am I letting you tackle this on your own."

He snorted. "Right. You can't fight, and you don't know anything about the Underworld. No offense, but you're just going to slow me down." He glanced up in the review mirror. "Best friend or not, you can't help me with this. Only Underworlders can."

I growled and crossed my arms. "At least explain—"

"No. I'm done talking about this." Marc punched the radio button on his console.

I started to yell at him, but a screaming-loud guitar riff drowned me out. Marc shifted, sped up, and wrapped both hands around the steering wheel.

I flopped back in my seat and shook my head. Fae, monsters, conspiracy. It was insane. I gave Marc a sideways glance. His face was tight, his eyes staring straight ahead at the road. He'd never told me, through all those years we'd been friends. Maybe that should have bothered me more, but it didn't. Marc and I'd been friends for years, long enough that I trusted him without question.

I drummed my fingers against the windowsill. He was probably right. I'd be in way over my head if I tried to help him, a liability rather than an asset. Still—

Brakes squealed. The chest strap cinched tight over my shoulder as the back end of the car jittered back and forth. Marc screamed something incomprehensible over the music. I snapped my head forward.

A huge black truck barreled toward us, the lights off, the windshield gleaming in the moonlight like the eye of a malevolent cyclops.

Marc cranked the wheel to the right. The truck clipped the front bumper, sending us into a spin. Marc jerked on the wheel again, trying to compensate.

I saw it coming. He was pulling the car too hard to the left. In my mind's eye I could clearly see the trajectory of the car, right into the guardrail—

I cringed.

The tires hit the curb, and my side of the vehicle slammed down into the ground. Glass breaking, metal crunching, the feeling of being trapped inside a carnival ride gone wrong. The air bag threw me back in the seat. Something smacked the side of my head, and my vision tunneled.

Silence.

Darkness.

I opened my eyes. I didn't remember closing them. Everything felt wrong—there was a heaviness at the crown of my head and my legs and arms seemed to be hanging toward the ceiling...

"Upside down," I said. "Of course. That would be just my luck."

I looked forward. I wasn't in the driver's seat. Who had...

Marc. His arms hung limply toward the ceiling, and his head flopped to the side. Was he dead? I took a deep, shuddering breath. No, I could see dust swirling in front of his mouth as he breathed. What were we doing here? The air was full of grit and dust and the smell of gasoline. I sneezed, felt my neck pop. Pain shot through my shoulders. My vision tunneled again.

I ground my teeth. *No, no, no!* I couldn't pass out. Had to get Marc out...

I reached up and braced myself against the ceiling with one hand. My hands trembled so much and felt so weak that I had to push as hard as I could to pop the seatbelt. I collapsed on the ceiling-turned-floor, bumping my shoulders again and feeling another, duller wave of pain. The interior of the car looked less crumpled than I would have thought. My window was webbed with fractures. I kicked it, and the glass crumpled outward.

I crawled out, bits of glass scraping into my skin through my jeans. Carefully, using the edge of the car as support, I pulled myself up and glanced toward the road.

We'd just missed the guardrail. There was a muddy track down a mild slope to the car. We hadn't rolled down, we'd flipped onto the roof and slid. That's why the car wasn't completely crumpled.

I hurried around to Marc's side of the car and paused.

There were no buildings around us. I frowned. That wasn't right. We'd been in Springfield the last I could remember, at the coffee shop. It had to be a weekday, otherwise the car would be locked up in the St. Bart's parking garage.

I shook my head, earning another jab of pain in my neck and shoulders. I kicked at Marc's window. It broke apart and I reached through and grabbed his shoulder. "Marc!"

His hand seized my wrist, his eyes opening wide in spiking shades of blue. I jerked back, but his hand tightened on my wrist, making me wince. After a second, the wild look in his eyes calmed, and he breathed out a sigh of relief.

"Josh. You're okay?"

"I think..."

A door slammed. I glanced over my shoulder. A truck

had parked at the shoulder, and I saw several figures hurrying down toward us. One looked huge...monstrous, even...why did that ring a bell?

"Get me out now!" Marc clawed at his seat belt.

"Whoa, careful, you're probably hurt!"

"Not as hurt as we're going to be if those guys get hold of us, genius!" Marc jerked at his seatbelt again. "We're dead. We are so dead. Scyrril's going to kill us."

"I'll just leave you here if you keep complaining..." My brain started to catch up to my mouth. *Scyrril.* My thoughts were fuzzy, but I knew he was bad news. I knew it.

I started to stand.

Hands jerked me away from the car, and an arm slid around my neck. I clawed at it. The world started spinning.

Marc screamed, and the sound shattered the night sky into thousands of glass shards. For the second time in the space of a few minutes, I blacked out.

chapter 3

Jostling and shaking again. Would this car wreck never stop? My eyelids fluttered.

My arms were twisted behind my back, most of my weight leaning on them. I shifted, trying to relieve the uncomfortable tingling, and pain screeched through my tense muscles. I groaned, felt something thick and fuzzy between my teeth. Cloth.

"Hey, the scrawny one is awake."

The scratchy voice was right in my ear. My eyes flew open and I instinctively jerked away to the left.

The guy sitting next to me grinned. He had the darkest skin I've ever seen—pure black—and a mop of dread-locked silver hair. He smiled, and a gold incisor flashed in the moonlight.

Fae. Monsters. My heart skipped a beat. *Car crash.* I could remember everything now.

The huge, hunched monster sitting in the seat in front of me looked over his shoulder. Blake—Scyrril. He grinned.

I probably had a bruise on my neck in the shape of his hand. I tried to snarl at him. The gag probably ruined the effect.

He laughed. "Let him stay awake. He doesn't have any idea where we are."

I looked out the front windshield. The headlights lit up a

hill and forest on either side of the road. Great, he was right. That was helpful.

Where was Marc? I took a longer look at the front of the van. Just a couple more fae freaks: one pale-skinned guy with a ponytail, and another dark-skinned fae with silver hair.

I twisted my wrists back and forth behind my back, grinding the gag between my teeth as the movements pulled at tight, bruised muscles. Whatever it was holding my wrists together—it had the sticky, flexible feeling of duct tape—yanked out a few arm hairs. I winced.

The bucket seat to the right was next. I could barely see the person slumped in it, but I recognized Marc's red jacket. We hit a bump, and his head flopped to the side. He had bruises on his right jaw and cheek and a nasty-looking cut across his forehead. The cut hadn't been there right after the wreck.

My stomach felt like it was rising into my throat. I forced it back down. Yeah, that'd be good, asphyxiating because I threw up while I was gagged. These guys would probably laugh as I choked.

The van took a sharp right, fishtailing a little as gravel crunched under the tires. I leaned to see out the front again, trying to spot any landmarks, and the guy beside me shoved my head into my lap. I bucked my shoulders, but he held me down by my neck and squeezed. It took all of a few seconds before I got dizzy and stopped fighting.

The van lurched to a halt. Doors opened and slammed and the sliding door on the side rolled open. Scyrril grabbed Marc and slung him over his shoulder. The dark elf beside me grabbed my arm and pushed me out the van. We stood in the middle of the forest, the van lights illuminating the shaded windows of a massive log cabin.

As we started for the house, I dug my feet into the ground, but it was gravel—easy for him to drag me through. My foot caught a root sticking out of the ground.

I stumbled to one knee. The dark elf wrenched my arms painfully to one side. He kept walking, and I staggered along until I could scramble up to my feet again.

Scyrril stopped near the front door and shrugged the shoulder Marc hung over. "He's waking up."

Sure enough, Marc's head was moving back and forth.

Scyrril knocked on the door, and it swung inward, a square of golden light spilling onto the front porch. Scyrril ducked inside. Marc's back grazed the top of the doorframe.

The dark elf shoved me in next. I jerked to a stop near the door, squinting in the bright light. The door opened into a huge living room, small clusters of leather chairs dotting the area. There was a fireplace at the far end, a bed of coals glowing inside, with several chairs and a leather couch parked in front of it. The chill hit me next—it felt much colder than the low sixties we'd had outside. I shivered.

Goosebumps popped along my arms as I noticed the fae sitting beside the fire, his chin resting on his steepled fingers. His silver hair picked up ruddy highlights from the fire, and again, I could see the graceful curving points of his ears. He looked a little like a modern-day Elrond in a fancy three-piece suit and tie. He stared at the fire, ignoring us.

My stomach heaved again, and my face tingled.

"My Lord Blodheyr?" Scyrril stepped forward.

The fae gave a sharp nod.

Scyrril dumped Marc onto the couch.

The fae behind me prodded me forward. Blodheyr nodded to the seat beside Marc. My legs felt a little sore as I sat, but I was either working out the stiffness or adrenalin had kicked in. I shifted to get more comfortable and realized my hands were shaking. Yeah, adrenalin. The fae untied my gag. I swallowed, trying to get the fuzzy taste of the bandanna out of my mouth.

Blodheyr eyed me, and then focused on Marc, who had stopped moving. He dropped his hands to his lap. "I hope you didn't damage him, Scyrril."

His voice was low, calm.

The pony-tailed fae stepped to Marc's side and slapped

him. I flinched. Marc's head rolled to the side and he blinked slowly. He brought his head up, wincing, and focused on Blodheyr.

His face went pale and his eyes widened.

Blodheyr smiled. It spread his lips out, making them look bigger and fleshier than they really were.

The sight turned my stomach even more. I hunched forward, biting back a groan, curling my fingers into my damp palms.

Heartbeats throbbed by as Blodheyr and Marc stared at each other. Finally, Marc spoke.

"I thought I told your pet troll that I couldn't break the cipher."

A growl bubbled in Scyrril's throat.

Blodheyr held up a hand. "Easy, my friend." He folded his hand together in a steeple, brought the fingertips up to rest under his chin. "You couldn't break a simple cipher, but your father could."

Marc snorted a laugh. "My dad was human. You know— not fae? Solving quantum physics while my mom's family was dancing around a bonfire at Stonehenge? You know fae suck at anything like that, Blodheyr."

The Unseelie's pale, bulging eyes shifted to me. The silver circles around his pupils flickered, just a little. The sight of the d'anam fuinneog made me shiver.

"This human can see through glamour," Blodheyr murmured. "Tell me, Joshua, are you feeling ill?"

I stared at him. "What?"

Blodheyr nodded. "Most humans have a fight or flight instinct around fae. They perceive us much the same way as animals perceive predators, and for good reason. This usually manifests in feeling sick to the stomach, nausea, trembling, sweaty palms..." His voice trailed off.

Adrenalin, I told myself. *It's the adrenalin.*

"It doesn't appear to be hitting you as hard as it does most humans, though." Blodheyr glanced at Marc. "He's not from a curator family, is he?"

Marc glared.

Blodheyr shrugged. "Answer enough. A human who can see through glamour, who can fully understand the Underworld around him, who is unattached in his loyalties, and is a master of technology. A mathematical genius—isn't that what you've said, Marc?"

He'd talked about me?

Marc's eyes narrowed. "No."

Blodheyr tapped his fingertips together. "I assume you're rejecting my proposal?"

Proposal? What proposal? I glanced at Marc.

He nodded, chin jutting forward. "You got it, crowbait."

The smile left Blodheyr's face. He pressed his lips together, then lifted two fingers of his right hand and made a slight waving motion.

Two of his goons grabbed my arms and pulled me to my feet.

"Hey!" I tried to pull away. Nausea pushed bile into my mouth.

They gripped tighter and steered me toward a hallway to the side of the fireplace.

"Josh, it's okay, don't get yourself hurt!" Marc yelled after me. "Blodheyr, I swear, if you hurt him, I'll have your head!"

The hallway was short, with several white doors breaking up the monotony of the dark wood paneling. The fae opened one, flicked on the light, and shoved me inside. The door slammed shut.

I took a deep breath and tried to relax. The room contained only a couple of chairs, a small table, and a bed. Paneled in the same wood as the hallway. Nothing very interesting. There was a curtained window high on the far wall, but with my hands tied behind my back, I knew I couldn't reach it.

The fae hadn't taken me very far down the hall, so I should have been close enough to hear a little bit from the living room. Especially if Marc raised his voice again. I knelt next to the door and pressed my ear against it.

Nothing.

I stood, wincing as the muscles in my legs burned. Every inch of my body ached from the crash and being manhandled by creatures that shouldn't exist. I flopped onto the bed. My rolling gut had eased a little, though I was still trembling. My brain felt like it was going ninety miles a minute on a freeway with no traffic signs.

We're gonna die. That fae dude is gonna kill us. Or torture us so Marc will give him whatever it is he wants. The thought sent panic jolting through me, and my breathing sped up.

Calm down, Josh. Chill. I closed my eyes. *Three point one four one five nine two...*

The familiar rhythm of pi calmed my pounding pulse and helped my breathing slow. Somewhere around the two-hundred-thirty-third digit, the door opened again. Scyrril shoved Marc through, then pulled the door shut.

Marc stood beside the door, a fresh cut over one eyebrow dripping blood down the side of his face. He lowered his head and refused to look at me.

"What happened?" I swung my feet to the floor.

He shrugged. "What always happens when you deny Blodheyr."

"Oh, wonderful. So you're not wanted by the Mob, just a fae Mob wanna-be."

"I'm not in the mood for this, Josh."

I laughed. "You're lucky. Neither am I. So care to tell me what's. Going. On?" I hoped my tone would get the point across to Marc. "Tell me what this cipher is. Why Blodheyr wants it. Why the heck you can't deal with it."

Marc sat down beside me and twisted around so I could see his wrists. "Let's get ourselves loose first, then I'll explain. Okay?"

I turned and pushed my hands up to Marc's. I scraped my fingernails along the tape on his wrists and found the seam. After picking at it, I was able to grab a loose corner and pull the tape off. As the last bit tore away, Marc grunted.

He shook his hands out in front of him, wincing.

I smirked, until he jerked the tape from my wrists. I pulled a sharp hiss in through my teeth and rubbed my arms.

"So, an explanation." Marc folded his arms around his legs. "You remember when my dad died earlier this year?"

Marc had received the phone call right before class, which was weird, because his family knew his schedule and were always really good about not calling him during school. He'd answered it and immediately gone pale, just like tonight when he'd seen Blodheyr. He'd left school for an entire week right before finals to be with his family.

I nodded.

"Did I tell you that we suspected he'd been murdered?"

The widening of my eyes must have been enough of a clue. He went on.

"The Underworld doesn't use a monetary system like we do. It's a system of barter and trade. We exchange our skills for something of equal value. I didn't know this before Dad died, but he'd exchanged his skills in codes and ciphers for enough money to send me to college." Marc brushed his hair out of his eyes and winced as his fingers ran across the cut. He pulled his fingers away, stared at the blood on his fingers.

"And Blodheyr was the one he traded them to," I said.

"Dad didn't know Blodheyr was Unseelie at first, or he never would have accepted the work. He must have gotten suspicious because, according to how Blodheyr tells it, he destroyed everything he was working on and refused to do any more."

"So Blodheyr killed him."

Marc nodded, his jaw tightening. He got up, walked to the door, and kicked it.

The door rattled under a heavy blow. One of the fae yelled something through the door. From his tone, I guessed he was cussing us out.

Marc backed away, his eyes narrowing as he scanned the rest of the room. He crossed to the one window in the room and pushed the curtains aside. Black-backed glass glinted past the heavy rebar dividing the window into five vertical parts. Marc reached past the rebar, unlocked the window, and shoved it open.

The sweet, heady smell of honeysuckle trickled in past him, coupled with the sounds of chirping crickets. Marc wrenched on the bars. They didn't move.

"Blodheyr wants you to finish what your dad was working on," I guessed.

Marc nodded again, sighed. "It's only one document in some kind of number cipher. I can't make heads or tails of it."

"Why are you working with Blodheyr when your dad—"

"Because I don't want to end up like my dad!" Marc snapped. He scraped both hands through his hair. "I left the Underworld for a reason, Josh. I can fight, but not well enough to survive in the Underworld. Besides, it's just so— dark. I'm sick of fighting. I wanted to just finish this job for Blodheyr, finish my schooling, and settle down in the Overworld."

I rubbed my wrists again nervously.

The color in Marc's eyes spiked to a light blue-gray. "The only problem with that was…I found notes from my dad on this final document. Not a key—not any clue on how to break the cipher—but he was scared about something. I think Blodheyr knows I have the notes on it, and he's getting tired of waiting. If I don't come up with something soon, I'm afraid…" He shook his head.

Blodheyr knew about me. About how good I was with math and computers. "You think he'll try to make me crack the cipher?"

Instead of answering, Marc turned to the window again and grabbed the bars.

"What—"

"Ssh." He held up his hand, squinting into the darkness.

For a second, I thought he was going to yank on them again, but instead he grabbed my arm and jerked me off the bed.

"Get down!"

chapter 4

The floor knocked the breath out of me. It smelled like blood and urine. I pulled my face away, gagging. I was doomed to keep shoving my face in horrible smells tonight.

Marc flopped down beside me, looking up through his bangs at the window in...what? Excitement?

"Close—" Marc started.

A piercing snap filled the room with blinding white light. I yelled and pressed my hands against my eyes. Tears streamed down my cheeks.

The door banged open. Hands grabbed my arms, jerked me to my feet, dragged me through the doorway. I banged my ribcage on the doorframe and yelped. I couldn't see anything but strobes of painful lightning. My eyes burned.

Behind me, Marc started to yell, but his voice was quickly muffled.

"Leave him!" Scyrril said.

The hands on my arms released. I staggered. A foot hooked my leg, knocked me to the ground. My head smacked into the hardwood floor, and pain flared through my skull. I heard a door slam open, shouts and yells, the clanging of steel on steel. Someone—not Marc—screamed.

I pushed myself up a little. Ghosts of shapes were starting to show up. I could see outlines of the furniture around me, but it was pale gray, washed out black, piercing white. Everything seemed reversed, a photo negative of reality.

A vehicle roared outside and gravel splattered the sides of the cabin as it took off.

I tried to stand and fell back onto my butt. The world spun around me.

Footsteps echoed on the porch, and I caught sight of three pale human-like shapes coming in from the gray of the night. I shoved my back against the wall, my breath catching in my throat. My gut wrenched.

They stood at the front of the room. My eyes weren't back to normal yet—I couldn't see details of their faces—but I could see points of reflective light, like animal eyes, flashing where eyes should be as they looked around.

"I see him," a female voice said, and the smallest of the figures started toward me.

"Check the hall," a male voice said.

The biggest of the shadows split off, walking past me and into the hall. The other two stopped, and the girl knelt beside me.

"Who are you?" I croaked, wishing my voice had come out stronger.

"Ssh, ssh. It's all right." Soft fingers brushed close to my eyes.

I flinched.

"Your flash-bang blinded him," she said.

"Blinded?" I didn't like how that sounded.

"Relax, dude." The voice was the first male voice I'd heard—gruff and ticked off. "Give him the eyedrops, see what we can get out of him. If he saw anything he could understand. Why'd you have to follow me anyway?"

The girl's hands tipped my face up. I felt something cool touch the corner of my eye and flinched away. "What are you doing?"

"You can either let her give you the eyedrops or you can wait twenty-four hours for the effects to wear off," the male snapped.

I submitted. The drops soothed my eyes, overflowing and sliding down my cheeks. I blinked several times and wiped my face with my arm.

Slowly, the colors blurred together like a little kid's watercolor painting, and the room came into focus. I was in the enormous living room, my back pressed against the wall next to the fireplace. Too close, in fact. The heat was making me sweat.

The two people crouched beside me were obviously fae. The girl had long jet-black hair, a jagged layer of turquoise-striped bangs slashing across her pale forehead. A black, spiral-twisted knife handle stuck out of the tall boots she wore over black, form-fitting pants, and she cradled a sawed-off shotgun in one arm.

The guy's pale blond hair jutted over his forehead in gelled spikes, and underneath, his bright green eyes flickered in jumps and starts. Those eyes looked hard and relentless, a little like Blodheyr's. In one hand, he held a sword, the point pressed into the wood floor to balance himself. Another sword was strapped to his waist under a black leather jacket.

He stood up and prodded my leg with the toe of his heavy motorcycle boots, the hems of his tattered jeans swishing. "Well, mud-eater. What are you doing here?"

"You friends of Marc's?" I asked. "Seelie?"

Pale violet color flared in the girl's purple eyes. She blinked once, her long lashes dark against her creamy skin. "You know about fae."

I nodded and pushed myself to my feet.

The two fae stared at me warily as they rose. The girl finally spoke.

"Yeah, we're Seelie." She poked the guy in the arm. "This is Eliaster. I'm Larae."

Eliaster glared at her. "You just give it up, just like that? Has it occurred to you—"

"That you could trust Overworlders a little more? Yes, it has." Larae flicked her hand at him. "Go find David. I'll talk to this guy."

"Freakin' idiots." Eliaster turned and stomped down the hall. "David?" he shouted, and slammed a door, making every window in earshot rattle.

Larae cleared her throat. "How do you know Marc?"

I brushed strands of hair out of my eyes and took a deep breath. My hands weren't shaking, and even my gut had settled down a little. "I've known him for years. We went to school together. He just started coming to my college."

Larae lifted her chin a little. "Saint Bartholomew's. You must be that genius friend he talked about."

"Oh, wonderful. Everyone knows about me."

She frowned. "How did the two of you end up here? What happened? I'm assuming you'll be able to make a little sense of what you saw, since you can obviously see our true selves."

I nodded. "Marc said it was because I'd been around him most of my life."

She cupped her hands around my face and stared into my eyes. My skin heated from more than the fireplace at my back. It was disconcerting to have this girl staring at me like this, her intense violet eyes scrutinizing me like she was staring through a microscope at a new bug or something.

"You're mostly immune." She dropped her hands and rubbed the sleeves of her thin jade-green blouse. "Still have stomach trouble around us?"

"A little."

Eliaster came back out into the living room, followed by the guy who looked like a body-builder, who must have been the David they'd mentioned earlier.

Eliaster grimaced. "Nothing to see and absolutely no clues as to where they went."

Larae bit her lower lip. The skin around her eyes crinkled. "I hope he has the good sense to give Blodheyr what he wants."

"Right, like that would solve anything." Eliaster grunted and stalked toward the front door. He let that one slam behind him, too.

"What's his problem?" I muttered.

"Pick something, and it's probably one of his many problems," Larae said, brushing her bangs from her eyes.

I frowned.

David chuckled. "Glad to find another human who is confused by the fae."

I jerked my head toward him. Sure enough, no weird eye-color thing, no pointed ears, no delicately sharp features or slanted eyes. David looked like your typical Midwestern corn-fed football player. Generally I avoided his type, but now, it felt good to see another human.

I breathed out a sigh. "Glad I'm not the only human to get mixed up with them."

David shrugged. "Sorry it had to happen to you. From what Marc has said, you sound like an okay guy." A swift wince crossed his square face. "Sorry. You forget most humans aren't as blunt as fae."

"Don't worry about it." I glanced over at Larae.

She folded her arms and was staring at the door.

"So, how do you guys know Marc?" I asked.

"I've known his family for years," David said. "Same for Eliaster."

Eliaster pushed the door open and jerked his head. "Are you guys going to stand there gabbing all night? Josh, you can explain to them on the way."

"The way? And how do you know my name?" I moved toward the door.

Eliaster rolled his eyes. "As in, wherever you'd like to go that would be safe for you tonight. And I know your name because, as you've probably discovered, Marc blabbed all over the Underworld about you."

"Oh." I scratched my neck, trying not to show how embarrassed I felt. *Duh, Josh. Stop acting like your average idiot.* "I guess my parents' house. The dorm wouldn't be safe right now."

"Score one for the not-so-genius." Eliaster hopped off the porch.

"Hey!" I growled.

David stepped past me. "Leave it. You don't cross Eliaster when he's in this mood."

I followed him outside. A black Porsche sat idling in the driveway. Eliaster headed past it, and I noticed a dark blue motorcycle with a snarling dragon's head on the gas tank lying on its side about fifteen feet behind the Porsche. Skid marks in the gravel showed where it had fallen and slid.

I glanced at David.

He shrugged. "He was moving pretty fast."

"I was hoping to lose you idiots," Eliaster snapped, righting the motorcycle.

The Porsche's driver door popped open. Larae glanced at Eliaster over the car's roof. "So you're following us?"

"Yeah." He pointed at me. "Fill them in. Don't leave out a single detail." He straddled the bike and kick-started it.

Larae ducked back inside the car. David opened the passenger door and moved the seat forward. I squeezed into the back. I wasn't very tall, but the front seats still hit my knees as I got settled. We pulled out of the cabin's driveway, and Eliaster shot past us, jacket flapping, gravel spitting from the back tire of his bike.

"I thought he said he'd follow us," I said.

David snorted. "Yeah, Eliaster says a lot of things."

Larae cleared her throat. "Okay, so, Josh, why don't you tell us what happened."

I leaned forward between the two front seats and started the story. David sat and listened impassively, his arms crossed over his chest. Once or twice, I caught Larae's eyes glancing in the rearview mirror.

When I finished, I leaned back and looked out my side window. The orange glow of Springfield's lights surprised me. We hadn't been as far away as I'd thought. Even more surprising was the grayish-pink streak coloring the eastern skyline.

I glanced at the clock on the dashboard. Six-thirty-two, it read. All this had happened in four hours? Unbelievable.

I glanced out the front window but didn't see Eliaster's motorcycle ahead of us. Where had he disappeared to?

"Hey," Larae said.

I looked up. Her violet eyes in the rearview mirror were focused on me. How was she doing that and still driving?

"Where do your parents live?"

"Republic." I gave her the address.

"Glad I asked now." She spun the wheel.

The Porsche smoothly and sharply turned onto the off ramp. Larae didn't slow down as we slipped through the residential streets. A few houses had the lights on in the kitchen or living room as we turned onto my family's street.

She parked the car at the curb near my parents' two-story ranch house. David pushed open his door, stepped out, and pulled the seat forward so I could squeeze out.

Eliaster pulled up beside the car on his bike. Somewhere along the ride he must have fallen behind us and I hadn't noticed.

"Hustle up," he growled. "We don't want to be seen."

I started for the driveway, ready to get away from the irritable fae. "Thanks for the ride."

Eliaster leaned over and grabbed my arm. His eyes narrowed. "Listen if you want to live, because you don't understand how the Underworld works. You can see through the glamour, and the fae are going to recognize that. Don't show off. Keep to yourself, ignore the fae as much as possible, and you might get lucky and live to die of natural causes. Got it?"

I tried to jerk away, my heartbeat sending sharp pulses into my neck. "What about Marc?"

"We'll find him. Don't you mess with it." Eliaster released my arm.

I stepped onto the lawn. Without a word, David got back into the Porsche and closed the door. Eliaster shot down the street, the car following him at the same breakneck speed.

They'd take care of it. Right. Let Grouchy-Gut and the other two sort it out. My stomach twisted at the thought of abandoning my friend, but I couldn't help. Marc and Eliaster were both right—I didn't understand their world enough.

I let myself into the house with a spare key and collapsed on the couch in the living room. If I was lucky, I could catch a few minutes of sleep before my parents came downstairs and found me.

After a moment, though, I got up and opened the side table drawer. My dad's tablet lay there, as usual. I pulled it out, started it up, and tapped the Internet browser. If I could see the fae now, I needed to know what I was dealing with.

chapter 5

"Josh?"

The voice was feminine, concerned. My eyelids twitched, but my car-wreck dream didn't want to let me go. I flinched as the window next to me splintered, and an all-too-real twinge in my neck made my eyes open a bit more.

A small-boned, gentle hand brushed my shoulder.

I yelled and jerked up, swatting the hand away. The tablet slipped off my stomach and clattered to the wooden floor.

My mom fumbled her coffee, nearly spilling it over the back of the couch. She took a step back and brushed her auburn hair back from her face. "What's wrong?"

I sat up, running my hands through my hair. My eyes were wide, and I looked wildly around the room. How...where was...

The familiar furniture of my parents' living room fell into place. I was lying on the couch, the entertainment center across the narrow room from me, teeth marks on the corner of the door from one of the twin's teething days. I swung my bare feet to the carpet. The movement made my neck ache again, and pain throbbed down my head and into my shoulders. I felt like I'd been hit by a semi-truck. Kinda had, in a way.

I winced and rubbed my neck. "What time is it?"

"Eight thirty. Are you all right? Your clothes…"

I got up, glanced down at myself. I was wearing an older, faded shirt that still looked fine, but my jeans were ripped at the knees and stained with what I guessed was blood. My blood. I vaguely remembered cutting myself as I'd crawled out of Marc's broken car window last night.

I smiled at Mom and headed past her into the kitchen. "I'm okay. They're just old clothes."

Dad sat at the kitchen table, his nose buried in some kind of business book, gray-touched brown hair combed back as usual, gel taming it into perfect place. He glanced up as I fumbled a coffee mug from the cabinet and poured myself a cup.

"Well, long time no see," he said dryly.

"Yeah, been busy." I plunked down at the table and gulped. The bitter black liquid scalded my mouth. I choked the swallow down. My burning tongue snapped me wide awake, and I remembered.

Marc. Eliaster, David, Larae.

Fae. Trolls.

Crap.

"We didn't hear you come in last night at all," Mom said, sliding into the seat beside me.

"I just got in about six-thirty," I muttered.

"Late night," Dad said, closing his book.

Uh-oh. I recognize that tone. I took another gulp of the coffee to cover the fact that my mind was racing for an answer. It was way better to lie than deal with the hassle of the truth—they'd think I was lying anyway.

Or into drugs. Yeah, that was exactly not the thing I needed my parents thinking. "It was kind of unexpected, actually. Someone broke into our dorm building early this morning." That was true, after all.

Mom's eyes widened.

I hurried to add, "Nothing was stolen, but they wanted everyone out while the police investigated. They probably think it's a student prank gone too far." True and probable.

"So I came here to sleep some more."

"You walked here?" Mom looked surprised.

"You should have called us," Dad said.

"I left my phone at the dorm." *True.* "A friend of Marc's dropped me off." *Also true.* They didn't need to know the whole story, just the basics. If I tried to explain everything.... Yeah, I could see that going over well. *Marc and I were kidnapped by trolls—oh, surprise, Marc's half-fae, in case you were wondering—and some nutcase Unseelie thinks I should be able to decipher some weird ancient document or whatever.*

Yeah, that was no good. My parents would think I was nuts.

Maybe I was nuts. In the light of day, Irish legends seemed a lot less likely than they had last night. But my neck kept twinging every time I moved. My brain was still foggy and felt distant, like it could float out of my skull at any moment. I rubbed the hairless spots on my wrists, mind flashing back to all the stuff I'd looked up last night.

Well, at least this attempt to convince myself Irish legends weren't real didn't include hysterics. I wanted to punch myself for how I'd acted last night.

I glanced out the window and nearly jumped out of my chair. One of the fae from last night—dark-skinned, white dreadlocks trailing down his back—was standing outside on the lawn, staring into the kitchen. He noticed me and grinned, a gold tooth flashing in the sunlight.

"Do you need a ride back to school?" Dad asked.

I snapped my attention over to him. "Uh, no. No, I—I'll be fine. I don't want to—"

The dark fae waved.

I blinked and tried to ignore him. "To, uh, make you guys late for work."

Mom's eyes narrowed just slightly. Oh, great, she didn't believe me. I raised the mug to my lips. *Please don't ask, please don't ask...*

Her eyes fell on the clock. "Dan, we'll be late if we don't

hurry." She got up and strode to the bottom of the stairs. "Matt! Ollie! Are you up?"

Oh, right. I'd forgotten my brothers' school ended for the summer before mine.

Matt's voice echoed down the stairs. "I am, but Ollie isn't."

Thud.

"I'm gonna kill you, Matthew Isaiah MacAllister!" Ollie's voice cracked in the middle of the yell.

"Boys!" Mom rolled her eyes and grabbed her purse from the bottom step. "Coffee is made, breakfast is in the fridge. Chores before video games, please." She turned back to me. "You're sure the break-in was nothing serious?"

"I'm sure, Mom."

Dad folded his paper and headed for the front door. "He's a big boy, Madeline. See ya, Josh. Be careful going back to school."

"Yeah, be careful." Mom kissed my forehead, and gave me a narrow-eyed glance that said she still thought I was lying about something, but dashed after Dad.

I yawned and dropped my forehead to the table.

Matt came clattering down the stairs, still wearing pajamas, his thick black hair sticking up on one side. He grunted at me and went straight for the fridge, pulling out the remains of a hashbrown casserole, dumping a block of it on a plate, and shoving it in the microwave.

Ollie followed a few minutes later, looking slightly more awake and actually dressed for the day in gym shorts and a t-shirt. "Mornin', Josh. Why're you here?"

I repeated the same story I'd told our parents.

"Break-in? And they're surprised it happened at a school for losers?" Matt shrugged. "Present company excepted. You should transfer to a different school."

"Why bother? I've stuck it out this long, and anyway I'll graduate at the end of this term. I'll get a master's at a different school." I glanced out the window. The dark-skinned fae was still there, his arms crossed, that stupid grin still on his face.

Yeah, as if I was going to live long enough to contemplate my future.

I went into the living room and grabbed my shoes, making sure to delete the browser history on the tablet while I was there. That might look suspicious, if my dad thought to check it, but it was better than any alternative I could think of. I came back to the kitchen and leaned against the wall to pull my shoes on.

"Leaving?" Ollie brought a plate of cold pizza to the table.

Matt's eyes widened. "Where was that?"

Ollie smirked. "Hidden from you."

Matt lunged across the table. Ollie jerked his plate of pizza away and tipped over his chair in the process. He hit the tile floor with a grunt. Matt grabbed the biggest slice and took a huge bite.

I shook my head. "Wow. Lindsay and I never fought over pizza when we were seventeen, you guys."

"No, you just locked each other out of the house and stuff," Matt said around his mouthful.

The thought made me smile. Lindsay was only eleven months older than me, and we'd had some serious sibling rivalry all throughout high school. *I should call her, see how the new artsy-fartsy job is going.*

Ollie reached across the table and punched Matt in the chest.

I looked out the window for the dark fae again. He was gone. Somehow I doubted he'd gone far. The twins continued their bickering as they shoveled their food into their mouths, and for a second I watched them, my throat clenching.

"I'm gonna head out now, guys," I said. "Don't—" *Don't what? Don't open the door for anyone who doesn't look human? Don't talk to strangers with pointy ears?*

"Sheesh, you're as bad as Mom and Dad," Ollie said. "We got it. Shoot first, ask questions later, blah, blah, blah."

"Not exactly…" I muttered.

Matt rolled his eyes. "Dude, we're seventeen, okay?"

I raised one eyebrow. "Really? Could've fooled me—I'd have guessed you at ten right now."

Ollie threw a chair cushion at me. "Dude. We got this."

I forced a smile. Maybe the best thing would just be for me to get away from them as fast as I could.

The twins said muffled goodbyes through full mouths, and I waved at them over my shoulder. I pulled the front door closed, hopped from the porch to the sidewalk, and started down the block, carrying my jacket under my arm.

As expected, a few minutes later I heard soft footsteps behind me. I gritted my teeth. Eliaster had said to ignore the fae, but ten to one he hadn't expected one of Blodheyr's goons to show up at my house.

I spun around and walked backward. "You trying to hide from me?"

The dark fae shook his head. "Still feeling queasy?"

A bit, but not enough that I wouldn't be able to run. Not that he needed to know. "What was the game, showing up like that?"

The golden incisor flashed as the fae grinned. "Just wanted to see the happy family."

"Well, stay away from them." *Oh, nice, Josh. Very macho and threatening. Idiot.* I grunted and turned back, just in time to avoid smacking into a street sign.

Goldtooth chuckled and caught up to me. "You don't seem to appreciate my restraint as much as you should, MacAllister."

"Hard to be impressed by a guy who thinks he can get what he wants by beating up and killing others."

Goldtooth shrugged.

We walked in silence for a time, the fae a step or two behind me and to my left. I could just see him out of the corner of my eye, which made me nervous, but no way was I letting him see that. We were close to one of the city bus stops when he spoke again.

"Blodheyr only took Marc because he's loath to let a

mud-eater in on his secrets. However, he will make an exception for you, Joshua. He's impressed by everything he knows of you. He wanted to make you an offer. Anything you want—be it money or power—in exchange for deciphering the code Marc spoke to you about."

I stopped dead and glared at him. "He missed his chance."

"What about Marc?"

I couldn't hide a wince.

The fae straightened his shoulders. "Blodheyr will free your friend."

I recalled what Marc had said right after Scyrril and his buddy had chased us. "Crows take you and Blodheyr."

Goldtooth's eyes flashed, and his jaw tightened.

"Oh, sorry, was that offensive? Oops." I stepped toward him and jabbed my finger at his chest. "In other words, not happening, buddy."

"You will regret this," he ground out between clenched teeth.

"Yeah, like that isn't cliché at all." I started to walk away and realized he was no longer following me. He stood on the sidewalk, hands clenched at his sides. It made my neck prickle, but I turned my back and walked away.

He didn't follow.

I stayed on high alert as I waited for the bus, and even on the bus itself, half-expecting another fae to pop up and try to kill or kidnap me. But the driver and my fellow commuters were all human, as were all the people waiting when I got off a few streets away from Saint Bart's. On the way there, I saw one fae across the street and tensed, but all he did was give me an acknowledging nod.

When I got to the side street of Saint Bart's, the same one Marc and I had barreled out of earlier this morning, I hesitated. The two security guards were there now, and neither one of them looked pleased by the pieces of shattered gate sprinkled over the street.

Before I could retreat, one of them looked up and saw

me. "Hey, MacAllister!"

Just my luck, it had to be Harris. I'd had a couple of run-ins with him before—namely, he was the one who caught me sneaking out the last two times. Way too late to run now, though—that would definitely earn me an escort to the dean's office.

I forced a grin. "Hey."

The guy waved his hand around. "Sorry about this. In the confusion of the break-in and all, I forgot to get a few students' signatures when they left campus. Yours was one of them. Do you have a second to fix that?"

What, was he playing around before nailing me? "Uh, yeah, no problem." I followed him up to the security booth, glancing over my shoulder at the dorm. There were several police cars still parked in front of it.

Harris squeezed inside and pushed a clipboard over the counter to me.

I tried very hard not to melt into a puddle of relief as I signed, put the fake time I'd left campus, and gave the clipboard back. "So, did the security cameras catch anyone?"

"Nah. The guy must have had technical backup. Every one of the camera tapes is full of static."

Or some weird fae power messed with them. Could they do that? I thought back over all the research I'd done this morning, but nothing had ever mentioned shorting out cameras as a fae power. I looked over at the camera attached to the corner of the security booth. Out of the corner of my eye, I could see Harris give me a strange glance.

My stomach sank. Just what I didn't need. Time to move out before he decided to question me further. "Hope you find him."

"Let me know if there's anything missing from your room!" Harris called after me.

I snorted softly. Yeah right. If there was anything missing, chances were it wouldn't be important to anyone but Marc. And me.

The side door I normally used was blocked off, pieces of

glass spraying the grass and sidewalk around it. I skirted around the building and went into the front door. Thankfully no one was in the lounge—almost everyone was out on the town. Hopefully my suitemate Brian was gone.

I bounded up the stairs two at a time and slunk down the hallway to my door. I unlocked it and started to ease it open, but the stupid hinge betrayed me with a loud squeak.

The door next to mine popped open, and Brian's chubby form leaped out. I swear, sometimes I thought the guy was stalking me.

His eyes were wide and round. "Dude! You missed all the excitement!"

I slid a foot into my room. "Really?"

"Yeah, the school had a break-in. The first in its history! We all had to assemble at eight in the theater—man, the deans were mad. Where were you?"

I glared at him. "Whatever happened to the 'don't tell me, if I don't know I can't get in trouble too' thing?"

"Well, yeah, but other people know you were gone. There's only a matter of time before folks start asking questions."

I smacked my hand onto my forehead. Great, apparently others aside from Harris had made the connections earlier. With my record of hacking and playing computer pranks on people, what was to stop everyone from thinking that I'd hacked the security system for the thief?

"Now you get it." Brian bobbed his head up and down. "Look, I know you wouldn't do it, not something this serious, but other people aren't happy with you. Joe, down the hall, you know? You did hack his computer and upload private photos to his Facebook. Tony isn't too happy either, not after—"

I glared. "If you talk to anyone about this, Brian, I swear, all of your grades will disappear. Got that?"

Brian's chin wobbled. "Now, see, this is what I'm talking about, Josh. You can't go around antagonizing everyone and messing with their..."

I stepped into my room and slammed the door. Brian kept squawking for a few minutes before he gave up. I heard his heavy footsteps trudge away from my door and down the stairs.

I groaned and slid to the floor. Great. This was way beyond a few pranks or messing with people I didn't like. I could easily be arrested for this.

No, actually, I can't be arrested. The evidence was circumstantial at best. Still didn't keep me from hyperventilating. I thumped my head back against the wall and pressed my hands against my face.

"Trouble, Josh?"

I looked up into the barrel of a pistol. I jerked back, smacking into the door. "I thought I'd gotten rid of you."

Goldtooth motioned for me to stand. He stepped in close and patted at my jacket pockets and jeans. I raised my hands so I wouldn't get in his way. My heartbeat thudded in my suddenly-dry mouth.

The fae finished searching me and stepped back. "You know what I want."

I swallowed, hard, and shook my head.

"Aiden's notes." Goldtooth waved his free hand around the messy dorm room. "We didn't have time to search last night before Marc came back."

The notes...I remembered what Marc had told me last night. He had his dad's notes about the cipher. And Blodheyr thought Marc had hidden them and told me where they were.

I cleared my throat. "Marc never told me about any notes." My voice still came out squeaky. Other than my pulse, I couldn't feel anything. Somewhere in the back of my head, a part of my brain was screaming and freaking out. But for the most part, I felt calm.

"That's to be expected, but you're his best friend. You should be able to guess where he hid anything valuable." Goldtooth motioned to the room.

I stood up and scanned the room. The troll hadn't gotten far in his search last night. A couple of Marc's desk drawers hung open, and a few things were scattered on the floor, but that was all. I was so screwed.

I crossed the room and started riffling through the open drawers. My hands weren't even shaking. How was that possible? I cleared my throat again. "So just these notes. I'd have thought that you'd be coming back for me. To make me work on that cipher."

I heard the fae settling on my bunk. Great, he was planning to be here a while.

"You know, since Blodheyr's so 'interested' in me and all," I muttered.

"The cipher will come later. These notes are important now."

The first phrase sent a slight chill through me. I forced my hands to keep moving through the contents of the drawers. Then I opened Marc's computer and turned it on. "Letting me go, that wasn't an accident last night? Did you do that deliberately because Blodheyr guessed I'd come here and search for the notes? You don't have to hold me at gunpoint, you know."

"A few of your abilities changed things."

What was that supposed to mean?

I spent the next two hours meticulously combing through all of our stuff. His computer was a total waste of my time— all he had on it were basic operating programs and school work. The textbooks we had scattered around the room revealed nothing more. The same with the entertainment center, our closets, and our bathroom. I even took the back of the TV off to make sure he didn't stick something inside there.

I did find a music CD I'd been missing, a half-dozen of my thumb drives, and the single thumb drive Marc owned. I flopped down at my desk, shoved my messenger bag off to the side, and fired up my laptop. A search through all of my files revealed nothing. I slowly went through each of my thumb drives, though each one was password protected and I doubted Marc could have gotten into them.

Sure enough, nothing new.

I inserted his thumb drive next. All that popped up were pictures of Marc and his family...before his dad died.

I glanced over at Goldtooth. He lounged on the bed, pistol in one hand, the other picking at his teeth.

I scrolled through the pictures. They all looked like they were from one event. There were pictures with Marc and his whole family. His mom and sister looked like they were ready to cry, but they still had big grins. His dad looked like Marc—dishwater blond hair falling back from a widow's peak, big grin, blue eyes—the only difference were the lines and wrinkles cutting through Aiden's features.

I remembered the last time I'd seen them, at Marc's high school graduation party, held at a restaurant here in town. That had been six years ago, but Aiden looked like he'd aged more than ten years since then. Maybe by this time, he'd already started working for Blodheyr.

The last few pictures were of Marc in action, wielding the katana I'd seen him use last night, in what looked like a sparring match between him and Aiden. Even in the pictures, his expert swordsmanship was evident. In one picture, he had his sword locked under the hilt of Aiden's sword, his free hand reaching out to push Aiden away even as he twisted Aiden's sword free. If he was this good and could defend himself that well, why did he ever leave the Underworld?

The final picture looked ceremonial—Marc and his dad both wearing their swords. In the previous pictures, Marc hadn't been wearing the metal bracelet that he'd had in college. In this picture, Marc's dad was holding his son's arm up, like he was a champion, and on Marc's wrist was that bracelet. Probably some fae coming-of-age thing.

I grunted and jerked the thumb drive from the computer. Nothing.

Goldtooth glared at me. "You're stalling."

"No, I'm not." I swiveled my chair, staring out over the room. How were Marc's mom and sister taking his disappearance? He never went a day without calling them.

Something similar to a rock settled in my gut. Had they known Marc was working for the same guy who had murdered his father?

I shook my head and shoved the thought away. *Not now. Think. Where else could Marc have hidden something? And how could I keep it away from Goldtooth if I did find it?*

My gaze fell on the entertainment center again, on the little white game box tucked under the TV. Marc had complained last night about the Wii not working—that's the excuse he'd used to sneak out. A game disc stuck out of the Wii, only the last quarter of it in the slot.

What was wrong with it? I chewed my lip. If Marc had hidden something in it…

A knock sounded on the door. I jumped and stared at it.

Goldtooth scrambled to his feet, hissing at me. "Get the door, stupid!"

I stood up, too slowly for him. He jabbed me in the spine with the gun. I gritted my teeth and looked out the peephole on my door.

The blond fae from last night, Eliaster, slouched in the hallway, looking bored. He glanced at the door, then kicked it a couple of times.

I pulled back, pulse hammering. "It's Eliaster."

Goldtooth's eyes narrowed, and he stepped to one side of the door. "Let him in."

chapter 6

I opened the door. Eliaster didn't even acknowledge me and stared into the room, scanning as much as he could see.

We stood silent for a few seconds, him ignoring me. I rubbed my fingers against my damp palms. How was I supposed to warn him about the Unseelie?

He finally met my eyes and sighed. "Are you going to let me in or not?"

I stepped back slowly, and my eyes flicked to the Unseelie waiting at the side of the door. Eliaster's face didn't change—he gave no indication that he'd noticed my look away—but as soon as he stepped inside the room, he ducked.

Goldtooth's pistol whipped inches over Eliaster's spiked hair. The gun cracked into the door frame, chipping the wood.

Eliaster grabbed Goldtooth's arm, twisting him away from the door. He slammed Goldtooth against the wall, his forearm against the Unseelie's throat. "What are you doing here?" he snarled.

I closed the door. "Aiden's notes. He thought I would know where they are."

"Anything else?" Eliaster asked.

I shrugged.

The Unseelie said nothing.

Without taking his eyes off Goldtooth, Eliaster grabbed my messenger bag and threw it at me. "Pack."

"What?"

"Get what you need. Now."

"Why?"

"Because I'd bet my weight in gold that he was sent to drag you back to Blodheyr." Eliaster stepped closer to the Unseelie, pressing his arm tighter against Goldtooth's throat. "Isn't that right, crow-bait?"

Goldtooth shrugged. "I was sent to persuade him to help his friend."

My stomach knotted. It didn't feel good to have my suspicions confirmed. I pushed open my closet door and grabbed a handful of clothes off the floor. "Where are we going?"

"We'll discuss it later," Eliaster said.

Goldtooth chuckled. "Taking in another stray? Didn't the last time teach you anything?"

Eliaster slammed his fist into Goldtooth's jaw, throwing him against the wall. The Unseelie slid to the floor, his eyes sagging shut.

I edged past them and grabbed my computer, slid it into my bag, went into the bathroom and grabbed a pair of tweezers.

"What are you doing?" Eliaster stepped closer to me, his hand twitching, like he was ready to grab my arm and drag me out of the room.

"Dude, chill. Half a minute." I crouched in front of the entertainment center and pulled the CD from the

Wii, then slipped the tweezers into the game slot. The space was just big enough for the tweezers to fit. I poked them back a little further and felt something stiff stop them.

Slowly, I maneuvered the tweezers around it and pulled the thing out. Sure enough, it was a couple of pieces of folded paper. I held it up to Eliaster.

He grinned. "Good one."

I stood up. "Now that the Unseelie is no longer a threat—why do you want me to go with you?"

"That's your problem. The Unseelie are always a threat. Blodheyr is always a threat, as long as you have this." Eliaster jabbed my forehead with his index finger. "He'll make do with Marc, but he really wants you."

I shoved the papers at him. "Take these and get out of here. I'll find somewhere to stay."

"Where?"

"Anywhere other than with you." I started for the door. Just as I reached for it, another knock sounded. I gritted my teeth and jerked it open.

Brian stepped back, holding his hands up. "Whoa, man."

"What do you want?"

"Someone, not me, told the dean you snuck out last night and hadn't been back until this morning. There are a lot of people talking about you. Rumors are starting to fly that you had something to do with last night's break in, and I got here just ahead of a couple of detectives, so you might want—"

I swore under my breath and slammed the door on him.

Eliaster blew out a long breath. "Next time, tell me so I have time to use glamour."

"Sorry, I'm just a tiny bit preoccupied right now." I rubbed my neck, then dragged my hands through my hair. "This is stupid. I can't be a part of this, I'll get eaten alive."

"Marc doesn't choose friends who are cowards," Eliaster said.

"I'm a computer nerd! I get revenge on people by hacking into the school database and messing with their grades. I can't do anything else! You know the reason Marc and I became friends? He got sick of seeing me picked on at school. You fae have that in common, you know—you can't leave well enough alone."

Eliaster stared at me, the muscles in his jaw working. His bright green eyes flickered once, twice. Then he shrugged, grabbed the papers from my hand, and walked to the window. "Fine. Stay here. Take care of your own problems.

Let your best friend die." He swung one leg over the window sill.

I stared at him, clenching my hands. *You are not going to guilt me into this. I can't do anything about it. Sorry, Marc. I can't.*

"We need your help. You could break the cipher faster than anyone I know. But, that's okay. The Underworld scares most humans, and rightly so." Eliaster looked me in the eye. "But if you think that by backing out of this, you're going to avoid the fae, you're wrong. We can tell those who can see through glamour, Josh. Like it or not, you have that curse for life now. There will be fae who come after you. Some will want your help. Some will see you as a threat. You're never going to get away from us for the rest of your life."

He dropped out of the window.

I slumped against the door and massaged my forehead. *I'm not making the wrong decision. I'm not. They can handle it without me.*

The thought of Marc being beaten and tortured sprang to my mind. I shook my head, shoved it away. Blodheyr wouldn't harm him. He wanted the cipher.

The Unseelie moaned and stirred. I jumped away. Great. What was I supposed to do with him?

Another knock on the door. Oh, wonderful. The detectives Brian had warned me about. I looked out the peephole. Two men in polo shirts stood outside, both with badges strung around their necks.

Behind them stood two Unseelie, screwing silencers onto their pistols.

Another knock. "Mr. MacAllister?"
Wonderful.
Goldtooth rolled over and sat up, rubbing his head.
Crap.
I darted for the window.

Eliaster waited, leaning against the side of a sleek gray supercar as I trudged down the street, my messenger bag slung over one shoulder.

He raised an eyebrow. "I thought you didn't want to come."

"Then why are you waiting?"

He smirked and circled around the car, pulling a key remote out of his pocket. The car's locks clicked.

I jerked the passenger door open and slid inside. "Just until that stupid cipher is solved and all this goes away."

"You don't want to stay and sort out your problem with the police?"

"Any explanation I give them will land me either in jail or a padded room in the mental ward. Probably both. I'd rather duck out and let them work out that I'm innocent on their own."

Eliaster handed me the papers I'd taken from the Wii, then started the car and pulled away from the curb.

They were smallish pages that looked like they'd been torn from a five-by-eight-inch notebook. The handwriting was slanted to the point of being sideways, but I picked through it slowly.

I'm working on a new project for Blodheyr. When he first brought it in, I was suspicious. The document is old—a hundred and fifty years old is my guess. Blodheyr wouldn't say precisely, nor would he tell me where he'd procured it. He gave me photocopies and asked me to let him know the results as quickly as possible.

The cipher wasn't hard to decode. Anyone who has gone through college-level calculus will recognize the pattern. Thank the Almighty that fae cannot wrap their minds around the higher maths.

But now I sit here at my desk, staring in disbelief and horror at the deciphered document that sits on my desk. Blodheyr has lied to me. I shouldn't be surprised at this, but I am. I ignored the rumors Eliaster brought to me when I should've been listening more carefully than usual. Why did I let myself get involved? I never should have allowed Marc to go to an Overworld college—I should have told him instead that he needed to tough it out here with the rest of us.

I can't fool even myself.

This document tells me the location of a relic that has been hidden from the Unseelie for decades. If they get hold of it, I shudder to think what they could accomplish with it.

I will burn my translation. I want to speak to a few people I know...maybe I can gather some knowledge of Blodheyr's plans, enough that Counselor Tyrone or one of the other Seelie leaders will listen to me. Blodheyr must be stopped from gaining this relic.

I flipped to the second page. It just held a short list of names.

Before I could speak, Eliaster said, "I looked at it already. I helped Aiden make that list."

"Why?"

"Because something's going down, and I thought he had a good shot at getting people to pay attention to it. Better than me, anyway."

I scanned the names. "So who are they, anyway?"

"Most of them are informants for the Seelie council members, either drifters—fae unaffiliated with a court—or Unseelie traitors. If any Unseelie got that list, half the world would be at war in less than a day."

What was I getting myself into? I rustled the pages to hide my growing discomfort. "So, what are we going to do now?"

"We're going to visit him." Without looking, Eliaster reached over and stabbed at one of the names on the list. *Angel.* "See what he can tell us. After that, we're going somewhere safe where you can work on the cipher in relative peace and comfort."

My phone beeped. I pulled it from my hip pocket and

glanced at the screen. A text from my sister popped up on the black background. *Mom & Dad told me 'bout break-in. U OK?*

I texted back. *Fine. Not a big deal. Bit busy, talk later, OK?*

'K.

"Who was that?" Eliaster asked.

"My sister."

"Don't tell her anything."

"No duh." I started to shove the phone back into my pocket, then hesitated. "Should we—you know—call Marc's family? His mom and sisters have to be worried sick."

"Already done."

Okay then. It was probably better they'd heard it from Eliaster than me, anyway. Knowing Marc's mom, she'd probably be even more worried if she knew how deeply involved I was.

We wound through Springfield and soon found ourselves on the east side. I scrunched down in my seat. This wasn't a good area of town, and no one in their right mind came here who didn't belong here.

"What are you doing?" Eliaster demanded. "Sit up before your spine breaks."

"No thanks. The last thing I want is to die from some gangster's wild shot."

Eliaster rolled his eyes. "There's a reason I drove this here instead of one of my more bland vehicles. People here know this car. They won't bother us."

I chewed the inside of my lip. What kind of person was known to an area like this?

We came to a stop, and I peered over the edge of the window. A strip mall sat in a parking lot across the street. Two of the four spaces were empty, and the other two looked like pawn shops, though it was hard to tell with the grimy windows. Paint had chipped from one corner of the cinder-block building, and grass grew in the cracks in the sidewalk.

Eliaster turned to me. "Angel's not fond of new people.

Try not to antagonize him—if that's possible for you."

I waited, but he pushed open his door. Apparently, that was all I was going to get. "How about giving me ideas on how to avoid antagonizing him?"

"Okay, here's one. Don't talk."

Eliaster got out of the car and I followed carefully. A few cars rolled by and one or two people strolled along the sidewalks. So far, everyone seemed to be ignoring us.

We had parked in front of a tall concrete-block building fronted with large metal garage doors. Now that I was out of the car, I could hear music—something with a loud, thumping beat and screaming guitar riffs—pounding from inside the building.

Eliaster punched in a code at the side of the building, and reached down and rolled one of the doors up. He ducked inside and motioned in me after him.

Inside, the music, mostly bass and drums now, was deafening. I clamped my hands over my ears. Bright, bare fluorescent lights hung from the ceiling above us. Directly in front of me were stairs leading up to a grate-floored loft that held a bed, desk, and a couple of bookshelves. A small kitchen area sat on the far wall, and underneath the stairs sat exercise machines—a weight bench, a treadmill and a bicycle. In between the exercise machines and the kitchen sat a cluster of four motorcycles, one of which had its engine strewn over the floor intermingled with greasy rags and tools.

Eliaster grabbed my arm and pulled me around the stairs to a better view of the exercise area. A man was doing pullups on a bar attached to the underside of the loft, hidden before by the stairs. His tattoos caught my attention—white ink on pure black skin, a graceful pair of wings that arched from his shoulders and upper arms to the waistband of his gym shorts. Each feather was outlined in incredible detail.

"Angel!" Eliaster yelled.

The guy dropped to the floor and spun around, grabbing a pistol that sat on top of a t-shirt.

I ducked behind Eliaster.

Eliaster held out his hands. "Whoa, whoa, it's me!"

For a second, the man stared at him, his eyes narrowed. Then he straightened and, pulling a remote from the pocket of his shorts, turned off the music. The silence seemed to ring in the empty space.

I lowered my hands from my ears.

"Eli," the dark-haired man said, grabbing a towel from the floor and wiping his face. He shot an annoyed glance at me. "Who's the newbie?"

"Josh." Eliaster jerked his head at me. "Meet Angel."

"I thought we had an agreement." Angel brushed past us to the kitchen area and grabbed a shirt from the counter.

"How long ago did Marc's dad talk to you?" I asked.

Eliaster elbowed me.

Angel glared at me before pulling his shirt over his head. "You're going after the relic."

Eliaster nodded.

"Are you going to talk to the curators?" he asked.

Eliaster shook his head. "Not unless I have to."

Angel crossed his arms and leaned back against the kitchen counter. Eliaster shifted his weight from foot to foot. For a moment, they just eyed each other, both tense.

Angel shook his head. "You should know better than to drag an Overworlder into this, Eliaster."

Eliaster shrugged. "We need him."

"For the cipher? You really think he can solve it for you?" Angel gave a half-chuckle, half derisive snort. "Look at him, Eliaster. He's scrawny, he jumps at the smallest thing. He's not gonna survive a day in the Underworld."

Excuse me? I opened my mouth.

Eliaster turned on me. "No you don't."

I stepped back and ducked, avoiding his hand. "Angel. You have a thing for fours, don't you?"

Angel's eyes narrowed. "Yeah, sure, kid."

I looked at the floor, letting mental pictures roll into my brain. "Four pieces of furniture in the loft—two bookshelves, desk, and bed. Four pieces of exercise equipment—treadmill, pullup bar, weight bench, bicycle. Four motorycles."

"That's easy. What's my password for the door?"

I thought back, trying to remember the tone of the buttons Eliaster had pushed. "Four-zero-nine-six. Still a progression of four—eight to the power of four."

Angel grunted, opened a cabinet, and pulled out a bag of coffee. "Not bad. You might get that cipher solved after all."

Eliaster rolled his eyes at me. "Can you tell us anything about the relic it points to?"

Angel's bare foot slapped a soft jig on the concrete floor as he measured out the coffee grounds and put it into his machine. He put everything away and turned to us, his dark eyes averted. "There have been…rumors."

Eliaster lifted his chin. "Yeah?"

"Nothing concrete. They say that *Fear Doirich Lucht Leanúna* are rising again. They're after a relic."

A faint flush rose to the back of Eliaster's neck. "The Lucht Leanúna? Are you sure?"

"The what?" I asked.

Eliaster scratched the back of his neck. Angel clenched his hands around the edges of the counter, his foot still tapping—*one-two-three-four-pause-one-two-three-four-pause*.

The coffee machine gurgled.

Eliaster jerked his head in a nod. "Thanks for the help."

Angel's foot stopped tapping. He turned his back on us and reached to open another cabinet. "Wish I could do more."

Eliaster shrugged and motioned for us to head to the door. He pulled open the garage door, and we slid underneath. Outside, the street was completely deserted.

I waited until we were in the car and driving away to ask again. "What was that Angel mentioned? The Lucht Leanúna? Sounds like some Gaelic tongue-twister."

Eliaster grunted. "Let me think, Josh."

"But—"

"Seriously. Shut up."

chapter 7

The car ran smoothly, so I was left to the clamor of my own thoughts as Eliaster wove in and out of the increasingly-busy Springfield traffic.

Maybe I shouldn't have run when I heard the police knock on my door. But what else was I supposed to do? The fae that had tagged along seemed prepared to kill, and I'd bet it wasn't me they were going to kill. By running, I'd probably prevented those detectives' deaths. That would have brought up a million more complications than simply disappearing.

I'd have to go back sometime and sort it out. I wasn't going to stay in the Underworld forever, despite what Eliaster seemed to be hinting. Maybe after I finished the cipher I could lie low for a bit, pretend I couldn't see the true forms of the Sidhé…

I snorted. Eliaster glanced at me, but I ignored him.

Why did I have to be the one who decoded the cipher? Surely the fae's resources weren't that limited. For Blodheyr, it was probably a matter of convenience—Marc wasn't doing a satisfactory job, but one of his friends had the perfect for it and would probably require very little persuasion. Eliaster's reasons probably weren't that much different.

I glanced at him out of the corner of my eye. The fae's

jaw was set as he shifted gears of the car, driving slowly through an upscale business section of Springfield. His eyes were a flat, perfect emerald green, no sign of the d'anam fuinneog. I'd only caught quick glimpses of it from him, not like Marc or Larae's prolonged, flickering eye-colors at all. My nausea was barely noticeable, but at the same time, I couldn't relax. Deep down, in the same part of me that had remained calm and controlled even at the wrong end of Goldtooth's gun, there was something about Eliaster that kept me wary.

Eliaster flipped the blinker on. I sat up as we pulled into a tan parking garage and followed the yellow arrows to a subterranean level. Only a few cars were parked in the long stretch of concrete rows.

Eliaster got out of the car and popped open the trunk.

I gave another glance at Aiden's notes as I got out of the car. "Where are we going?"

"Somewhere safe. You'll decipher the document, and maybe that will be enough to convince my dad Aiden was being serious. Obviously his evidence wasn't enough the first time around." Eliaster hefted a duffel bag out of the trunk and slung it over his shoulder.

"Who's your dad?" I ran through the notes.

"Counselor Tyrone."

"Counselor," I said under my breath. "Okay. Sounds important."

Eliaster growled. "Unfortunately, yes. C'mon."

The elf dude had super-hearing. Right. Of course. I scanned the garage. The only exit was the ramp we'd just come down, though I supposed a door could have been hidden from my line of sight by one of the thick concrete support pillars that dotted the level.

Eliaster walked to the wall and opened a breaker box. Instead of switches, the inside of the box had a flat black screen, similar to a turned-off computer screen. Eliaster pushed his hand against it, and the blackness moved like mist, engulfing his hand up to the wrist.

The wall shivered, and a section soundlessly wheeled open, creating a gap large enough for a Hummer to squeeze through. I stepped back, my jaw hanging loose. A tunnel stretched out behind the wall, snaked with dripping pipes and thick electrical cables, lit by glass globes hanging from the ceiling. A musty, wet smell wafted out of the tunnel, and a cool, damp breeze brushed my face.

Eliaster started down the tunnel. I jogged after him. The door wheeled shut almost on my heels.

It didn't look or smell as bad as I anticipated. I caught the occasional scummy drip of water in my hair, but other than that, the interior of the tunnel smelled like a mix of a cave and the ocean. Salty and musty. Not as bad a combination as I might have thought. Eliaster strode several paces in front of me, hands jammed in the pockets of his black leather jacket, shoulders hunched.

I tried not to snort. He looked like the broody lead in some teeny-bopper drama movie.

Eventually our tunnel expanded as other small tunnels converged. It became crowded. If I ignored the pointy ears and glamour-ghosts of everyone around us, I could imagine I was back on an Overworld street. The jeans, boots, jackets, and t-shirts all looked surreally familiar. Even the occasional trench coat, robes, or all-leather could be explained away.

The other creatures made it impossible. A few trolls, similar to Scyrril with their scaly skin and bony protrusions along the back of their skulls. One or two mangy cat-like creatures scuttled in and out of the crowd, sometimes on all fours and sometimes on their hind legs. A small group of beings with thick-set bodies, papery skin, mashed facial features, and little hair walked apart from everyone else, darting their round eyes back and forth among the crowd.

Eliaster elbowed me in the gut. "Stop staring. You're the freak around here."

"It looks like a comic convention," I whispered.

He glared. "Don't say that to anyone, or you'll get your head knocked off."

"You Sidhé are very fond of threatening things like that."

He rolled his eyes and kept walking.

"So..." I jerked my head at the parchment-skinned beings. "What are they?"

"Goblins." Eliaster brought one hand out of his pocket and used his thumb to gesture to one of the cat-like creatures. "Those are..."

"*Cat-sidhé*," I said. "Type of goblin, right?"

Eliaster nodded approvingly. "You did your homework, Genius Boy."

Well, I hadn't stayed up for two extra hours this morning for nothing, at least. "Please don't call me that."

"So, do you know what a *faoladh* is? Selkie? *Droch fhola*?"

The last phrase caught my attention. "Drok-o-la? Oh please, don't tell me you have bloodsuckers. If the word gets out, every teenage girl for miles around is going to flock to the Underworld in hopes of finding an undead boyfriend."

Eliaster's grin had a nasty edge. "I don't think they'd like it if they found one. Droch fhola are monsters, plain and simple. Though lucky for you, there hasn't been one sighted since before Bram Stoker's lifetime."

"Charming."

We rounded the corner and I stopped, staring at the sight spread out in front of me. We'd stepped into an enormous cavern—it seemed like it went on forever under the glow of enormous orange globes hanging from the fifty-foot ceiling. Thick cables and pipes crawled up the walls and looped across the ceiling, stalactites dripping from them. Houses shot up between rambling, non-linear streets paved in a variety of things—cobbles, wood scraps, tarmac, and dirt.

"Whoa," I muttered. *This is amazing.*

Eliaster looked at me like I'd grown horns—or whatever the fae metaphor for that look was, since horns probably weren't all that strange to him.

I followed him in a kind of daze, craning my neck as I stared around me. It was so weird to see normal houses of all types, ranging from cottages to castles, stuffed into a cavern that could have given the Son Doong a run for its money. Thankfully we didn't have far to go, just a turn or two on an extremely winding street—if I'd been in top form I probably would have made a sarcastic comment about it.

"So," I said, turning my attention back to Eliaster. "I may not have found out about different types of Sidhé, but I did discover a few things. For example, does salt really work to repel you guys?"

He snorted. "Yeah, and we flock to people who set out bowls of cream. Does this look like *The Elves and the Shoemaker* to you?"

"Excuse me for only finding out about all this stuff yesterday, Mister Snark." I sighed. "Okay, what about iron?"

"Now that is real. If it touches full fae, it makes us sick and weak, and if it cuts us, it burns like hellfire. In general, though, the ancient legends got more twisted up in the telling and translating. I wouldn't rely on those as your single source of info."

I rubbed my fingers against my palms. "So, crows aren't considered evil omens?"

Eliaster stopped dead in the middle of the street and turned to me. "Okay, what did you say? And who did you say it to?"

"I may have told Goldtooth to go to the crows."

"I'm not sure if I should tell you that was one of the stupidest things you could do, or if I should be relieved you've got a bit of fight in you." Eliaster started walking again.

"So it's really offensive."

"Fae burn their dead. To tell someone to go to a bird that desecrates the dead by eating their flesh is offensive to the extreme. You're lucky Goldtooth had orders to take you alive, otherwise he might have stuffed his gun in your mouth and ended you right there."

I snorted and looked away, mostly to hide the unease that kept growing in my gut like one of those expanding sponge toys dropped in a glass of water.

We stopped at a big Victorian-style house painted blue and yellow. People seemed to prefer bright colors here in the Underworld—it was sandwiched between a hot pink cottage and a lime green cracker-box-shaped house. Eliaster stepped up onto the porch and knocked on the door.

Larae barreled out of the house. She planted her fists on her hips and glared at him. "What is the meaning of sneaking off without telling me? *Again*, I might add."

Eliaster rolled his eyes again—it seemed to be his automatic response to anything and anyone—and tried to edge around her.

"Not this time, Eliaster." She poked him in the chest with a long manicured fingernail. "We agreed to keep each other in the loop. You broke that trust." Larae's gaze fell on me, and her lips pinched together. "And why is he here? I thought you said no Overworlders! In fact, as I recall, you threw a hissy fit about Josh getting even marginally involved."

I was going to shrivel if she kept that death-ray glare trained on me any longer. Thankfully she looked back at Eliaster, her eyes starting to flicker between a deep purple-red and a lighter violet.

"Does the word 'cipher' ring a bell?" Eliaster said. "None of us can break it. Maybe Josh can. Besides, if we didn't grab him, Blodheyr would have."

After a few more seconds of staring each other down, Larae turned and stomped back into the house. Eliaster grabbed the screen door to keep it from slamming and motioned me inside. Larae pounded her way up the stairs at the side of the entry.

The house smelled like a used bookstore—that dusty, musty, cigarette-smoke-soaked-paper scent. My shoulders relaxed a little. The front door opened into a long, thin hallway painted white and lined with framed photographs and paintings of ethereal landscapes.

At the end of the hallway, a door swung open, and a tiny lady with a fluff of platinum-silver hair stepped out, dressed in khakis, a purple blouse, and a bright-red apron. A smile broke over her wrinkled face at the sight of us.

"Hey, Roe." Eliaster gave her a big, genuine grin, and gave her an enthusiastic hug.

"Eliaster." She kissed his cheek and turned to me. "Who is your friend?"

Oh great. Little old lady kisses. "Uh, my name's Josh."

She gave me a hug. Okay, maybe the kisses were only for people she knew. I gingerly patted her shoulders.

"He's Marc's buddy. Genius Josh," Eliaster said.

Did *everyone* down here know me by that nickname? Marc's butt was getting kicked when I found him.

The woman nodded. "Marc spoke about you often. I'm his grandmother, Roe. And you all must be hungry. I was just getting lunch out of the oven." She moved to the bottom of the stairs and called up, "Larae? Lunch, dearest."

"Not hungry," Larae yelled down, her voice muffled.

The woman shrugged and headed back into the kitchen.

Instead of following her, Eliaster pushed a side door open. "We'll eat in the library. Get a head start on this cipher."

I followed Eliaster into a room with wood paneling barely visible between rows of bookcases. A couch, several overstuffed chairs, and a coffee table were drawn up in front of a fireplace about ten feet long. David, who was stretched out on the couch, twisted his head around.

"Hey, you're back. Wondered where you'd gotten off to." He levered himself up.

I sighed and collapsed into one of the overstuffed chairs by the fireplace. Eliaster dumped his duffel bags on the floor and took the chair opposite me. He kicked off his thick-soled boots and stretched his socked feet out to the fire. The firelight gleamed off a small, leaf-bladed throwing knife strapped to his ankle.

"Amazing how quiet it can be when no monsters are chasing you," Eliaster muttered.

I chuckled.

Eliaster gestured at the bookshelves. "Everything you need is there somewhere."

I glanced at them. Every shelf was stuffed to overflowing, books stacked two rows thick and papers crammed into every available inch. "Anything more specific than that?" I didn't exactly want to go digging around in a fae's private files.

"For goodness sakes, Eliaster. Let the boy relax for a few minutes." Roe elbowed the door the rest of the way open, a tray stacked with steaming sandwiches balanced on one hip.

David stood from the couch and took the tray from her.

"Thank you, David. I'll go get drinks. Coffee, anyone, or would you prefer tea or water?"

"Coffee," Eliaster and I said at the same second.

"Lots," Eliaster added.

She chuckled and left the room.

David grabbed a sandwich from the tray and gestured at me with it. "So Eliaster disappears and a few hours later, comes back with you in tow. How did you convince him to let you come?"

I shot Eliaster a glance. "He didn't really give me much choice."

"I take it you'd rather have taken on those Unseelie by yourself." Eliaster left his chair, grabbed a sandwich, and sat back down. He pulled an onion ring off the sandwich and flicked it at David.

"Hey." David picked the onion up and threw it back, clipping Eliaster's ear-point and leaving a smear of mayonnaise.

The fae's nose wrinkled and he wiped the offending glob from his ear.

Roe pushed open the door with another tray. She pressed one hand to her hip and raised her eyebrows. "Please tell me I didn't just see two grown men having a food fight in my library."

"No, ma'am," David said, grinning.

She put the tray on the coffee table and poured mugs for

all of us. "So, Eliaster, did Aiden's notes tell you anything?"

He nodded. "The coded document tells where an old fae relic might be found."

Roe tipped her head to one side as she took a sip of the coffee. "That doesn't seem within Blodheyr's normal range of interests. Is it valuable, something he could sell on the black market?"

"Oh, I'm sure it's valuable, but I don't think he'll be selling it. The Lucht Leanúna are back, and—"

Roe stiffened and her face went pale. "They're not."

"Aiden had a list of informants that, I'm assuming, he asked questions of. Angel is one of them. Before we came back here, Josh and I talked to him. He said the Lucht Leanúna wants the relic. Angel has no reason to lie to me."

"He's Unseelie."

Eliaster frowned. "Not anymore."

"I don't think your father will believe that."

Eliaster lurched upright. "I don't need my father's help with this."

I watched them stare at each other, looking like big cats ready to pounce. David looked back and forth between them, his sandwich forgotten in one hand.

"Did I miss something?" I injected as much sarcasm into my voice as possible—not hard. It was getting old for the fae to keep rambling about something I didn't understand.

Eliaster sank back into his seat with a groan. "Lucht Leanúna. The Followers."

I glanced at Roe.

She sighed. "To understand why the Lucht Leanúna are so feared, Josh, you have to understand our history. Back in the old days, the Sidhé lived in a different world. Tir N-iall, the Other Land." Her voice softened a little. "That's our true home. It's where Sidhé belong. We visited this world often—maybe too often—and grew to love it also, but never as much as we loved Tir N-iall."

Roe's voice sank into almost a singsong, as if she was reciting a story she'd heard a thousand times before. "One of the fae, Fear, learned to mask his d'anam fuinneog. He began studying the forbidden arts of sorcery, twisting his glamour to evil purposes, and learned to summon sluagh and demons to his will. He killed our king and set himself up as ruler of Tir N-iall. The land withered under him. Those who opposed him began calling him *Fear Doirich*—the Dark Man.

"And then we discovered he wasn't content with ruling Tir N-iall. He would rule all the worlds, and his next conquest would be this one. For some time, he'd been sending some of his loyal followers to earth to act as false gods. My ancestors retaliated by trying to close the paths. It wasn't easy. Fear Doirich's people fought back, and in the struggle, such great glamour was used that it destroyed all the known paths. Since that day, no one has passed between the worlds."

Roe's voice died, and she looked down into her coffee cup. David resumed eating his sandwich. Eliaster stared into the fire, gnawing at his thumbnail. I realized I was leaning forward, biting my tongue against all the questions rising in my throat. The fae had lived in another world? What had it been like? I was picturing a beautiful land, the basis for all the fantasy stories I'd ever read as a teen, full of soaring mountains and rolling plains.

Roe cleared her throat. "The Lucht Leanúna are followers of Fear Doirich that wish to find ways to open the hidden paths again, or make new paths. There used to be many of them both in the Seelie and Unseelie courts, but the two factions united and destroyed them—we thought. Every few years rumors rise again, but we've always been able to prove them just that—rumors."

"I told you," Eliaster muttered. "I told you all years ago that Blodheyr was involved in something nasty."

Roe gave him a sharp glance. "This is not a time to bring up a personal vendetta, Eliaster."

His jaw clenched. He looked back into the fire.

David grunted. "So they think this relic will...what? Help

them open a path to Tir Ni-all again?"

"Can't be," Eliaster muttered. "It would take some serious glamour to make something like that."

"So maybe something that would allow them to communicate with Tir Ni-all, then?" David rubbed his chin. "Or something that could create a new path?"

"That's impossible," Roe said sharply.

Eliaster grunted.

"So let me get this straight." I rubbed my head, trying to grasp everything I'd just learned. "In short, you just dragged me into the biggest mess in fae history."

"That might be slightly exaggerated," Roe said.

"Nah, I agree with him." David leaned back into the couch cushions. "I've more experience with fae and the Underworld than Josh, and I don't even want to be involved with this."

"But if Josh doesn't help us…" Roe pursed her lips.

I dug my fingers into my hair. Right, that was the kicker there. The more I heard about this, the more I knew I couldn't leave Marc to Blodheyr. Nor could I just walk away from the cipher and leave the fae to muddle it out on their own. If Blodheyr *was* associated with this Lucht Leanúna, then my world was in danger of being taken over by someone who rivaled Sauron.

"All right, you'd better get me the stuff for the cipher." I sighed. "But once I finish it, I'm done. Out of here. I'm perfectly happy to go back to being the oblivious hobbit who stayed in the Shire while Frodo went on the insane quest."

David clapped me on the shoulder. "Good. Get out while you can."

Eliaster and Roe shared a disbelieving look. My smile died, and I curled one hand into a fist. I would get out. I was not going to spend the rest of my life constantly looking over my shoulder like this.

Roe stood up, pulled a folder from one of the bookshelves, and handed it to me. "This is all we have."

I opened the folder. It contained a few pages of plain

printer paper. "I'll start work on it right away."

"Please do." Roe pressed her lips together. "I hope you can help us. And my grandson."

Yeah, you and me both.

chapter 8

David and Roe cleared away the coffee and sandwiches, leaving me room to spread the contents of the folder over the coffee table.

The cipher document was a half-page of numbers arranged with five numbers to a line, with the end of each number denoted by a period.

819. 263835. 23790. 690729. 2145.
23790. 426894. 23790. 312. 263835.

And so on. Some of the numbers got up into the millions.

It looked random to me, not a sign of the pattern that Aidan had written about. I scrubbed one hand through my hair. Why had Eliaster and David thought I could do this? For that matter, why had *I* thought I could do this? I was a math nerd and a hacker, not a cryptologist.

I dropped the cipher on the table and started in on the report. Within a paragraph I realized two hours of sleep wasn't going to get me through this thing.

The thing was textbook-dry, just a simple statement of the facts of where the document was found, what state it was in—even the mentions of 'traps' and 'snares' were put in the most boring way possible. Only one thing interested me—a photograph of the stone they'd broken through to excavate the document. It had a series of horizontal and vertical slashes in it. In the margin of the photo, the words '*The wise Keeper knows the fathers of Our Lord the Christ*' were written. A translation?

A snore cut through the gentle crackling of the fire.

I glanced over at Eliaster. His legs were slung over one arm of his chair, and his head dangled over the other. One arm hung off the chair and the other was tucked up, cradling his swords to his chest like a little kid would cuddle a favorite stuffed animal. He snored again.

I yawned. That was just cruel. "Eliaster."

Snoring.

"Eliaster!"

More snoring. He shuffled his body so that both arms hung over the seat of the chair. One sword hilt dug into his shoulder.

I rubbed my eyes and yawned again. He was going to make me fall asleep before long.

The door creaked open and David stepped back inside. He made a face at Eliaster, then grabbed a pillow from the couch and threw it across the room. It smacked Eliaster in the face. In a split second the fae was on his feet, one sword half-drawn.

"Hey!" I curled my feet onto the couch, ready to duck if he started swinging.

David burst out laughing.

Eliaster glared at him with red-rimmed eyes.

"Really?" He grabbed his boots and pounded from the room.

I snickered. "How does he keep from getting killed if he sleeps that heavily?"

"He doesn't."

"Doesn't what?"

"Doesn't sleep. At least, not much. Seriously, I've never seen him sleep more than an hour, and that never at night. Too paranoid one of the Unseeelie he's ticked off will try to cut his throat." David snuggled into the chair, crossed his arms over his chest, and yawned. "Unlike me, Eliaster can survive on little sleep."

The door swung open again. Larae hesitated. "Oh, I didn't know you were working already, Josh. I'll leave."

"No, it's all right."

She crossed the room, but instead of sitting on the chair that Eliaster had vacated, she flopped down on the floor next to David's chair. "Have you figured the cipher out yet?"

"He's been working on it for ten minutes, Larae," David muttered.

She elbowed his leg.

I rubbed my eyes as I picked up the papers. "And for half of that, I had a snoring fae distracting me. I'm not even sure what kind of cipher this is yet. Marc's dad said they could be recognized by anyone who had taken higher mathematics, but that still leaves a ton of possibilities." I scratched the side of my face. "I read through the report on finding the document. It had this photo with it." I handed her the picture. "Do you know what the scratches in the stone are?"

She bit her lower lip. "Ogham, looks like. Celtic runes."

"So the phrase underneath is a translation."

"I'm not very good with ogham, but that seems to be the likely conclusion." Larae rubbed her earlobe. "The fathers…like, Christ's ancestors?"

"I guess."

She stood up and pulled a leather-bound book from the shelves.

"Do you think that's the cipher key?" David asked.

"It seems fairly obvious, and usually cipher keys are a bit harder to figure out than that, but there's no other reason for that phrase to be there. If nothing else, it's a start." I blinked against the grainy feeling of my contacts and squinted up at him. "Remind me why you're not doing this again?"

"We tried. Ever since his dad died and Marc found his notes, he's had Larae, Eliaster, Roe, and me working on this. We've kept our ears to the ground, but until today we didn't know who to talk to." He chuckled. "Besides, higher mathematics, remember? I lost too many brain cells playing high school football to understand any of that stuff."

I snorted. At least he seemed more respectful than most jocks I'd come in contact with.

"Here we go," Larae said, holding the book up. "A list of Christ's ancestors in the book of Matthew. Do you know what we're looking for?"

"The cipher is in numbers, so the clue should be in numbers," I said. "How many ancestors did Christ have?"

Larae ran her finger down the page, muttering under her breath. "Thirty-nine."

Bingo. Cipher key accessed.

"Is this really going to help?"

I ignored her. Okay. I stared at the page, absorbing the numbers into my brain as my mind wandered. No thirty-nine. What was this supposed to be, then? Maybe the phrase wasn't the clue. But if it wasn't, what was? How was I supposed to find it? Maybe the number thirty-nine was a clue that would lead me to another clue, which would lead to another... which would make this entire thing far too Indiana-Jones-like.

Fae were supposed to like riddles and games, right? Not ciphers and insane adventures. I swore under my breath.

At the top of the page, I deconstructed the second number down to single digits. Two. Six. Three. Eight. Three. Five. Two-hundred sixty-three thousand, eight-hundred thirty-five. Big number.

All the numbers made me think of Angel and his obsession with fours. What made a person think that one number was lucky, or better, than the others?

I scribbled *thirty-nine* on the page in the upper left-hand corner, then in the opposite corner wrote *Angel*. Keeping track of my thought process always helped, no matter how tangential the thought.

If thirty-nine was the beginning of the cipher, it would correspond with the letter *A*. In most ciphers, the vowels were left out, so what I really needed was the number for the letter *B*. How to get that number?

On a whim, I divided thirty-nine by four. Nine point seven five. Nothing there.

Larae's voice snapped my concentration. "This isn't going to help, is it?"

I glanced at her. Her lips were pressed tightly together, quivering, and she clenched her hands together in her lap like she expected a lifeline to be between her fingers.

"It might," I said.

"But it didn't. It wasn't the key, was it?"

"I don't know yet."

"I don't want to sit around waiting," she muttered.

"Give it time," I said. "There are probably a million different ways I could take this."

"What about a computer program to decipher this? Couldn't you—"

"First I have to know what kind of cipher it is," I told her. "You're just going to have to be patient with me for a bit."

She pressed a hand to her mouth. "I know, I just…Blodheyr could be torturing Marc right now. I've seen that, Josh. Marc could even be dead."

I cringed, and my gut turned. I shifted and reached out, carefully patting Larae's shoulder. "I know it sounds weird, but take comfort in the thought that Marc's probably too valuable for Blodheyr to kill."

"Just yet, anyway," David said.

Larae smiled at me and grasped my hand, meeting my eyes. "Thank you for saying that, Josh. But I still can't just sit here. I just have to feel like I'm some good, you know?"

She was hanging onto my hand way too long. I dropped my gaze and eased my fingers free.

"What do you think we should do?" David asked.

"I don't know." She looked around the room, then snatched the list of Aiden's informants from the coffee table. "Has Eliaster talked to any of these guys yet? Maybe one of them will have heard something."

"Just Angel," I said.

"Maybe I should go talk to the others, then," she said.

David frowned. "I don't think that's a good idea. Those are Eliaster's informants."

"Since when do I care?" Larae stood up.

"You just going to make him ma—"

She slammed the door behind her before David could complete the sentence.

He sighed again and stood. "If I can't talk her out of it, tell Eliaster where we went, all right?"

I nodded. "I'll keep working. That phrase had to be the key somehow."

David left the library, and I heard his voice start up again in the hallway.

I sighed and slumped into the couch. This was going to be a very long day. I let my brain go blank and just stared, slowly memorizing the entire cipher.

The front door creaked, and I heard two sets of steps on the porch. So they were going somewhere.

Another set of steps in the hallway caught my ears. I stood up and opened the library door. Eliaster stood at the foot of the stairs, watching out one of the door's side windows as David and Larae walked away.

"Where are they going?" he asked.

"To talk to some of the other informants on Aiden's list. I don't think she has much faith in my ability to decipher the document. And really, I'm not sure—"

"Back in a second." Eliaster spun and took the stairs two at a time.

I pulled the green-checked window curtain back into place. As I did so, I noticed a rim of black around the inside of the window casing, closest to the glass. Mold? That didn't fit the cleanliness of the rest of the house. Paint, maybe? I tapped the line with a fingernail. No, it was metal.

Eliaster came down the stairs again, sat on the bottom step, and started pulling on his boots.

"Where are you going?"

"To follow them."

"Really? Come on, Eliaster, you guys are on the same team. Shouldn't you trust them to be able to do their jobs?"

"It's doing their job I'm worried about." He stood up and started buckling his swords around his waist.

I glanced at the door. I knew I should be working on the cipher more, but I was already stuck to the point of becoming frustrated. Maybe if I went with them, and we talked to some of the informants together, I'd hear something that could jog my mind and help me with the cipher.

Eliaster caught my eyes as he opened the door. "Stay."

I rolled my eyes "Dude, do I look like a puppy?"

Eliaster stared at me for a moment, his eyes narrow. "Don't you have a cipher to be working on?"

I tapped my head. "It's memorized, and I'm stuck."

He rubbed his forehead, muttering under his breath in Gaelic.

"If I can talk to some of these guys, I might find out some stuff to help with the document. Clues as to what kind of cipher they used, that sort of thing. Aiden wouldn't have—"

"All right, fine, come with me. But you have to do exactly what I say, all right? No goofing off, no wandering away by yourself."

I grinned, trying to look innocent. "What makes you think I would do that?"

He shot me an *oh, please*, look and grabbed a backpack that sat on the lowest stair. As he left the house, he rubbed his hand along the hilt of his left-hand sword.

This time, I paid a little more attention to the winding streets, keeping a careful track of the twists and turns that led back to Roe's place. The high cavern ceiling was illuminated by the hanging orange globes, casting a sunset glaze over everything.

The streets were not as busy around what I guessed was the residential area. As we turned off onto a wider road, the sidewalks became more crowded. A few motorcycles and mopeds buzzed by, leaving a trail of dust in their wake, but I didn't see a single car, even a small one.

The Market was located in a huge open area about a fifteen-minute walk from Roe's house. Tall wooden gates separated it from the houses and buildings outside. As we stepped inside those gates, I had to do some fancy footwork to avoid tripping over my own jaw. The place was huge. I'd never seen anywhere so full of noise, chaos, and color. Everywhere I looked there were fae, pushing and crowding each other through the narrow, twisted paths between vendor booths and tents. Women in long skirts, men in robes, men and women in leather pants, jeans, t-shirts, vests, duster-length coats, tanktops, Converses, high heels, heavy-soled boots—every fashion imaginable mixed into one giant melting pot.

My vision blurred, and I stopped walking, wondering if my contacts were going haywire on me again. When I squinted, I realized that it was the glamour ghosts of everyone's faces, turning everything into a fuzzy watercolor, even the lights and bright fabrics of the Market tents.

Even as amazing as it all was, as soon as I realized I was surrounded by fae, my shoulders tensed and my gut started turning. I clenched my hands and found my palms sweaty. No one touched me as they walked by, but I still felt closed in. Panic swelled in my throat. I took a very deep, deliberate breath, then slowly let it out.

Eliaster put his hand on my shoulder. "You doing okay?"

I nodded, not trusting my voice.

He squinted at my face for a moment, frowning. "You're pale."

"Says the guy who lives underground."

"Come over here for a second."

He pulled me to the side, dodging an amorous fae couple who'd apparently decided that the middle of the road was as good a place for a make-out session as any. Eliaster stopped at a clear space near the gate. There were no fae within five feet of us. The panic died down, even though I still felt like puking.

"You're not from a curator family, are you?" Eliaster

asked, scanning the crowd.

Blodheyr had asked the same thing. "What's that supposed to mean, anyway?"

"Most humans have a severe fight or flight reaction when they're around Sidhé. Kept them safe, I guess, especially back when the paths were open and Sidhé glamour was stronger. Curators are the members of certain Irish-descended families who don't have that reaction. They used to fight side by side with the Seelie, especially in our efforts to repulse Fear Doirich, but lately they're more scholars."

"Of—"

Eliaster stiffened, and he lifted his chin. I followed his gaze and spotted David and Larae disappearing into the thick of the Market.

"They must have stopped on the way here." Eliaster jogged forward, shoving between two dark-skinned fae.

I skirted around them, offering an apologetic smile at their grumbling, and ran after him. David and Larae, both dressed in dark jeans and t-shirts, easily blended into the crowd. If I'd tried to follow them on my own, there's no way I could have kept track of them.

We speed-walked through streets lined with booths clustered shoulder to shoulder and hung with colored cloth, signs, wares, and garish Christmas lights. Some were the size of a Wal-Mart Supercenter, others barely as big as my dorm room.

Hawkers jumped and pranced in front of their booths, their hoarse voices adding to the chaos: "Freshly slaughtered buffalo steaks here!" "No better electronics than mine!" "Weapons, swords, knives, shotguns, pistols—all here!" I could smell the tang of the blood on the buffalo steaks, mixing with the heady perfumes of the lace-draped booth next door. Gunpowder from the weapons booth gave an acrid undertone to the dust raised by hundreds of feet.

I stopped in front of the weapons booth, ogling the broadswords, scimitars, and rapiers laid in shiny rows on the tables.

Eliaster pulled me after him. "Uh-uh. The last thing I need is you lopping off your own head with one of those things."

To one side of the weapons booth, a group of fae clad in black leather stood around one of their number, who was swinging a huge broadsword over his head. I stumbled over a chain dragging in the packed-down dirt street, nearly knocking over a group of raggedly dressed people—humans and fae. A whip-wielding troll shoved them along. The monster snarled as I passed, making me jump.

"Slaves?" I whispered to Eliaster.

"In some ways, the Underworld typifies the darkest of the human world. There's not as much room for a glossy veneer here as there is…" He jerked his head upward.

Two guys on a street corner caught my eye next. One of them, a human with black dreadlocks, was handing off a package of white powder to a nervous, twitching fae. When they saw me staring, the dealer put his hand on the butt of a pistol protruding from his waistband.

"Don't look too curious." Eliaster guided me to the opposite side of the street.

"What about law enforcement?"

He barked a short laugh. "My dad and his kind are about the only type of law enforcement you're going to find around here. From what I understand, they tried implementing some patrols and policing, but there was enough opposition even among the Seelie that any effort was quickly dismantled."

We stopped beside a bright yellow-and-red tent that had the sides folded up, revealing tables packed with a random assortment of clothing, shoes, backpacks and bags, and personal care stuff like deodorant and toothpaste.

"They went in there? Why would they go in there?" I asked.

"Sometimes informants are extremely paranoid. I've had to meet in all sorts of crazy places—there was one guy who wanted to meet in the paper products section of the local Wal-Mart." His lips twitched into a thin smile. "*That* was an adventure."

Oh-kay. I followed him inside the tent. The interior was dingy white canvas, light provided by thousands of white Christmas lights strung along the ceiling. Chairs and tables crowded the inner part of the tent, and a long wooden bar ran along the far side of the tent, backed by ice chests and racks of bottles. I could smell the alcohol from the entrance. Shop and drink at the same time. Handy.

Fae and humans were packed into the space. I saw a half-dozen illegal-looking deals as Eliaster and I wove our way to the bar, though I pretended to not notice. The fae girl behind the counter flicked her long hair over one shoulder, smiled at us, and pulled two glasses from under the bar.

Eliaster waved them away.

The girl pushed her lips into a pout. "You sure? Two fine lookin' men like—"

"We're just here looking for a couple of friends. David North and Larae Ó Dáleigh?"

The girl sighed and replaced the glasses under the counter. "Larae went straight through and out the back." She nodded at a doorway on her right. "David's still in here, as far as I know."

I looked over my shoulder at the tall rows of shelving. He could be anywhere in there. I rubbed my forehead. "Sheesh."

Eliaster grabbed my elbow and steered me out the back door. "You stay here. I'm going to circle around and see if I can pick up the trail in the back."

"I thought you didn't want me by myself."

Eliaster gnawed one side of his lower lip, glancing over his shoulder at the street beside us.

I shook my head. "Seriously? I was joking. Go find her, if that will make you feel better."

He shuffled his feet, like he was ready to take off but couldn't quite make himself go. "I know, but...I need to know what they're up to, both of them, but you're right, I shouldn't leave you by yourself..."

The press of people in the street cleared for a moment,

and I saw Larae talking to a vendor on the other side of the street.

Eliaster groaned. "Just stay there. It will take me all of a minute and you'll slow me down." He ducked into the crowd.

I shuffled my feet, watching the streams of fae and human as they moved past the tent. No one approached me or even looked at me, but I still felt antsy. Why had Eliaster been so torn over leaving me alone? It wasn't like I was a toddler and would wander off.

A hand tapped my shoulder. I yelped and nearly tripped over my own feet as I whirled around. David stood in the alleyway between the two tents, grinning.

"What are you doing?" I hissed.

"C'mon. You don't think I can tell when people are tailing me?" He pulled me into the alley. "I know what Eliaster is trying to do. He's trying to buddy up to you, make you think there's something weird about Larae and me. He's over-paranoid—always has been, always will be."

I frowned. So far it sounded like David was the one trying to buddy up. "Okay, why are you telling me this?"

"I want you to understand I'm not doing anything weird. You and I are humans—not fae, not even curators. We need to stick together. The fae don't care what happens to us as long as it furthers their own agendas." David glanced behind me. "So, are we good?"

I crossed my arms over my chest.

"Look, I just want you to avoid what happened to me when I was a newbie. It wasn't pretty."

He sounded truthful enough, and what he said made sense. Still...

He looked at my empty hands. "Eliaster didn't even leave you with a weapon? Yeah, he sure cares about what happens to you."

I jutted my jaw forward. "He said he'd be right back."

"Don't defend the idiot." David reached under the hem of his t-shirt and pulled a pistol from a concealed holster. "You ever shoot a pistol?"

"I grew up in the redneck capital of the world. Of course I've shot a pistol." Once, but he didn't need to know that.

David chambered a round and handed the gun to me. "Good. I'll see you around." He pushed past me and disappeared into the crowd.

Okay, David, I'll play. Human against fae, we can do that. This place would have to be pretty terrible if I couldn't trust another human. I crossed my arms again and tucked the gun close to my side, careful to keep my finger off the trigger.

A couple of fae approached the tent entrance, talking back and forth in Gaelic. One wore a bandolier of knives over his white t-shirt, his hair buzzed short on the sides but with long bangs that covered his left eye. The other wore a black vest, exposing the Celtic whorl and knot tattoos covering his arms and torso.

Tattoos elbowed his buddy and nodded to me. "Look at that, Ghurdan. The little mud-boy thinks he's all tough."

I stepped back, making sure I was well out of their way, and looked away. Maybe if I didn't acknowledge the jab, they'd leave me alone.

One of them stepped closer and shoved me away from the tent. The hope popped like a soap bubble.

I turned around and held my hands up, making sure to keep a tight grip on the pistol. "Look, I'm just waiting for someone. I don't want any trouble." *Nice clichéd line, Josh.*

Ghurdan mimicked me. "He doesn't want any trouble, Llew. If you don't want any trouble, mud boy, go back up to the Overworld where you belong."

I glanced around the street. Everyone was completely ignoring the two fae. Neither David nor Eliaster was in sight. Llew grabbed my shirt and yanked me nose to nose with him. I slammed the pistol into his gut, using it to shove him away.

He let go, huffing out a sharp breath.

I stepped back, raising the pistol with both hands. "Stay away from me." *Yeah, another cliché. How much you wanna bet he's not gonna listen to this one either?*

Ghurdan drew a dagger from his bandolier and licked it. The piercing in his tongue grated against the blade.

Llew flicked his bangs out of his eye and reached down to his side, drawing my attention to the sword he wore. I groaned and clicked the safety off the gun. Before I could move my finger to the trigger, Llew drew his sword and slammed the blade into the pistol. The gun snapped from my hands. My fingers went numb. Llew grabbed my shirt again and pressed the edge of the sword into my throat.

I grabbed his wrists and squeezed as tight as I could. His grip relaxed a bit, but not enough that I could pull free. "What did I do to you?" I demanded.

"Llew!" Eliaster shouted from behind us.

The fae spun, dragging me along with him. I stumbled. He yanked me to my feet, my shirt twisting around my neck. He moved the sword from my neck to my exposed stomach. The cold edge sent a shiver down my spine.

Eliaster closed a hand over the hilt of one of his swords. "Answer his question. What did he do to you?"

"Should've known you'd be along to save the pretty little Overworlder, just like you always do." Llew spat.

Spittle sprayed the side of my face. The pulse in my neck hammered, fighting against the tightened shirt neck.

Eliaster lowered his head. His voice deepened to a snarl. "Answer the question, Unseelie."

"You draw on us, and I'll take your head, stuff it, and use it as a paperweight," Ghurdan said.

"Ha. Get in the back of a very long line, crow-bait."

Ghurdan took a step forward. Llew moved his sword from my belly to in front of his friend, holding Ghurdan back.

I punched my elbow as hard as I could into Llew's diaphragm.

The fae grunted and crumpled. Ghurdan roared and sliced at me with his dagger. I jumped back, tripping over the rough ground. Eliaster dove forward, smacking Ghurdan in the side with his sword. It knocked him several steps away from me.

Llew scrambled to his feet, and the two Unseelie circled Eliaster, who calmly straightened and drew his second sword. Ghurdan and Llew both lunged at the same time, dagger and sword coming in at opposite sides.

In one fluid motion, Eliaster ducked Llew's sword, dropped to one hand, and spun, taking out Ghurdan's legs. Ghurdan landed flat on his back, his head thumping into the dirt street. Llew sliced downward. Eliaster parried and rolled onto his feet out of Llew's reach.

The Unseelie pressed forward. Steel on steel rang over the Market noise. Llew pushed Eliaster further out into the street. The pedestrians calmly stepped out of their way. Some continued on, and some stopped to watch. The two fae broke apart and circled for a brief second, then dove at each other again.

Ghurdan staggered to his feet and drew another dagger. He pulled his arm back.

"Eliaster!" I yelled. I dropped to my hands and knees, feeling along the ground for the pistol.

A *thwick* jerked my attention back to the fight. Ghurdan dropped in a pouf of dust, Eliaster's sword sticking halfway out of his shoulder. He curled onto his side, teeth bared, eyes screwed shut in pain.

Llew glanced over his shoulder. His swing faltered. "Ghurdan!"

Eliaster slammed the flat of his blade into Llew's knees. Llew dropped to the ground. Eliaster kicked him in the chest, and Llew rolled close to his friend.

Eliaster's hands shook as he grabbed Llew's hair and jerked him to his knees. He shoved his face close to Llew's, teeth bared. "Don't come near me again." He let go and stepped back, pulling his sword from Ghurdan's body. Ghurdan's eyes flew open and he screamed. Blood gushed from his now-open wound.

I looked away, tasting bile at the back of my throat.

"Come on, Josh."

I left David's pistol lying in the dirt and scrambled after

Eliaster. He shoved his swords in the sheaths and walked away. I glanced over my shoulder. Llew was crouching beside his friend, pressing his hand over Ghurdan's. He looked up, and even from that distance, I could see the murderous rage burning in his eyes as he stared at Eliaster.

We slid down a narrow passageway between two tents and emerged in another dirt street. Eliaster glanced up and down. There was no one around. He stopped and rubbed his face, smearing streaks of dirt over his cheeks. Light green spikes of color gleamed in his eyes.

"Are you all right?" I asked.

"Yeah." Eliaster reached for the silver cross around his neck. He bent his head and pressed his hand with the cross in it to his lips. His fingers trembled.

I stepped back, and my legs nearly buckled from under me. I looked down at my own hands. They were shaking as well. My pulse still throbbed loudly in my head, and I felt cold. I reached up and rubbed my neck. The skin felt raw where Llew had twisted my t-shirt tight.

"Who were they?" I asked.

Eliaster straightened. "Couple of Unseelie thugs who have it in for me."

"What do they have to do with—"

"As far as I know? Nothing." He dropped the necklace back underneath his shirt and started walking again.

I caught up with him. This time, instead of pulling ahead and letting me follow him, Eliaster stuck close to my side. As we got to a busier area, and people crowded us from every side, one of his hands strayed to his sword hilt.

After a few minutes, I said, "If those Unseelie are after you—"

"Then they attacked you to get to me," Eliaster said quietly. "I know. Trust me, you're still safer with me around."

I was beginning to doubt that. *Is David right?* I blew out a deep breath. For now, I had to stick with him, because it was the only way to find Marc.

We reached an intersection with a big purple tent on one

corner. I recognized it from earlier. Rather than head back toward the Market gate, however, Eliaster turned and headed back, deeper into the Market.

I jogged after him. "Where are we heading now? Back to Roe's?"

Eliaster shook his head. "No. Time for you to really learn what being part of the Underworld means. Time to get you a sword."

chapter 9

A sword?

Man, would it be cool. For a split second, I let myself imagine wielding a slick metal weapon, kicking, flipping, and bloodlessly beheading a hundred baddies. *More like you'd be the one getting beheaded, idiot. You've seen too many cheesy kung-fu flicks.*

The image of Ghurdan slumped on the ground with a sword sticking out of his back popped into my mind. My gut turned. I shook my head. This wasn't a good idea. I'd end up cutting off my own head or something equally stupid, just like he'd said a while ago.

"Are you coming?"

I looked up and realized I'd stopped in the middle of the street. A few fae stepped around me. Eliaster stood on the edge of the street, glaring at me. I hurried over to him, and he started off, again staying by my side.

"I don't need a sword. I'm not going to be doing any fighting."

"Right, like you did back there?"

I groaned. "Why a sword? Can't I just have a gun?"

"Speaking of, who gave that to you?"

"David."

Eliaster growled. "He should know better. As for why you need a sword rather than a gun, most fae carry swords. Even if they carry guns, they tend to reach for a sword first. You'd blend in much better carrying a sword. Plus, as Llew demonstrated, swords are much better in close combat. Therefore, you need a sword."

"Oh," I muttered.

Eliaster quickened his steps until he was walking several paces ahead of me, as usual.

As we reached the heart of the Market, I noticed more and more permanent buildings—most just a simple wooden frame with roll-down canvas sides, but there were a few dingy brick buildings and one bar that looked like it had been cobbled together from scraps of corrugated metal and steel beams. This place looked worse than a refugee camp—but, if Eliaster had told me the truth, the fae were the original refugees.

Eliaster ducked down an empty side street, then paused outside an open-sided building with scraps of metal cluttering the tables within. A fire framed in a brick oven-like structure crackled, throwing shifting shadows over the interior of the building. The light flickered off the dull, dark metal of an anvil sitting in front of the fireplace. The back of the building was closed off, and a door was set to the right of the fireplace.

Eliaster pounded his fist against one of the wooden supports. "Opti! Are you here?"

The door swung open, and a tall, heavily-muscled man with hair that stuck out in every direction poked his head out. He grinned. "Eliaster!"

Eliaster started to step inside the shop and stumbled. He jerked away. "Where is it this time?"

Opti pointed into the rafters. I looked up and could make out the faint glimmers of a chain hanging around the perimeter of the building.

Eliaster sighed. ""Josh, meet Opti—one of the best swordsmiths around, even for being only half-fae."

Opti nodded in acknowledgment of the introduction, but stayed beside the door. "What can I do for you, Eli?"

Eliaster nudged me in the side. "Josh needs a sword."

Opti looked me up and down. His eyebrows drew together, a deep U-shaped wrinkle appearing between them. "Do you really think that's a good idea?"

"Yeah."

"I don't like the idea of a novice carrying one of my swords."

Eliaster raised his eyebrows. "Oh come on already! I might as well have been a novice."

"But you had at least grown up around the art. I can tell this one hasn't handled a sword in his life."

Um, hello, dude? I'm right here.

Eliaster slapped his hand over my mouth. "No, Josh, playing with sticks in the back yard doesn't count."

That hadn't been what I was going to say. I punched him in his exposed ribcage.

"Ow!" He jerked his hand away to cover his left side.

"Crow-bait," I muttered.

Opti burst out laughing. "Not many Overworlders have the guts to say that to a Sidhé's face. I'll give you one of my swords. Eliaster, you'd better keep an eye on him, before he goes charging out to take on Fear Doirich himself."

Eliaster rolled his eyes but, strangely, stayed silent.

"Now, which hand is your dominant?" Opti asked, motioning me inside.

"Left." I stepped into the building.

Opti pulled out a tape measure. "Stand still. Has Eliaster told you what kind of weapon you're getting?"

"Umm, a sword."

He pulled the tape around my waist. "Yes, but not any type of sword. Up until twenty or thirty years ago, the Seelie court didn't allow any fae to carry unconcealed weapons in the Overworld. Put us at a distinct advantage, of course, since the Unseelie do whatever they want. So I came up with a sword that incorporates some of the characteristics of fae glamour into the metal." He pressed the tape against the outside of my right leg. "Basically, unless you know someone is armed and you're specifically looking for the weapon, you won't see it."

That must have been how I'd missed Marc, Eliaster, and Llew's swords at first. "Like a perception filter."

His forehead wrinkled and he frowned. "What?"

"Uh…yeah, forget I said anything. So, with the glamour, how does that work? Magic?"

Opti's frown deepened. "That's a question a full fae is more qualified to answer. What we call magic and what they call magic…it's not necessarily the same. Better you ask Eli…if he'll give you a straight answer." He stood up and brushed off his hands. "I have something that might work— let me grab it." He disappeared into the back room of the shop.

I glanced at Eliaster. He was leaning against one of the shop's supports, his arms crossed casually over his chest. I pointed up into the rafters. "Iron chain?"

He nodded.

"Smart guy."

"More like paranoid."

"Says the dude who doesn't sleep when he's in the Underworld."

A quick grimace crossed Eliaster's face. "Opti has no reason to fear anyone. He's one of the most gifted swordsmiths in North America. Me, on the other hand—well, let's just say I've pissed off more than a few powerful Sidhé over the last few years. I have a reason to be paranoid."

I resisted the urge to roll my eyes. "I thought half-fae couldn't use glamour. How does a half-fae make glamoured swords?"

He lifted one shoulder in a half shrug. "Glamour is part of what you humans would call 'fae magic'." He used his index fingers to make quote marks in the air. "Opti can't use it himself, but he has enough that he can imbue the swords with it."

"And magic is…?"

"The way some fae react with their environment. It's … hard to explain."

I switched back to the first subject. "So why doesn't Opti get rid of the iron at least for you, if he's your friend?"

Eliaster gave a bitter, grating burst of laughter. "Opti isn't my friend. Here's a good, general rule to keep in mind in the Underworld. Just 'cause you're on the same side doesn't make you buddies. Got it?"

A shiver prickled my spine. Was that Eliaster's shot across the bow, warning me not to rely on him too much? Did that mean that once I was no longer an asset to his little team, he'd stab me in the back? His eyes were calm, his face relaxed but impassive. He didn't look like he'd just delivered a warning, but it might be such a part of his everyday life that it didn't faze him any more.

Opti came out with the sword and handed it to me. I couldn't help but grin as I ran my thumb over the soft leather sheath and bronze-colored hilt. The sword was a little longer than the length of my leg between hip and knee. I squeezed my hand around the leather grip, then carefully drew the sword and weighed it. It was a bit lighter than I'd expected, but still heavy enough that I'd feel it after swinging it around for a few minutes.

"So, what do you want for this?" Eliaster asked Opti.

"Why don't you teach a month's worth of lessons to some of my customers?"

"Too much. How about once a week for a month?"

"Please. You think that everyone can make glamour swords as good as mine?"

I sheathed the sword. "You don't have to trade for me, Eliaster. I can do it myself."

Eliaster snorted. "You can pay me back."

I tried to protest more, but the two ignored me and continued bartering. Eliaster finally walked away with promising to come in once a week for three months to teach, as long as his other work didn't get in the way. Opti seemed more than satisfied as we walked away, me fumbling to strap the sword belt around my waist.

"Treat that sword as befits the tool of a hero," Opti said to me as we left the shop. "Remember, you're the first Overworlder to own one. Don't take that privilege lightly."

"I'll try," I told him. "Thanks."

Opti waved the words away and disappeared into the back of his shop again.

I caught up to Eliaster, who was waiting for me on the corner. We walked for a few minutes in silence. The clunk of the sword against my leg felt good, and despite myself I grinned.

Eliaster cleared his throat. "Now, about payment."

I groaned. "I should've known you wouldn't let it rest long. What is it? Some fae oath that will make me your slave for the next seven centuries?" I remembered reading about deals like that. And David's words rose to my mind.

Eliaster grinned and shook his head. "Nah, nothing like that."

"You're enjoying my ignorance, aren't you?"

"There are times." He turned serious. "All I ask in payment is that you swear on your honor to keep the fight against the Lucht Leanúna going."

I laughed. "Yeah, I think you'll be around a good long while to ensure that that happens."

His eyes narrowed. "You can't count on anything around here. I'm being serious, Josh. You need to take this seriously, too."

I stopped dead in the street and faced him, feeling blood rush to my face and neck. "Look, I can accept that the Underworld is never going to leave my life now. I accept that fae will forever be trying to kill me or ask me for help. But you didn't want me involved in the first place. All of a sudden, you want me to be your protégé. What is your deal?"

Eliaster's lips parted. His eyes narrowed. He shrugged and walked past me, the shoulders of his black leather jacket drawing together close to his ears. "Forget it."

I pulled at the buckle of the sword belt. "If that's the condition that this comes with..."

Eliaster shook his head again. "No. You'll need that—hang on to it. Consider it a gift from someone concerned about your welfare."

He shouldered his way into the crowd. I shrugged and followed him. Fine, I'd hang on to the sword until this was over. But I wasn't going to be indebted to him forever. When Marc was rescued and the relic found, Eliaster would find the sword with his stuff—or maybe stuck in his back, if he kept annoying me. He couldn't ask me to keep fighting for something that wasn't my concern.

I was not a hero.

Thirty-nine.

I tapped my pencil against the paper. Addition hadn't worked. Subtraction wouldn't work, for obvious reasons.

I glanced up at Eliaster, who slumped in his customary over-stuffed chair by the fire. The fae hadn't moved or even looked at me since we'd gotten back. In fact, he'd acted like a pouty five year old. Totally pathetic. How had even-keeled Marc been friends with this guy?

Thirty-nine. Thirty-nine.

The numbers in the cipher whirled around my head. What glued them together? They were so ... random. No pattern that I could see thus far.

I looked at the earlier work I'd scribbled down on the side of the page. Thirty-nine. Angel...why was he on...right, Angel and his numbers.

Wait. Angel liked fours *and* progressions of four—I thought of his passcode, eight to the power of four. Maybe the key to this cipher was in a progression of numbers.

So, 39 + 39 = 78. 39 + 78 = 117. I scanned through the entire code, running my finger along the line of text.

And found 117.

I stared at the text. No way. I kept going with the calculations. 39 + 117 = 156. I ran through the numbers.

No good.

If it wasn't a progression of thirty-nines ... I added 78 + 117 = 195. That occurred several times within the cipher text. And 117 + 195 = 312, which also occurred several times within the text.

I smacked myself in the forehead. "Idiot!"

Eliaster snorted. "You're just now realizing this?"

I thrust the papers toward him. "It's similar to a Fibonacci sequence! That's why the numbers go so high."

He raised his eyebrows. "I hate to ask, but what is a Fibonacci sequence?"

"You wouldn't know unless you'd taken higher math," I said. "I'm an idiot for letting it stump me for so long, but I've never seen a Fibonacci sequence that didn't start with three...though thirty-nine is a progression of three. Thank you, Angel."

"Can you just tell me—"

"Fibonacci sequences are sequences where all the numbers are the sum of the two numbers before it." I held up the page with the key phrase on it. "Christ's 'fathers' number thirty-nine. Thirty-nine and thirty-nine equal seventy-eight, which corresponds to A. Thirty-nine plus seventy-eight equals one-hundred-seventeen, which is the next highest number, so it would equal B. Seventy-eight plus one-hundred-seventeen equals one-hundred-ninety-five, which is C..."

I flipped the sheet of paper over and began working out the numbers. Within twenty minutes, I had the entire alphabet, from A to Z, in a sloppy row on the page. I showed it to Eliaster.

He clutched his head in both hands. "I got it! Don't make my head hurt any more than it already does."

I grinned.

It took me no time at all to convert the numbers to letters. Within twenty minutes, I had the back of a page covered with consonants in groups of five.

THLST KPRNT HYRFR LRDGH TNSVN TNNLG HTFTH RCNTD SCVRS RGRDN GTHRL LCNRH NDSHS DCDDT PTTHR LCNDR SFKPN YNHDD NPLCT HSWHS KTWLD BWSTR MMBRT HLSTG RLDDN GRNVG HTNSV NTNXX.

As I stared at the letters, the triumph I'd felt at cracking the cipher withered like old lettuce. Technically, I'd known all along this was what I'd find. Confronting it was different. *I hate word puzzles.*

I glanced up at Eliaster. He was asleep again, his head tucked under his arm. No help from him. I sighed, scanned Roe's shelves until I spotted a dictionary, grabbed it, and spread the cipher out on the coffee table. I picked the first combination of letters—THLST—and flipped the dictionary open to T.

By midnight, I'd figured out that it was actually two words, 'the' and 'last'—and not much else. David and Larae still hadn't shown up. Eliaster had woken up and, upon discovering that I hadn't finished the cipher, reverted back to his usual cranky self.

Roe pushed the door open. She had been in and out since supper, checking up on my progress. She'd always had an encouraging word, but pep talks every thirty minutes were starting to get old. This time, however, she just sat down on the couch beside me and folded her hands in her lap.

I sighed and threw the papers onto the coffee table. They slid across it and off the other side.

"Nothing more?" Roe asked.

"No." Why was my brain blinking in and out today? Absolutely ridiculous. Now I really felt stupid. I'd figured out a Fibonacci sequence, but I couldn't solve a few scrambled letters.

The front door clicked, and a moment later Larae and David came into the library. Larae flopped into the chair opposite Eliaster's and dropped her bag at her feet.

"Find out anything?" Eliaster growled, leaning forward.

"Not a thing, no thanks to you," she snapped.

"Oh, it's my fault that your informants are lame?"

"If you hadn't followed us—"

Roe sighed. "Please, Eliaster. Larae. Can we just put away the pettiness for a little while?"

Larae crossed her arms. "A couple of the guys on the list said that they've heard increased rumors of the Lucht Leanúna. My own guys told me no way that there's anything to those rumors. So basically, we're back to where we started, hoping that Genius Boy can figure out something."

I grabbed my work papers from the floor and shoved them at her. "I've gotten something accomplished."

She eyed the papers, then muttered, "How long until you're done?"

"Who knows."

"You're stuck again? Really? Marc always told me you were smart—for a human, anyway."

Eliaster snorted.

Larae turned on him. "Oh come, on, really? Why do you always have to be so melodramatic?"

Eliaster pointed at himself. "Who, me?"

"I didn't hear anyone else throwing a temper tantrum."

"Why do you always have to be a pain in the butt?" Eliaster snapped back.

I took the opportunity to slink out of the room and flop on the bottom step of the entryway stairs.

Had Marc ever added that last bit—*for a human*—when talking to his fae friends? I smoothed the cipher over my leg and tried to ignore the sounds of Eliaster and Larae's bickering in the library. Did it matter? It wasn't going to make me stop trying to help.

Not that I was doing all that much good.

The library door opened, releasing the sound of hard-edged Gaelic words, and Roe and David came out into the hallway. David made a face as he stepped around me and headed up the stairs.

Roe patted my shoulder. "I put toiletries and an extra

towel in the last bedroom on the left upstairs. Perhaps going to bed would be the best thing right now."

"Maybe."

Roe reached out and grasped the edge of the papers. I tightened my grip. She raised her eyebrows, the soft lines of her grandmotherly face turning sharp. I let go.

"I appreciate your worry about Marc—but between that and those two..." She nodded at the library. "I'm sorry you were dragged into this, Josh. I know you don't want to be here."

I shifted, looked down at my hands. "It's okay."

"Is it?"

I nodded, pressing my lips together. It wasn't okay. I wasn't okay. But the faster I finished the cipher, the sooner I could get out of here.

She sighed. "Sleep well. I pray that it refreshes your mind."

"Thanks."

She headed down the hallway to the kitchen.

I rubbed my hands over my face. My stomach growled, but there was a knot in my gut the size of my fists. I couldn't eat right now.

I stood and trudged up the stairs. The upper story of the house stretched away from the stairs in a long hallway. I walked past four doors, all shut, to reach the open doorway of my bedroom. As promised, Roe had left towels and bathroom essentials on the dresser tucked under the sloped blue ceiling. I kicked off my shoes, peeled off my socks, and curled my toes into the thick, plush gray carpet.

Like Roe said, maybe sleep would help. I moved my messenger bag from the bed to the floor, then pulled off my jacket and tossed it over my bag. It landed with a dull smack, and I saw the corner of a green CD case sticking out of the pocket.

Where had this come from? I hadn't stuck it in there, had I? I tried to remember if I'd felt it banging around in my pocket within the last couple of days. Then I remembered that there had been dozens of times someone had bumped into me in the Market today. It could have gotten stuffed in my pocket at any time.

I booted up my computer.

A light rap on the door frame made me jump and drop the disk.

"Oh, sorry." Larae stepped hesitantly into the room. Her hunched shoulders gave her crossed arms a softer look, like she was trying to keep warm. "Getting ready to go to bed?"

I nodded. "Yeah. I'll work on the cipher some more, but I think my brain needs some time to process everything that's happened before I'll get much more work done on it."

She nodded and glanced away, looking past me to the black and white sketches hanging on the wall over the bed. "I feel as though I should apologize for my earlier comments. It was stupid of me."

I shrugged. "Believe me, I'm getting used to not being trusted."

"But Marc trusted you, and that should have been good enough for me." She stepped toward me and laid her hand on my arm. "I'm sorry. I know you wouldn't abandon Marc."

Prickles of heat washed over me, emanating from the spot where her nails brushed my skin. Her big violet eyes looked way too soft, and gentle fluctuations danced in the irises. She leaned toward me, her body inches away from my torso. The knot in my gut got heavier.

I moved my arm away and scratched my neck, making her hand slide off. "Yeah. Yeah, I just didn't feel like I could—you know..."

She smiled and reached up, brushing my cheek with the tips of her fingers. "I know. You have the makings of a hero more than you realize, Josh."

I stared after her as she left the room. What had just happened? No, dumb question. I knew what had just happened. Larae—my best friend's girlfriend—had just hit on me. I sat on the bed and dug my fingers into the edge of the mattress. Why?

"Nice little show." Eliaster stepped up to the doorway and leaned against the jamb, grinning. "Gettin' all cozy, are we?"

I growled under my breath. "Don't tell me you have laser vision."

He laughed. "Nope. Came up to the door when you two were busy gazing adoringly into each other's eyes. Or, more correctly, Larae was gazing adoringly, and you looked like a rabbit about to get run over."

"Thanks. You could've rescued me."

"Nah." He stepped into the room and closed the door after him. "Now do you believe me that there's something weird about those two?"

I wasn't ready to make a final judgment on David yet. That was partially because he felt safe—he was another human, after all. Someone like me who had been through all of this, someone who had survived it and adapted to it. Maybe I could do the same.

Larae, however…

"You said she was Marc's girlfriend."

"They certainly seemed infatuated with each other. Sickeningly so. Always purring over how nice the other looked and how sweet they were. I 'bout had to puke a few times." Eliaster flopped onto the floor and leaned his back against the wall. "Curiously enough, I saw her pull a similar stunt with Marc once or twice. Big doe-eyes, hand on the arm, soft voice, the works. It was gross. Can't believe Marc always fell for it."

"So why was she pulling the sweet-and-innocent act on me if she's Marc's girlfriend?"

"Surely you can't be that dense. Have you ever had a girlfriend?"

Dating had been misery for me in high school, so I hadn't even tried in college. Not that I was going to tell him that. Time for a subject change. "Look, as much as I'd love to get all chummy and discuss my love life, we've got bigger problems." I held up the CD. "I found this in my jacket. I think someone stuck it in my pocket at the Market."

Eliaster stood up and hovered over my shoulder as I inserted the CD in my computer and clicked 'play' on the video command screen that popped up.

Blodheyr's face appeared on the screen, his silver eyes seeming to bore into me even out of a computer screen. He leaned forward on a desk and steepled his fingers underneath his chin. "Joshua."

I glanced at Eliaster. His eyes were so narrow I could barely see the color spikes in his irises, and the rest of his face was as expressive as a stone carving.

"Most businessmen will start out by telling you how patient and flexible they will be, especially when they're trying to work with a freelancer like yourself. However, I have never claimed to be a patient man.

Marc is performing adequately, but it has taken a lot of..." The Unseelie paused, leaned back in his chair, and reflectively smoothed the front of his shirt.

"...persuasion, to get to this point. I want results, and I know that you can produce them.

"If you think that Eliaster Tyrone can protect you, you are gravely misinformed. Eliaster suffers from an overinflated sense of duty to Overworlders, as if the fae owe you something. I suffer under no disillusions, and I owe my allegiance to no human who's been dead for the last two thousand years." He cleared his throat, lowered his hands to his desk. Not a single movement he made seemed superfluous.

Blodheyr glanced off to the side as if gathering his thoughts for a moment.

"This guy..." Eliaster muttered.

"I will not be beaten, Joshua. I hope you understand that." Blodheyr picked up a blank sheet of paper from his desk and started fiddling with it. "I will find a way to acquire your cooperation."

I rubbed my sweaty palms against my legs.

He tore a long, precise strip from the paper. "It will not be pleasant for you unless you come voluntarily, though I doubt that you will, given your actions thus far. If this is your course, then so be it. Just be cautious." Another tear, and his eyes came up, staring directly into the camera. "And Eliaster—this is strike two. Next time, I will flay you alive."

The screen went dark.

Eliaster's jaw bunched. "I have to tell Roe about this." He started for the door, then paused. "For what it's worth, however sweet and innocent Larae may seem, I think she's trying to manipulate you."

Right. "And you're not?"

Eliaster met my eyes, then stalked from the room.

chapter 10

After Eliaster left, I went to bed and, despite Blodheyr's threat, fell asleep immediately. The next morning I woke at seven and quietly sat on the edge of my bed, feeling rested but achy, as if I'd slept too heavily for too long. My neck cracked as I stretched, but most of my bruises from the wreck and getting manhandled had eased.

The house had that still, expectant air that old houses do in the morning, before anyone has gotten up. The musty smell was a bit heavier. I pulled my feet back onto the bed, opened my laptop, and replayed Blodheyr's message with headphones stuck on my ears so I wouldn't disturb anyone.

The tone of Blodheyr's voice made my skin crawl, but the words and his actions seemed more appropriate to a campy James Bond villain.

Blodheyr wasn't stupid. Why was he trying this kind of scare tactic? And why was Eliaster the only one of my teammates mentioned? He talked about Eliaster's overinflated sense of duty to Overworlders, so maybe he figured that Eliaster would have appointed himself my guardian. That bothered me. Eliaster seemed to be the one in charge, and if our enemy knew him that well...

"I hate this," I muttered, standing up again and grabbing

my jeans from the desk chair. As I pulled them on, I noticed a folder lying partially under the door. I picked it up and flipped it open. The cipher. Roe must have slipped it under the door while I was still asleep, knowing I'd want to work on it as soon as I woke up this morning. I smiled and settled back on the bed.

The night of sleep had done something for my brain, just as Roe had told me it would. Slowly, painstakingly, I began to see words in the letters that had made no sense last night, and I made good headway by the time Roe knocked on the door at eight.

I scanned the cipher as I rolled out of bed, ran my fingers through my hair, and pulled on a wrinkled blue t-shirt from the wad of clothes in my bag.

By the time I got to the downstairs hallway, I could smell bacon. The kitchen door was open, and I could hear Larae and Roe talking over the sound of frying meat and pancakes.

Eliaster stumbled from the library, wearing the same jeans and black shirt he'd worn since I'd first met him at Blodheyr's cabin. His eyes were bleary and bloodshot.

"Morning, sunshine," I said.

He grunted and brushed past me, dragging a hand over the fine stubble on his face. I rubbed my own cheek and found the beginning of something that wasn't quite a beard, but was too long to call scruff.

A shave and a shower needed to happen soon. Preferably, immediately after breakfast.

I stepped into the kitchen. The upper half of the walls were papered in a muted green and pink plaid, and the lower half of the walls were covered in white wainscoting. A table with built-in white benches stood right next to the door, one of the benches almost blocking the door. Roe stood past it at the gas stove, wearing a blue apron and stacking pancakes onto plates sitting on the counter beside her.

Eliaster and David both sat on the far side of the table, so I slid into place between Larae and the wall. She smiled at me, and the warmth of a blush spread over the back of my neck.

"Morning, Josh." Roe put plates piled with pancakes and bacon the table. "Did everyone sleep well? You didn't sleep in the library again did you, Eliaster?"

He nodded.

"Did you actually *sleep*?" she asked, placing a full cup of black coffee in front of him.

Eliaster shrugged and chugged the coffee. "Couple of hours."

"Weirdo," Larae muttered, but she had a note of humor in her voice.

"I worked on the cipher for a bit this morning," I said around a mouthful of bacon. "Got some of it done—I think another few hours and I can finish it."

Larae clapped her hands together. "Excellent!"

"Well done, Josh," David said, grinning. "I guess we'd better start getting stuff together, planning out our next steps."

Eliaster nodded thoughtfully. "Maybe it's time to think about some defense training for you, Josh."

I tried not to grin as I stuffed a huge bite of pancakes into my mouth. I still wasn't totally excited about the deal that came with accepting the sword, but at the same time, I wasn't going to pass up a chance at actually learning how to use it.

Roe caught my eye and motioned to the coffeemaker. I nodded, and she passed me a cup.

"Are you sure that's a good idea?" Larae asked Eliaster. "Even if you start today, he won't have time to learn much. He's going to be more of a liability in a fight."

"What if there's another cipher? Or some computer hacking?" Eliaster scratched his neck. "Josh's skills more than outweigh the liability of inexperience in fights. We need him."

"You assume that he's staying," David said, glancing at me, eyebrows raised.

I hesitated. This was David giving me an opportunity to back out, to bail. Sticking up for another human, like he'd said.

But I might need the skills Eliaster could teach me, especially if, like everyone kept saying, the Sidhé were never going to leave me alone after this. And, as always, the thought of taking off and abandoning Marc when I still might be able to help him made my gut turn.

"I'm staying," I said.

David frowned.

Roe smiled and patted my shoulder. "Thank you, Josh."

I shrugged again and started stuffing my mouth with food. It wasn't like I was being heroic.

We finished the rest of the meal in silence.

Afterward, I retreated back upstairs, grabbed the toiletries Roe had left out for me, and took a shower in the bathroom at the far end of the hall. The pipes were old, and made a rattling sound as soon as I turned the handle on the tub, but the water was hot and blasted out of the showerhead in a stinging rain. I hurried through the shower, dressed in clean clothes—well, cleaner, I guess. After I finished shaving, I realized the shirt I'd grabbed had come from my pile of dirty laundry.

Oh well. It wasn't like anyone would care too much.

I settled down in my room again and resumed work on the cipher, carefully unscrambling the letters. Occasionally I heard someone talking or moving around downstairs, but it was quiet for the most part. If I ignored my surroundings, I could almost pretend I was back in my dorm room, finishing up some homework in a mad scramble before class…if the class was something like Codebreaking 101.

Finally I penciled in the last word and checked over the cipher one last time. I stretched, my shoulders and neck popping, and glanced at the clock. One-thirty. As if in response to the red numbers on the desktop clock, my stomach growled.

I went downstairs. Everyone was in the library again.

David and Roe had their noses in books. Eliaster was sleeping again. Larae was curled up in the armchair opposite him, chewing on the eraser of the pencil she held. A copy of the cipher sat in her lap.

"I got it!" I waved the paper over my head.

David poked Eliaster's arm with his foot. "Hey, Sleeping Beauty, wake up. Josh says he's got it."

Eliaster sat up, rubbing his eyes. "Yeah? What does it say?"

I read off the message. "'From the Museum director in the Year of Our Lord 1871, in light of the recent discoveries regarding the relic in our hands, has decided to put the relic under safekeeping. Those who would seek it would be wise to remember the lost. Nov 1871.'" The two X's at the end had turned out to be fillers, letters placed there to finish out the last set of five.

I set the message on the table and looked around the room. Larae had her lower lip fixed between her teeth. David and Eliaster looked disappointed.

"Are you sure that you translated that right?" David asked.

"Yes," I said defensively. "The letters didn't make sense in any way except this one. Why? What's wrong?"

"More riddles," David muttered. "After protecting the location of the relic with a cipher and everything, couldn't they just state straight-out where it is? It's not even the fae who wrote this, it's the curators. Humans. They should be on our side."

Larae tapped her lips with her pencil. "Leave the heavy thinking to someone who hasn't had two concussions, David."

The look David shot her was startled, almost hurt.

Larae straightened. "What happened in 1871 that was significant for the Sidhé, Roe?"

"Before November 1871," Roe added. "That was…let me think…the year of the Great Chicago Fire. In early October. That's it, I think. It was a very quiet year, quite unusual for back then."

" 'Those who would seek it would be wise to remember

the lost!'" Eliaster repeated, his voice rising.

"The Lost Tunnels of Chicago!"

Roe's eyes widened just a touch, and she pressed her lips together tightly.

Larae paled. "Oh no. I'm *not* going there!"

I was tired of hearing my voice asking questions, but I said it anyway. "What are those?"

"The Chicago fire was started by a fae relic, and it blazed both above and underground. Many of the tunnels were decimated. As the city was rebuilt, some of the tunnels were cleaned out and rebuilt as well, but the majority of them were left untouched," Eliaster said.

"They're haunted," Larae said. "Everyone knows that ghouls and *béan sidhé* live there now, not to mention the souls of those who died in the fire. I've even heard the *dullahan* has been sighted there."

Eliaster groaned.

David leaned toward Larae. "Besides, who says we're going there?"

Eliaster swung his head around. "What?"

The single word was sharp, a razor blade cutting through the room.

David's shoulders hunched. "I haven't heard a thing about going anywhere. As far as I knew, this entire mission was to find a way to rescue Marc. Right, Josh?"

I tried not to growl under my breath. Crap. Why did he have to put me on the spot like that? "I have no idea. I've done what I was supposed to do—I deciphered the document."

"But Eliaster never told you that we might be packing up and going somewhere?"

I gritted my teeth. "No, he didn't say anything about going anywhere. But again, I didn't ask."

"Would you have come if you knew he wanted to drag you on a trip?"

Eliaster stood up. "What is this, Twenty Questions?"

David rose, his head leaning forward just a little as he

glared at the fae. "Maybe you should have told us your plan in the first place. Come to think of it, Eliaster, what is your plan? All we've heard from you is, get the cipher finished, get the freakin' cipher finished. Well, it's finished. What now? You don't honestly think that going after this relic will help Marc?"

"You don't honestly think that we can do nothing?" Eliaster shot back. "You've heard the rumors. The Lucht Leanúna want this thing for something. Can we really just sit and let them take it?"

"You can't leave Marc!" Larae clenched her hands. "We could find the relic after we rescue him. Then the Lucht Leanúna would really be stuck."

Larae had voiced my thoughts. I crossed my arms over my chest and waited for Eliaster to reply.

The blond fae gnawed on his lower lip. He took a step to the side, as if beginning to pace, then jerked back into place. His hands worked into fists, then relaxed, then clenched again. He looked over at Roe.

She shook her head.

"Give me a bit to think." Eliaster walked out, his shoulders hunched and his hands stuffed deep into his pockets.

Larae growled and tucked her arms around her body. Tears glimmered in the corners of her eyes. "No, no, no. He can't abandon Marc. He can't."

Roe scooted across the couch and put her arms around Larae. She glanced up at David and me and made a shooing motion toward the door.

David brushed his fingers against Larae's shoulder, then held the door as I walked out. He let it slap shut behind him and rubbed his neck. For a moment, we just stood beside each other, awkward and quiet. Then he shrugged.

"Want to start on those defense lessons?" he asked.

I nodded. It would be good. And after hearing Eliaster contemplate abandoning his friend, I needed to hit something. Might as well make it useful in the process.

David headed into the kitchen. A door at the back, beside the fridge, opened up to a wooden staircase and a cement-block room. The basement had been turned into a full gym. I stepped off the stairs onto the floor padded with thick foam and rubber mats. David continued flipping lights on, illuminating the punching bags set up in one corner. A weight bench and treadmill were in another. The main portion of the floor was left open, and the reason was pushed against the wall opposite the staircase.

Racks on the wall held wooden and metal weapons, mostly swords but some maces, knives, and a few odd-looking things I couldn't identify. A tall metal gun safe stood beside the weapons rack.

David stepped up to the safe and started to punch in the code.

I cleared my throat. "If it's all the same to you, I'd rather not bother with guns anymore."

"Are you scared after the mess at the Market the other day?"

I gritted my teeth. "I'm not scared. Eliaster said that guns are basically worthless in close combat, and that not many fae carry them."

David dropped his hand from the safe. "And you trust Eliaster?"

I frowned. Truthfully, I didn't much trust any of them. Roe, maybe, and that was because she didn't seem to care about anything other than finding her grandson. It felt like everyone else had an agenda, even though I couldn't name those agendas.

David snorted. "Eliaster's fae. He doesn't care what happens to humans as long as his little agenda is fulfilled. Teaching you the sword is worthless. You don't have one, and it would take you too long to learn how to be of any use in a fight."

"I do have one. Eliaster got a glamour sword from Opti."

"What are you, his pet project?" David shook his head, turning to examine the practice swords lining the weapons rack. "Eliaster is…different than most fae. He's viewed as unorthodox because he worked with curators and has been known to get protective of humans."

"Well, he needs to figure out that he's not my mommy."

"When Eliaster gave you the sword, did he ask for anything in return?"

"Why does it matter? You're not my mommy either."

"Fae tend to twist words so they always get a good deal. I hope you didn't agree to anything stupid."

"For once, can't someone give me the benefit of the doubt? Even if I don't know much about the Underworld, I can still put the meaning of a sentence together." My mind raced. I hadn't really promised anything—had I? Eliaster had wanted my word that I'd continue fighting against the Lucht Leanúna, and I had refused to give it to him. *I hope that was it.*

David sighed. "Well, I guess there's no reason not to teach you the sword, then. I'm guessing you've never picked up a sword before."

"Closest I've come is some throwing knives my parents got me when I was a kid."

"Yeah?" David raised an eyebrow. "Any good?"

"I got them confiscated after a week because I thought it might be fun to use my sister's teddy bear as a target. My dad sort of conveniently forgot where he hid them."

He chuckled and gave me a squinty, appraising look, then pulled a medium-bladed sword from the weapons rack. "This is a good beginner sword. It's not too heavy, and can be used with one hand or two."

He tossed it across the room. I held my hand out to catch it and the hilt bounced off my knuckles. My fingers went numb.

"Ouch!"

David chuckled. "Pick it up. Let's get going on this."

I leaned down and wrapped my hand around the hilt, flexing my fingers. The grip felt a little strange, meant for a different hand. The weight did feel similar to my sword. I'd definitely feel it in my arms and shoulders after a while of swinging it. The edges of the blade were blunt.

Something smacked my leg. I yelped and dodged away, narrowly avoiding another swipe from the flat of David's blade.

David grinned, blue eyes twinkling. "Pay attention."

"Not fair." I spread my feet to shoulder width and crouched down a little, holding the sword out in front of me with both hands.

"Get used to it. Fae don't play fair."

For the next hour, David had me hopping and dodging as he tried his best to land more stinging blows. He enjoyed it way too much, but he also taught me a few things—how to hold the sword and how to block without sending a shiver of pain through my arms. I didn't land a single blow on him, but my sword struck plenty of other things—the walls, the floor, and more often than not, my own shin.

After a bit, I noticed David had certain forms he was going through. There were only so many different ways to swing a sword, and each had a recognizable pattern, something I could remember and a trajectory I could trace.

After a while, I could predict what he would do next, which height he'd strike at and what kind of swing it would be. I even managed to land a couple of strikes on David as I recognized openings in his defenses.

After a particularly good whack on his leg, David stepped back and lowered his sword. He wiped sweat from his forehead.

I rose from the crouch I'd maintained. My thighs and shoulders burned, and my hands trembled just a bit as I braced myself with the sword. "How did I do?"

"Pretty good, for a first timer."

"Your patterns are predictable."

David paused slightly as he put away his sword. "How so?"

I racked my sword next to his and took a deep breath, trying not to grin. Yeah, not so useless in a fight after all.

"You just go through various patterns—well, I guess they would really be called sword forms. You even use the forms in predictable ways. If you'd change up the patterns you use, just a little…"

David patted my shoulder. "Wait 'til you get a little more practice before you start critiquing, newbie."

As I opened my mouth to snap, the door creaked above us, and Larae came down the stairs, chewing on her lower lip.

"What's up?" David asked.

She nodded to the weapons' rack. "Good thing I didn't have access to that a little while ago. I'm pretty sure Eliaster would be missing an appendage."

David laughed. I chuckled nervously as the fae girl turned her deep, violet eyes on me. What did she want now? Out of the corner of my eye, I saw tension appear in David's neck and shoulders. He looked away, running his hand through his hair.

She rubbed her arms. "I want to talk about a rescue mission for Marc."

"Um, didn't Eliaster say he'd think about it?" I asked.

She frowned. "That's Eliaster-speak for 'no chance in any world, Heaven, or Hell'. But we can't just leave Marc! I don't feel right about that, and I can't believe Eliaster would either."

Don't feel right about that? I'd been expecting a much more impassioned argument for saving her boyfriend.

"Eliaster's an idiot," David said.

Larae rolled her eyes. "Oh please, David, don't bring your alpha-male arguments into this."

He held up his hands. "Hey, I'm on your side. So do you have a plan at all?"

I took a few steps away from them. Part of me wanted to stick my fingers in my ears and chant *la-la-la* so I couldn't hear them. If I didn't know what they were planning, Eliaster couldn't get mad at me.

"Josh." Larae's hand landed on my arm.

I jerked and spun around.

She stepped back. "Do you want to be a part of this? If you don't, I think you should leave so you can't tell Eliaster what we're planning."

"That's a good idea." I rubbed my neck and winced as my fingers hit a raw area from yesterday when Llew had twisted my shirt around my throat.

Larae and David were silent for a moment, both watching me. I tried not to squirm under their gaze. Did I really want to be a part of this plan? Eliaster would kill us if he found out—and in the back of my mind, I cringed at the thought that the usually-exaggerated phrase just might, with Eliaster, be literal.

But I couldn't reconcile abandoning my friend. Marc had never backed away from helping me. The most notable memory I had of that was when we were ten, and two boys a grade older had tackled me on the bus. Marc hadn't hit his growth spurt yet and was a good head shorter than both those boys, but he'd calmly dropped them both with sucker punches to the gut.

This is different. Marc has trained his entire life to fight. I haven't.

David dropped his shoulders like he was disappointed and nodded to the stairway. "It's right there."

I stiffened. "I'm not lost. Look, I'll go. I think it's a bad idea, but I'll go, because I owe Marc that much."

David glared at me. "You think it's a bad idea to rescue your best friend? If you think that, why are you bothering to come?"

"Relax, David. I understand his misgivings," Larae said.

Yeah right you do. I bit my tongue.

Footsteps clomped down the stairs, and Eliaster came into view. He squinted at us suspiciously. "What are you three up to?"

David waved his hand. "Just finishing up a training session. Josh said you'd gotten him a sword, so I thought I'd show him the basics."

"So I'll have to retrain him the right way? Thanks a lot."

"I learned a lot," I said. "Figured out some of the patterns, that sort of thing."

Eliaster frowned. "That's because David sticks to the patterns like it's a religion."

Odd thing for him to say, given that cross he wears.

"It's a starting point at least," Larae said.

Eliaster grunted. "Maybe so. At least this will serve him better than leaving him with a pistol."

David raised his eyebrows. "Like it was a better idea to leave him unarmed?"

"It drew attention to him, David, and I had to deal with it." Eliaster sighed. "Look, I know you guys are wanting a decision on whether or not to go after Marc. I'm still thinking. I need to gather more information before I say yes or no. I'm going to go talk to Angel and a few other guys. Tell Roe not to wait up for me." He turned and headed back up the stairs.

As soon as the door shut, David put his arm around Larae's shoulders, pulled her closer to me, then put his other arm over my shoulders. I tensed. His arm was heavy, and with his bulky frame, it made me feel like a David chumming up to a Goliath.

"Tonight," he said in a low voice. "We'll head out tonight."

chapter 11

I hunched in the back seat of Larae's Porsche, watching the shop lights speed by. David and Larae sat in the front seats, both preoccupied with their own thoughts. Larae held her sawed-off shotgun close to her body and absently rubbed a thumb up and down the barrel. Outside, the city flowed by in a wash of golden streetlights and neon signs.

I wore the sword Eliaster had given me on my hip. *Please, please don't let me have to use this.* Tension coiled around my muscles at the thought. *This is insane. Why did you have to agree to go? You're not a hero. You can't even use this sword—you might as well be unarmed.*

Okay, enough. I had to stop analyzing this before I chickened out.

"So," I said. Neither David nor Larae acknowledged me. I kept going. "How do you guys know where to find Marc? It can't be common knowledge where Blodheyr keeps his prisoners."

"It's common knowledge that he owns a loan shop near the pink strip club on south Campbell," Larae said in a flat voice. "We'll start there and see if we can find anything. If not..." Her voice trailed away. Her hands tightened around the shotgun.

David took up her thought. "If not, we'll have to start from square one again, and hope Eliaster gives us enough time."

"Doubtful. That selfish *amadán* doesn't care about anything other than his conspiracy theories," Larae muttered.

I fingered the raw area on my neck and looked out the window. We rumbled up to a stoplight. Beside us, a fae in a pickup revved his engine and motioned to David, egging him on to a race.

Just how many fae were there in Springfield? I scanned the sidewalk. Most of the shops were closed at this time of night, but in the parking lot beside us, under a light, I could see a group of five teenagers playing hacky sack. Two of them were fae. Across the street at a gas station, a fae girl stepped out of her car, her glamour image blurring her real face.

I frowned. Did every city have this many fae? Were we humans really so oblivious? Another shiver crawled over my skin.

The light turned green, and the Porsche glided forward. David ignored the roaring engine as the truck blazed ahead.

A couple of blocks went by without any more fae sightings. The pink strip club came into view, the neon lights clashing with the orange city-glow of the clouds overhead. We pulled past it and into the next lot. A small group of shops sat beside a fence that separated the parking lot from the strip club. Two pawn shops bookended the group, and in the middle was a bar with one boarded up window, and a shop with the words

24-Hour Loans: Quick Cash emblazoned above the door in broken neon lights. All but the loan shop lights were dim.

"Cheery place," I muttered.

David parked close to the loan shop. He turned in his seat. "You hang back, Josh. Even if you are some human fighting prodigy, you're not ready for a fight yet, and Eliaster would have my head if you got hurt."

"Fine by me."

He raised an eyebrow. "What is, hanging back, or Eliaster having my head?"

"Either one."

David guffawed. I tried to laugh, but it sounded more like a whimper.

Larae pushed her door open and slid her seat forward. As I crawled out, the sword hilt snagged on a seatbelt, jerking me to a halt. I freed it and trotted after David and Larae as they headed around to the back of the shops. As we walked, Larae unzipped her backpack, removed several throwing stars, and slid them into loops on the sleeves of her jacket. She loaded her shotgun and ratcheted the cartridges into place.

David unzipped his jacket and withdrew two pistols from a shoulder holster.

I rubbed my sword hilt, full-out vampire bats fluttering in my gut.

Behind the shop, there was another fence. The tiny space had just enough room for one car and three Dumpsters. Larae glanced into the car while David went straight to the shop door.

"How are we going to get in there?" I asked.

David tried the knob. The door swung open, silent and smooth. He grinned at me and ducked inside.

Larae and I walked after him. The door opened into an employee area with a battered TV with a converter box perched on the top, a scraped-up refrigerator, and a depressing table and chairs set. A closed door to our right had the word *Office* on it, and an open doorway ahead led into the shop area.

David glanced into the brightly-lit shop. The place was sparse, with a dingy carpet, a few chairs, and a Formica counter that housed a computer and a couple of desktop calendars. Underneath the counter, shelves were stuffed to overflowing with boxes and file folders.

Larae reached around David and turned the lights off in

the front of the shop. "Where's the employee?"

David jerked his head toward the office. "I'll check in there. You two take care of the stuff up front."

I headed straight for the computer. It was on, the desktop background a shot of a skimpily-dressed woman reclining on a couch of dollar bills. I followed the wires to a power strip at the back of a shelf and pulled the plug.

Larae knelt beside me and started digging through the boxes.

I turned the computer box on its side. "You don't happen to have a screwdriver, do you?"

She pulled a multi-tool from her hip pocket and handed it to me. I flipped the Phllips-head screwdriver out, unscrewed the sides of the box, and pulled out the hard drive.

"What good is that going to do us?" Larae asked, riffling through a folder. She growled and threw it to the side.

Before I could answer, a body came flying through the doorway. The guy crashed onto his back and laid still, blood trickling from his nose. David stepped into the shop, flexing his hand and wincing.

"You didn't…ahhh…" I started.

"He'll wake up with a headache and maybe a broken nose," David said, rolling the guy on his side. He pushed past me and crouched beside Larae. "There's another computer in the office, if you're done with this one. I'll help Larae here."

I nodded, stuffed the hard drive into my pocket, and went back through the break room to the office. There was another door in the office, leading into a bathroom. The office was just big enough for a tall safe and a desk, both stacked with more folders and loose papers.

I ran my hand through my hair. If clues to Marc's whereabouts were hidden in the paper files, we were screwed. We could probably go through the files for years and not see it all.

A blinking icon on the bottom of the computer screen caught my eye. I grabbed the mouse and hovered over the icon.

A pop-up window announced, *Security alarm has been triggered.*

"Um, guys!" I poked my head into the break room.

David looked out from the shop. "What?"

"Your buddy must've triggered an alarm before you got to him."

David swore. "Any countdown or clock or anything that lets us know when backup will get here?"

"Nope."

"Let's get moving, then. Larae! Hustle up!"

I tipped the computer onto its side and pulled the hard drive. Just as I was moving it back into place, the back door crashed open. Four fae with swords stormed into the break room. From somewhere in the front, David starting cursing. I slammed the office door.

Seconds later, it shuddered. I threw my weight against it, my felt-soled sneakers sliding on the carpet as the fae pushed. I was never wearing Converses on a covert mission again. Something broke in the shop. Larae's voice rose, screeching in Gaelic.

I stumbled as I lost my grip on the door. Goldtooth stood in the doorway, grinning.

If I get through this, I'm buying myself boots. Maybe with built-in spikes. I shuffled backward and drew my sword, brought the weapon up at an angle in front of my body. The blade stayed steady in my hand.

"Nice to see you again, Josh." Goldtooth's eyes flicked to the sword, and his grin stretched wider. "One of Opti's? My, my, Eliaster really must think highly of you. How cute." He drew a long knife from his belt and edged forward.

I gripped my sword with both hands. "No verbal sparring this time, huh?"

"I must admit you're my better in that. We'll just go straight to the physical sparring this time." He lunged, sweeping the knife up under my guard.

I jerked back and knocked his hand out of the way with my hilt. The Unseelie recovered and came at me again. I caught his knife stroke. The tip of my sword sliced into the wall. Goldtooth scraped the knife down my sword blade and slashed the back of my arm.

I hissed and stepped back. The heel of my back foot thudded into the wall. Stinging pain ran along the shallow cut. He shouldn't have been able to come near me with that knife, but the length of my weapon was no longer an asset in the cramped office. I mentally cussed out Eliaster for telling me a sword would be more useful than a pistol.

Goldtooth didn't attack, but stayed alert, his dark eyes on my weapon. He knew he had me cornered. I squared my shoulders, inched the sword a fraction higher.

Over his shoulder, I caught sight of turquoise and black striped hair.

I dropped my sword and held up my hands. "You know what? You're my better at fighting. I'll readily admit that."

Goldtooth snorted. A throwing star zipped past his neck and hand and buried itself in the drywall by my shoulder. Blood welled along two thin cuts on the fae's neck and hand. He snarled and spun, only to smash straight into the butt of Larae's shotgun.

He crashed to the floor, blood running over his lips and chin.

Larae turned and headed for the back door. I grabbed my sword and headed after her. As we stepped into the alley, David came barreling after us, a fae with a raised sword chasing him. Larae raised her gun to her shoulder. David ducked. The Unseelie took a faceful of pellets and dropped. Acrid smoke drifted into my face as the sound of the shot bounced back and forth between the walls of the narrow alley.

I rubbed my ears. Even in the aftermath of the shotgun blast, I could hear the wail of sirens. They were dangerously close. I ran around the side of the building. Two black SUVs were parked at the pawn shop curb, both with their driver-side doors hanging open, one still running. David and Larae ran past me, heading for the Porsche.

"Come on!" David yelled to me.

I jerked one jacket sleeve over my hand, leaned inside the still-running SUV, and plucked the keys from the ignition. I stuffed them into my pocket, then checked the other vehicle. That driver had been smarter—they'd taken the keys with them.

The sirens were louder now. I glanced up, saw flashing blue and red lights bouncing off the pale pink strip club walls. David revved the Porsche's engine. I ran over and clambered inside, squishing past Larae to the back seat. David peeled out of the parking lot as she slammed the door. I twisted in my seat and watched as three police cars squealed into the opposite side of the lot.

My heart pounded so hard I almost expected it to burst. I sank against the seat and took a deep breath. I held up my hands. Just like the last two times I'd been in danger, they were just now beginning to shake. I'd always been able to compartmentalize very well, but I'd never expected that I could just shove away any fear reaction until the danger was over. I dropped my hands to my legs, clenched handfuls of my jeans. Was I turning into some kind of psycho?

"Never a dull moment," David said cheerfully.

"Well, at least we got the computer hard drives," Larae said. "Eliaster won't kill us for nothing."

"Small comforts," I muttered to myself.

I ditched the SUV keys in a trash can outside the ground level of the parking garage. We sneaked back through Roe's front door at three in the morning.

Roe wasn't there, waiting for us, so I guessed she'd gone to bed. I crept up the stairs, cursing every creak, collected my computer gear, and headed back down to the library. Larae and David were crashed in their usual spots. David already looked half asleep, his arm tucked under his head. Eliaster's chair was vacant.

I settled in on the couch, plugged in the hard drives, and started combing through them. For all the trouble we'd been through, there wasn't much on them. The shop computer mostly had games on its hard drive. The office computer had a few more programs I expected for a business computer, including an accounting program, but that was no good.

I needed to dig into the very core of the hard drive, to access data that I wouldn't be able to access through normal means. I shut down the external hard drive reader, opened my word processor, and began to lay down lines of code. It would be a piece of cake to write a simple program that could crawl through the hidden data, extracting passwords and cached and deleted files from the hard drives.

Larae looked over my shoulder. "What are you doing?"

"Writing a program to access some data."

"Did you find anything on the hard drives?"

"Not yet."

She groaned. "Please don't tell me that was a worthless risk."

"Don't rule it out yet." I squinted and double checked the last couple of lines. "I might be able to dig up passwords, deleted files, all sorts of stuff. Just give me a little time."

David chuckled. "You say that a lot."

I pursed my lips and glared at him over the edge of the laptop screen. "That's because you people keep asking me to do things that take time, but you expect immediate results."

The front door rattled under a couple of heavy blows. I jumped, nearly dumping the laptop onto the floor. Larae went into the hallway. The door creaked open, and Eliaster's voice exploded into the house.

"What were you thinking?" he bellowed. The library door slammed open and he stomped inside. "Out of all the freakin' stupid things you could do—"

"What did we do?" Larae demanded. "For all you know we've been sitting here quietly all night!"

"Strike three." Eliaster ran his hands through his hair, making the blond spikes stand up even more.

What was—oh, right. Blodheyr had said something on the video about 'strike two' for Eliaster. "What moved you up to strike three?" I glanced at David and Larae's puzzled faces and remembered we'd never told them about the video.

"You brilliant people did, apparently. Whatever happened, Blodheyr thinks I'm responsible, and that makes the third time I've meddled with his plans."

Roe shuffled into the room, tying the belt on her bathrobe and yawning. Her white hair fluffed around her face like a cloud. "What's going on?"

Eliaster grabbed my arm and pulled me off the couch. I grabbed my computer and just managed to prevent it falling to the floor.

"Get your stuff. We're leaving right now." He spun to Roe and gently put his hands on her shoulders. "I'm sorry, but I think you'll have to come too, just for now. I think I lost it, but I don't want to take chances."

She gripped his hands. "Lost what, Eliaster?"

"Yeah, how about you actually explain something for once rather than leaving us all in the dark?" David said.

"Please, guys." Wild, random spikes of color shot through Eliaster's eyes. He gave Roe a gentle push toward the door. "Just get going."

Larae stared gap-mouthed at him.

"Oh, how the mighty has fallen," I said, stuffing my laptop into my bag. "You actually said please, Eliaster. Sure you're not coming down with something?"

He stepped to the front of the room and edged back the curtain over the window. David shrugged at Larae, and they left to grab their stuff. I slung the messenger bag over my shoulder and joined Eliaster at the window.

The street outside was light with the dull orange night-glow of the light globes. Thin lines of light showed from other houses on the block, outlining windows that had heavy curtains or blinds in front of them. The street was deserted except for one black-cloaked figure walking down the center of the road.

Eliaster tensed, and one hand crept down to a sword hilt, gripping it so tight his fingers whitened.

The figure's head turned from side to side as it strode down the road. It passed a bit of light from a window, and that brief second, I saw the flash of long, glistening claws emerging from the cloak's sleeves.

Eliaster dropped the curtain back in place, his jaw muscles bunching. He went into the hall. "Roe!"

She came down the stairs, dressed in khakis tucked into rugged knee-high boots, and a dark button down shirt. She held a large, colorful tote tucked under one arm. David and Larae stood near the front door. Larae was peering out of the door window.

She turned to Eliaster, eyes wide. "He sent a sluagh for us?"

"For me. He told me he would, one day, if I didn't stop interfering." The tinge of fear had disappeared from Eliaster's voice. His eyes had calmed, and his face was set in hard, impassive lines.

"Do we have time to lay down a couple of knots?" David asked. "Slow it down a little, anyway?"

"We shouldn't have to," Roe said. "The windows and doors are lined with silver. It can't cross those lines."

I looked over Larae's shoulder. The thing—the sluagh—had paused in the street, facing the door. The head shifted, and a cold chill struck through my skin, to my bones. Somehow, even though I couldn't see into the dark depths of the hood, I knew it had just made eye contact with me. Some part of me, deep inside my chest, clenched like a fist, squeezing a small gasp from my lungs.

Roe gave me a concerned glance, then put her hand on Eliaster's arm. "We're safe here. You can relax."

He shifted free of her touch. "Let's get in a back room anyway, away from the windows."

We'd just started toward the kitchen when the front door crashed open, making us all stagger back. The sluagh stood in the doorway, clawed hands raised. Its hood had fallen back.

The thing's face had skin stretched tight over its skull, spurs of bone like a hooked beak lined with sharp teeth overhanging the mouth area. Sunken cavities marred either side of its face where cheeks should have been, and fine white wisps of hair hung over its shoulders. The eyes were black, but seemed to glow from deep within. The effect was like a dark, unholy anti-fire, not providing light, but instead sucking it into the shifting darkness.

My gut clenched tighter as it made eye contact with me, and I doubled forward, gasping in pain and clutching at my heart, but still unable to break eye contact. Rushing, like ocean waves, filled my ears. Over the noise, I could vaguely hear Eliaster yelling something at the others. The sluagh reached toward me, clawed appendages nicking into my shirt.

Something in my chest tugged hard, sending a burst of sharp, clarifying pain through me. I grunted, pushed back against whatever it was that dragged me closer to the sluagh.

Eliaster lunged between us, the fireplace poker clenched like a sword in one fist. He slammed the poker into the sluagh's side, and it shrieked—an impossibly high, harsh cry that like a bird of prey.

The pain in my chest eased.

Eliaster shoved me. "Move!"

We dashed through the house and out the kitchen back door. As I clattered down the back steps, I realized Eliaster wasn't with me again. I spun around, the glass door slipping from my hand and swinging shut.

He burst into the kitchen, running too fast to stop. He wrapped his arms around his head and crashed through the door. Glass sprayed across the alley, and he rolled off the back steps, knocking me off my feet.

Larae grabbed my arm and tugged me up and after her.

We dashed down the alley. Roe led the way, zigzagging through the streets with a spryness that belied her age. After several blocks, she ducked into a narrow alley between a tall, sky-blue Victorian house and a rickety wooden fence.

David stepped to the back of the group, pulling a pistol from his jacket and poking his head around the corner we'd just turned.

Eliaster stumbled to a halt and doubled over, pressing his hands to his thighs. Blood streamed in ribbons from gouges on his arms and congealed on the right side of his face.

"The sluagh?" Larae demanded, voice pitched high.

"Down for the count." Eliaster spit to the side, and a red stain appeared in the dirt. "Didn't kill the sucker, but that iron poker sure didn't feel good either."

"That was stupid, using iron when it makes you weaker," David said. "The sluagh could've sucked your soul easy, if it had dodged your attack."

"The bet paid off, though, and I'm still standing." Eliaster grinned, revealing bloody teeth.

Roe crouched in front of him and gently touched his chin, coaxing him to look up. She pulled a handkerchief from her pocket, clicking her teeth against her tongue as she dabbed blood from his face. "I don't even understand how the sluagh got in. Those silver wards…it should have worked. And all the doors and windows were closed."

"I'm sorry," Eliaster whispered. "For bringing it down on you."

She made an impatient tsk. "You needn't apologize to me."

He pushed her hands away and stood. "We need to keep moving."

Larae hitched her backpack higher on her shoulder. "No arguments here."

"Where are we going?" David asked. "You're not going to find a place in the entire Underworld where you'll be safe."

Eliaster smirked. "Sure we are. Unfortunately, it's only slightly more pleasant than facing the sluagh."

Roe raised her eyebrows. "You really must work on showing your father more respect, Eliaster."

Larae frowned. "We're going to your dad's?"

"It's the only place we'll be safe long enough to regroup

and think up a new plan." He started limping toward the Market. "Forward ho."

chapter 12

We exited the Market by a different gate than the one we'd come in, and I could tell we were in a different section of the city. The houses were bigger and further apart, and a few had moss growing in front of them so it almost looked like a yard. Eventually, the houses were spread out by several acres each, looking like an upscale Overworld suburb. Hedges of moss-covered rocks separated the properties. More orange light globes hung from this section of the city, making it almost as bright as Overworld daylight.

We trudged along the loosely graveled road until we reached a fenced-in property. A whitewashed Tudor mansion stood behind the fence, several hundred yards of moss separating it from us. A flicker moved on the roof, and I squinted. Against the dark roof of the house, next to one of the several chimneys, I could just barely make out the dark-clothed shape of a man cradling a weapon to his chest.

Another dark-clothed fae stepped into view just inside the gate, a rifle slung over one shoulder. "Eliaster."

Eliaster walked over to the gate. "Hey Lúkas. Open up for me and my friends?"

"Your dad didn't mention that you were coming here today," Lúkas said.

"My dad doesn't rule my day. Won't be here long,

promise."

Lúkas raised one eyebrow, then stepped to the side. His hand disappeared briefly behind one of the gateposts. With a creak, the black gate swung open. He motioned us inside.

Just like most of the other houses, the yard was made with a spongy, bright green moss. As we crunched along the white gravel drive, a sprinkler system popped up and began shooting water over the moss. I looked up at the roof again and noticed that the sniper was watching us. He noticed me and tipped his head.

I lowered my eyes.

A few steps from the front door, Eliaster stopped us. "Okay, guys. Let me talk. The last thing my dad will want is all of us trying to explain things to him."

"He's not going to be happy to hear you explaining it to him either," Larae said.

Eliaster's jaw tightened. "Thanks for that." He turned and smacked his fist against the door.

Another armed guard opened the door and nodded. We stepped inside to a wood-paneled foyer. The white marble floor was slick under my feet. I looked around the room, noting the niches for expensive looking paintings and the thin side tables, each tastefully decorated with one or two knick-knacks. Two cameras were mounted on the ceiling and trained on the door. There were probably plenty more both inside and outside that were better concealed.

"Got enough security?" I whispered to David.

"Counselor Tyrone is a bigwig among the fae leaders worldwide. He's made a few enemies in his time."

If his dad was so influential, why did Eliaster strike me as a bit of a drifter, not really tied down anywhere? Why wasn't he working with his dad in fae politics? I nearly had to bite my tongue to not ask the questions. Instead, I kept looking around the foyer.

Open doorways on either side showed what looked like a formal dining room and a ballroom. A closed door nestled to one side. Curving above it stretched a dark stone-and-wood staircase. The entire place looked rich and classy without being in-your-face.

"Swanky joint," I murmured under my breath.

"Built on blood and gravestones," Eliaster growled. "Don't be fooled."

The door under the stairs opened and a slim fae with red-blond hair stepped out. At first glance, there wasn't much resemblance between him and Eliaster. The fae turned his bright green, piercing eyes on our group. Those were recognizable eyes.

He frowned as his eyes fell on me. The look—eyebrows and lips pinched together, stern and irritated—made me want to squirm. I held myself stiff.

His gaze moved to his son. "Hello, Eliaster."

Eliaster squared his shoulders and clasped his hands behind his back, like a soldier about to give a report to his superior. "Sir."

They faced each other for a moment, stiff and formal. I shifted my weight from one foot to the other. David cleared his throat. Neither fae flinched.

Yeah, this wasn't awkward at all.

Roe stepped forward and extended her hands. "Cormac."

Tyrone smiled with just his lips, the expression not touching the rest of his face, as he took her extended hand. "I'm sorry my son dragged you into his latest escapade, Roe."

"No one drags me anywhere, you should know that by now. What Eliaster isn't telling you is that he had no intention of mixing you up in this until a sluagh came after him."

Eliaster grunted in protest.

Tyrone's jaw clenched, and a flicker of the same angry fire that burned in Eliaster came into his eyes. He glanced at one of his bodyguards and jerked his head at the door. The man left, and Tyrone glared at his son. "Anything else I haven't been told about?"

"No, sir."

"Good. Now what else do you need?"

Eliaster started to speak, but Roe interrupted. "A safe place to regroup and decide our next step, Counselor."

Tyrone stepped to the side and gestured at the door underneath the staircase. We filed past him into a large library. It reminded me a little of Roe's place, but this room was in perfect order, books filed correctly on the shelves, leather armchairs arranged in a stiff semi-circle around the fire, and no loose papers on the shelves or tables.

Tyrone waited until each of us had found a seat, then strode to stand in front of the fire. He looked at Roe, his face impassive. "Please, tell me everything."

She started all the way back to the spring, with Aiden's death. Apparently, Marc had found Aiden's journal entry as he'd gone through the stuff in his dad's study. He'd immediately taken it to Eliaster. Roe and Larae had been brought in right away, with Larae asking David to help some time later. But nothing had really happened until a couple of months ago, when Scyrril had approached Marc with the same offer Aiden had been given.

As he listened, Tyrone's lips compressed and his eyes narrowed. When Roe finished, he remained silent for a moment, staring at the floor, the knuckles of his right hand rubbing against his chin.

"I'd heard you'd been busy, Eliaster," he said finally. "I didn't think it was beyond your usual picking at scabs of wounds that should have been long healed. But messing with Blodheyr, of all people... And then to drag an incompetent Overworlder into this..."

Hey now. I glared at the counselor.

Eliaster folded his arms across his chest. "This proves what I've been saying since Iain died."

At the name, a swift wince crossed Tyrone's face, gone so quickly I wondered if I'd imagined it. "As I've said before—I only repeat it for the benefit of all of you—" His gaze swept the room. "The Lucht Leanúna are dragged into it every time there's a rumble of unrest. Roe, you know that as well as I. Seelie and Unseelie alike are far too superstitious when it comes to the Dark Man."

"I'd like to think so, Cormac, but this feels different than anything I've ever heard before," Roe said quietly. "With Blodheyr searching for this relic... And I'm afraid that this is no normal relic."

"What do you mean?" Tyrone demanded sharply.

Roe licked her lips and looked down at her clasped hands. For a long moment, she was silent, but when she finally did speak, her voice was soft. "Back in the nineteen-twenties and thirties, the curators put a ban out on all fae relics. It was around the same time as Prohibition." She smiled faintly. "You can imagine how that went over with the fae. Alcohol and their precious relics, banned at the same time."

Tyrone nodded. "It was a madhouse."

"Don't I know it. At one point, a dear friend of mine, Owen Craig, discovered that the curators were intent on finding one relic in particular. A very old, very powerful relic that, if the wrong people found it, could easily destroy both worlds. A pathstone."

The room went silent. I glanced from side to side. David looked just as confused as I was, but every fae in the room—Roe, Tyrone, Eliaster, and Larae—had gone pale, their bodies stiff.

"A...pathstone," Tyrone finally said. "Did you ever..."

"No, we never found it. At least, we never found this particular one."

"Then how do you know for sure that this—"

"Because Owen and I were told, although not in so many words, that others possibly existed." Roe sighed. "I don't know for certain that this is a pathstone, but I'm willing to place a very large bet that it is."

"And if it is a pathstone?" Eliaster asked. "The paths are lost, aren't they?"

"We thought pathstones lost as well," Roe answered.

"Still, it's just one stone," Larae said. "And you said earlier that no one would be so foolish—"

"It can still create plenty of havoc," Roe returned sharply. "Believe me. I've dealt with this before. If it is a pathstone…" Her lips pinched together, and she shook her head. "As for no one being that foolish…well, I've been in denial far too long, I'm afraid."

Tyrone let out a deep breath and looked at Eliaster. "Do you have any proof that Blodheyr is connected to the Lucht Leanúna?"

Roe, Eliaster, David, and Larae all looked at me.

I held my hands out. "What?"

"Did you find anything on those computer hard drives?" Larae asked. "Anything that would implicate Blodheyr as one of the Lucht Leanúna?"

"I haven't had time to dig into them," I said.

"Hard drives?" Tyrone asked at the same time. "So that's why the Sluagh is after you."

"Hey, this one? Not on me." Eliaster jerked his thumb at David. "Ask that genius. Blodheyr's assuming it was my fault."

Cormac pinched the bridge of his nose between his finger and thumb. "Thankfully, the *rath* is warded against sluagh, so you did something right." He sighed. "I'll give you asylum for a few days. We'll see if I can convince Blodheyr to call his monster off, but that's as far as I'm getting involved. Fix this. And try not to do anything else stupid." He turned and left the room.

I glanced at Eliaster.

He ran his hand through his hair. "Okay. Josh, see what you can dig up from those hard drives. Try to find anything that could link Blodheyr to the Lucht Leanúna. Larae, why don't you help him. David, let's start planning a trip to Chicago."

"What about rescuing Marc?" Larae asked.

Eliaster stared at her. "Yeah, 'cause that went so well the first time!"

She frowned. "I'm not leaving Springfield without him."

"For the love of…" He pressed the heel of his hand

against his forehead, and for a second, he looked a lot like Tyrone. "Just help Josh, okay? We can discuss this later."

Roe stood. "Your father has a much more extensive library than I do. I'm going to refresh my memory regarding the pathstones. I might be able to find something useful."

Eliaster nodded as he and David headed out of the room.

I pulled my laptop out of my bag and turned it on.

Larae leaned on the arm of the chair beside me.

She was way too close. I shifted away from her and said, "There's not much you can help me with now. I just need to finish coding the program that will dig into the hard drives and pull out info."

"What should I do then?" she asked.

"You can come help me," Roe said, standing.

Larae headed over to the shelves with her.

I brought up the file I'd been working on when the sluagh interrupted us. The thought of that thing's pale, cadaverous face sent a shiver through me. As if trolls and goblins and creepy Unseelie weren't bad enough. What other monsters would we discover on this little adventure? I didn't remember a mention of the sluagh in my online research. What other monsters existed that the legends hadn't mentioned?

I shoved the thought out of my mind and concentrated on my coding. Larae and Roe searched the bookshelves, occasionally bending over the same book to discuss something in low tones. After about an hour I laid down the last line of code and plugged the hard drives in to run the program. The last thing I remembered was checking the time on my laptop screen—four-thirty a.m.—and leaning my head on the arm of the chair. *Just a quick nap...*

Larae woke me at noon, waving a plate of sandwiches under my nose. "You missed breakfast. Roe wouldn't let us wake you."

I grabbed a sandwich and stuffed a bite into my mouth. "Did you check the computer? How'd the program work?"

Larae shrugged. I picked the laptop up and brought up my program. A list of hidden data files popped up.

We spent the afternoon combing through the files. At some point, Roe joined us in the library, but I didn't see Eliaster, David, or Counselor Tyrone for most of the day. Toward late afternoon, Larae and I struck pay dirt with old memory files that contained passwords to various websites accessed on the loan shop's office computer. One of them was a forum board called The Tree of Life.

"Let's check this one out," I muttered, typing the forum's address into my web bar and hitting Enter.

"Why that one?" Larae asked, leaning over my shoulder.

I shrugged, using the movement to mask moving away from her. Blodheyr hadn't struck me as the forum-frequenting type—none of the fae did—but it held more intrigue than, say, the Amazon and Barnes & Noble accounts I'd seen passwords for. The Tree of Life sounded like something fae would be interested in.

The forum popped up in my browser, a dark gray background with silver letters. I scrolled through the boards, then randomly clicked on one titled *Tír Ni-all go Brách*. A popup window asked for a password. I typed Blodheyr's into it, and after a moment, the website let me through to the message board.

I scanned the posts, entered by people by the names of 'Silverhand', 'Bloodheart', 'Maev', and 'Carman'.

As I went past a post by the 'Carman' user, Larae inhaled sharply through her teeth.

"What?" I scrolled back and read through the message.

We are close. Soon, we will be able to bridge the worlds. A few more months...maybe a year, at most. Doirich will be our king once again.

A chill raced over my skin. Could it be that blatant?

"Why would they put this on the internet?" Larae asked.

"It's not going to flag anything," I said, scrolling through the rest of the messages. 'Carman' was the most blatant of the posters—the rest merely spoke in vague terms about the coming of their king. And by the language used when they directly addressed 'Carman', I guessed he—or she—was a leader.

"Yeah, there's nothing here that would flag anything," I repeated. "No one would be able to access this website except the feds and hackers, both of whom would probably assume this is just a text-based role-playing game of some kind."

A reply to one of Carman's posts caught my eye.

My lady...So it was a woman...*we are working diligently on your orders in our search for the pathstones*...

My hands tensed on the keyboard. I turned to Larae. "Go find Eliaster. Roe!"

Larae dashed for the library door, and Roe hurried to my side. "Yes?"

I angled the laptop toward her. "Who is Carman?"

Roe's face, already pale, drained of any color until her skin tone was the same as the sluagh's. She spoke in a soft, hesitant voice. "Carman was Fear Doiricht's wife and battle-mate. We thought she'd perished in the battle to close the paths."

I pressed the heels of my hands to my eyes. "Ah, c'mon, you've got to be kidding me! Doiricht's wife is leading this pack of lunatics? I don't suppose this could get any worse?"

"Not really." Roe leaned closer to the screen. "And they're looking for more than one pathstone."

"Of course they are. Let's just make it a freakin' happy-go-lucky Indiana Jones adventure all over the world!" I shoved the laptop away from me, stood, and started for the door.

Larae and Eliaster came in. I glared at Eliaster. He raised his hands and started to say something. I shouldered past him and stepped into the hall. Before the door shut behind me, I heard Roe beginning to explain to them.

The hall was empty, save for the two guards sitting on either side of the door. I restrained my urge to punch the wall and, instead, settled for growling and running my hands through my hair.

It was just my luck that this whole thing became more

complicated at every turn. I paced in a tight circle, clenching and unclenching my hands. That wasn't helping. I spun around and kicked the leg of a table. The vase on top—probably some priceless fae collectible—clunked over on its side.

I cringed.

One of the guards lurched up to his feet, hand going to his sword, but he didn't move toward me.

"If you're going to break something, I'd prefer you do it in my personal gym and not the front hall," Counselor Tyrone said.

I spun around. Tyrone stood a few feet away, his hands clasped behind his back. What was it with fae and their inclinations to sneak up on people?

"Sorry," I muttered.

The library door opened, and Roe poked her head out. "Cormac? A moment?"

Cormac nodded to her, then raised his eyebrows as he looked back at me.

I nodded. I couldn't go back in the library, not with angry, nervous energy buzzing through me like this.

He gestured to the guard who was still standing. "Show Josh to the gym before he destroys anything." He walked into the library and shut the door after himself.

The guard gestured for me to follow him and opened a door on the opposite side of the hall. We walked through a formal dining room, big enough to fit at least twenty people, and into a small sitting room stocked with a glass-fronted liquor cabinet and plenty of comfortable chairs. The guard nodded to a door that inconspicuously blended into the paneling at the far side of the room.

I opened it and stepped into a room the size of a small gymnasium. The floor was covered in blue foam pads. A rack of practice weapons and a punching bag hung on the wall across from me, and to my right there were several wooden dummies, hacked and scarred from swords and arrows. The rest of the floor was open, probably for martial arts or sword form practice. It was probably four or five times the size of Roe's basement gym. I could see why Cormac had directed me here.

The door swung shut silently behind me as I crossed to one of the wooden dummies. I closed my hand around my sword hilt, and the metal rasped as I drew it. In the artificial light of the room, the blade looked almost yellow.

I clenched my hands tight around the sword hilt and gave a guttural yell as I lunged at the dummy. My blade flashed, bit into the wood, and swung away again. I struck head, shoulders, torso in a random pattern. I fell into a rhythm of the forms that David had shown me. I ducked and darted around the dummy.

Finally I stopped, slowly becoming aware of the burning in my shoulders and legs. I pressed the sword point into the floor mats and leaned on the hilt, my chest heaving. My shirt was soaked in sweat, and my hair dripped into my eyes. How long as I been in here?

My anger had evaporated. Of course, none of the fae had known exactly what we were getting into. In a way, we were all playing catch-up to the Lucht Leanúna.

And Eliaster *had* warned me.

Out of the corner of my eye, I saw the door open. Eliaster edged cautiously into the room.

I lunged and slammed the point of my sword into the heart of the wooden dummy, driving the blade deep. I released the hilt and stepped back. "What do you want, Eliaster?"

The fae moved to the side of the dummy and studied it. "I take back what I said about David teaching you swordplay. Looks like you've learned something after all."

I wrenched the sword free. "Didn't know you were one for chitchat."

Eliaster rolled his eyes. "Roe told my dad what you found."

I straightened my shoulders. "Oh yeah? What'd he say?"

"He didn't give you any compliments, if that's what

you're wondering."

"No, I'm learning to expect that from you people."

Eliaster smirked. "Set your expectations low enough that even us fae can achieve them."

"Do you have anything relevant to say?"

"Okay, fine. He wants us to leave for Chicago as soon as possible. The conversation you found on that forum that hinted at multiple relics really has him worried."

I sheathed my sword and looked him in the eye. "Yeah, and what about Marc? Larae's going to kick up a squall if we leave without making a rescue attempt."

Eliaster's jaw bunched and he glanced down at the ground. He rubbed the back of his neck. I narrowed my eyes. He looked as if he was trying to decide something…something to tell me, maybe?

"What is it?" I asked.

"Nothing."

"Eliaster, I swear, if you're lying to me…"

"You'll what? Rescue Marc on your own? The best chance of doing that is finding the relic." Eliaster left the room, his shoulders hunched.

chapter 13

We met the next morning in the library, just Roe, David, Larae, Eliaster, and me. Cormac had wisely opted out, since Larae was seething.

"He can't just order us to do something!" she growled, slinging her backpack against the couch cushions, then flopping down between it and my messenger bag.

"Well?" Larae picked up a pen from the side table and threw it across the room at Eliaster. "You can't be happy about this. Since when do you listen to your dad?"

He looked up. The dark circles under his eyes looked more pronounced this morning. "Just because we don't get along doesn't mean I don't agree with him once in a while."

"You act like you don't even want to rescue Marc," she muttered, crossing her arms.

Bright green flickered in Eliaster's eyes, and he turned his gaze to the side.

I frowned. Again, he couldn't be more blatant about the fact that he was hiding something from the rest of us. What was he not saying? Why was no one else asking this?

Roe cleared her throat. "I'm not going with you, of course."

"No one expected you to," David said.

She raised an eyebrow, her lips twitching into a smile. "Are you implying something, young man?"

He grinned. "Not at all."

"So what will you be doing?" I asked.

"Research. I'm going to see if I can find anything more about these other relics. Maybe I can guess at the Lucht Leanúna's end game. It's time we were on a level footing with them."

Eliaster abruptly stood and shouldered his backpack. "Let's not waste any more time then."

Roe gave me a hug as the others walked out of the library.

"You be careful, Joshua MacAllister. You've been a good friend to my grandson, and I've grown fond of you myself these last few days."

I hugged her back. "No promises, Roe. I'm only an Overworlder out of his element, after all."

"Nonsense talk, that is. You'll do fine." She patted my shoulders.

When I stepped out into the hallway, David and Larae were already outside. Cormac Tyrone and Eliaster stood close to the front door.

"—tell them," Cormac was saying, his tone urgent. "You can't expect to be—"

Eliaster caught sight of me and stepped away from his father. "Sorry, Da. Not gonna happen." Without looking at me, he pulled the door open and stepped outside.

Cormac sighed and nodded to me. "*Go gcumhdai Dia thu*. May God protect you."

Was that directed to me, or all of us? I settled for nodding to him, then hurried out after Eliaster. He was heading to a large metal garage tucked partially behind the side of the house. David and Larae stood in the driveway.

"Where's he going?" I asked, jerking my head at Eliaster.

"He wants to ride one of his bikes. Says he can't handle being cooped up in my car for hours." Larae jingled the keys to her Porsche in one hand. "Hey, Eli, should we wait for you?"

Eliaster paused in unlocking the garage's side door. "I'll catch up. You guys have a bit of a hike anyway."

Larae nodded and started for the gate. I tagged after her, gnawing on the inside of my lower lip, wondering if I should tell her and David about the snippet of conversation I'd caught between Cormac and Eliaster.

Why couldn't he just trust us?

As I clambered into the back seat, Larae popped the trunk of the Porsche and stowed her and David's backpacks.

"Want me to put your bag back here?" she asked.

"Nah, thanks. I'll probably end up working on my laptop some." I had a few papers due in a week. Maybe I could salvage my college career if I got them turned in on time. *Not. Why even bother?*

Larae slid into the driver's seat and tossed a water bottle at me, setting two others in the cup holders in front. "Just don't drink it all before we leave town. We're not taking many potty breaks."

I opened the bottle and took a drink. I'd never liked the taste of bottled water, but this one in tasted like chemical waste. I looked at the label. It was some cheap brand I'd never heard of. I scraped my tongue on my teeth, recapped the bottle, and stuck it in the pocket in the back of the passenger seat.

Larae pulled out of the parking garage.

Ten miles outside of Springfield, Eliaster flew past us on an expensive-looking, all black speed bike. Larae muttered something under her breath and accelerated. The countryside flew past, and eventually the hum of the tires on the road lulled me to sleep.

When I awoke, the melon-colored sun hung over the western horizon. Evening already? I glanced at the dashboard clock. Just after seven. I sat up straight, my neck stiff and uncooperative. My legs were cramped from sitting in the tiny backseat of the Porsche.

"Hi, Sleeping Beauty," David said, twisting in his seat to look back at me.

"Hey." Despite how long I'd slept, I didn't feel rested at all. I squirmed, trying to find a more comfortable position. My legs weren't just cramped, they'd fallen asleep. The seatbelt tightened as I squirmed. *I need to pee.* "Hey, are we close to a rest stop at all? Where are we?"

"In central Illinois," Larae said.

"Gotcha." I yawned and rubbed my eyes. "Man, I'm groggy." My mouth was dry too. Despite needing a restroom stop, I picked up my water and started to uncap it.

A white sediment had settled at the bottom of the clear plastic bottle. My skin went cold, and I slid the bottle back into the seat pocket. As I looked up, I saw
Larae staring at me in the rearview mirror.

I forced a grin. "Figured maybe getting a drink before I go to the bathroom was a bad idea."

She chuckled. "You must need to go bad. Hint taken. There's a rest stop coming up soon." She switched lanes.

I leaned my head back against the seat, my mind racing. I had never slept that well in the car before, but I'd just attributed that to being sleep-deprived for the last few days. That white powder, though…could it have been some kind of drug? It would explain the grogginess and the way I didn't feel rested despite having slept so long.

Had the water bottle been open when Larae had handed it to me? I thought back but couldn't remember. Who would want to drug me? The obvious answer was Larae, or David, or both…they were awfully chummy all the time. So the real question was, why?

Were we even in Illinois? Trying to be casual, I sat up and peered through the back window. My anxiety eased a little when I spotted Eliaster on his bike about ten yards back from the car.

Larae pulled off the highway into the empty parking lot

of a rest stop. Eliaster followed. As soon as she'd parked, David got out of the car and folded his seat forward. I almost grabbed the water, but what excuse could I have for carrying that into the restroom with me?

Telling Eliaster would have to wait. I jogged through the small, tourist-geared lobby of the rest stop to the bathroom and took care of business. David and Eliaster came in as I was leaving. When I stepped back out, I could see through the glass front of the building that Larae wasn't at the car either.

The lobby was well-stocked with several vending machines, shelves of pamphlets about local attractions, and a couple of water fountains. The main area was mostly clear, with a few benches. I flopped down on a bench and yawned again. My muscles were still stiff, and I was starting to get light-headed.

Eliaster stepped out of the men's restroom. "What're you yawning about? Larae just said you've slept most of the trip."

I grunted. "Funny, considering I think she caused the sleep."

Eliaster's eyes flickered. "What are you talking about?"

Just at that moment, Larae came out of the women's bathroom.

Eliaster walked over to a vending machine and started putting coins into the slot.

"How much longer 'til Chicago?" I asked Larae.

"A few hours, I think. Should get there late tonight."

Eliaster came back and handed me an energy drink. "While we're waiting for David, let's go do some sword work."

Larae frowned. "Here?"

"There's no one else here. Besides, I want to get a feel for the damage David's done before we get into any hairy situations."

Larae rolled her eyes and sat down on a bench.

I popped the top on the can as I followed Eliaster outside and around the building. There was a small open area behind

the rest stop, half dirt and half straggly grass. A rusty swing
set was to one side, and I could see a sandy patch where more
playground equipment used to be.

Eliaster drew one of his swords, then motioned for me to
do the same.

I gulped from the energy drink. "I thought you were just
saying that. I feel like a rubber band."

He shrugged. "May as well. Tell me about your
suspicions first, though."

I took another swig. "Not much to tell. When I woke up,
my mouth felt all dry, and I didn't feel rested. Plus, I never
sleep well in the car—there's no way I slept all the way from
Springfield to...wherever we are—"

"Just outside of Springfield, Illinois."

Ha, nice. "I wouldn't have slept that long without waking
up in the car. I've never done that, no matter how tired I am."

Eliaster's face settled into a passive stare. "That could all
be coincidence. You've had a rough few days."

"Could be, but coupled with white sediment at the bottom
of the water bottle that Larae gave to me? Don't think so."

Eliaster grunted and rubbed his chin. "Sneaky *siabrha*.
What is she up to? Could be David too, I suppose."

"Or you."

He gave me a glare.

I tossed the empty energy drink can at the Dumpster
sitting at the back of the building. It bounced off the rim. I
turned back to Eliaster. "You're still not being truthful. I
heard what your dad said to you this morning. What are you
not telling us?"

"It's none of your concern."

I mustered all the sarcasm I had. "Really?"

"Yes, really."

"Liar."

"I don't lie."

I turned my back on him and started toward the parking
lot. "Whatever."

Eliaster's feet pounded the ground behind me. I spun in

time to see his sword swing. I ducked and jumped back, drawing my own sword.

"What is wrong with you?" I hissed.

He lunged forward. I jerked back, knocking his sword to the side. The glittering edge sliced past a fraction of an inch from my face.

My momentum dumped me onto my back. I rolled to my side, saw Eliaster coming toward me. I got to my knees, slashed out at his feet. He jumped back, giving me a split-second longer than I needed to stagger to my feet.

"Need a tip?" he taunted, circling me.

I brushed hair out of my eyes. "No."

"Treat the sword as an extension of your arm. None of this flailing around, using your wrist to move the sword. A cut must come from your shoulder and elbow, like so." Eliaster jabbed at my side.

I twisted away and shifted the grip on my sword. Before he could jab again, I swept out, imaging that my sword was my hand, grabbing for his arm. Eliaster was right—the motion felt much smoother.

Until he parried.

A sharp, numbing pain jolted up my arm. I hissed through clenched teeth, shuffled backward to shake off the pain.

Eliaster wasted no time in his next few moves. His sword hammered at me, barely giving me enough time to recover from one blow before I had to parry the next. Unlike David, he didn't stick to a pattern. Yet I managed to hold my own, watching for the small telltale signs of where he was going to strike—a glance, a tiny movement. Within minutes, sweat was dripping down my face despite the cool evening.

"You might want to stop," Larae said somewhere behind me. "There's a van pulling into the rest stop."

I glanced over my shoulder at her, letting my sword arm sag. The next thing I knew, I was on my back. Eliaster's foot ground into my chest, and his sword rested on my Adam's apple.

"Had enough?" he asked.

"Get away." I shoved his foot off my hest and rolled to my side, panting for breath.

He grabbed my arm and yanked me to my feet, whispering harshly, "If you don't believe me, fine. But just know—if I didn't want to protect you, you'd be dead."

" 'Kay, boys, seriously. Show's over," Larae said. "Let's go."

I jerked away from Eliaster and started after her.

"A piece of advice, Josh?" Eliaster asked.

"Sure," I growled, slamming my sword into the sheath.

He shook his head. "Never mind. I don't dole out advice where it's not welcome."

We rounded the building. David hopped up from the hood of the Porsche.

"Ready?" he asked.

Larae tossed him the keys, then looked at me.
"You're not setting foot in my car like that."

I looked down. A coating of old grass clippings and dirt clung to my clothes. I shook my head and headed back for the restroom. As I opened the lobby door, a cool breeze rolled over my sweaty skin. I shivered.

Yes, looking over my shoulder at Larae had been stupid. I slammed into the men's bathroom and grabbed a wad of paper towels from the dispenser. At least my adrenaline was pumping enough that I no longer felt the sleeping drug's after effects.

I ran water on the towels and began wiping down my face and neck. As I swept off my clothes, one of the stalls opened and a preteen boy stepped out. He gave me a suspicious glance as he ran his fingers under the faucet for a few seconds, then wiped his hands on his jeans as he left the bathroom.

I slung the towels in the trashcan and stared at my reflection in the pocked mirror. What was Eliaster hiding, and why did he feel the need to attack me when I called him on it?

No, he hadn't really been attacking me. Just toying.

Reminding me that he wasn't my friend. I slammed my palms against the counter. What would it take to get him to trust me? Idiot fae.

I grabbed the door handle. As it cracked open, I heard a small sound—a whimper.

Normally, I wouldn't have paid it any attention. But given all that had happened in the last twenty-four hours, my suspicion snapped to attention.

I peered around the door. It was dusk outside the building. I could see David, Larae, and Eliaster standing under the streetlight by the car. David and Eliaster looked like they were arguing, as usual.

The men's bathroom was at the end of the building, with the women's bathroom to the right and water fountains between. Most of the building stretched to my right. Among the benches, a half-a-dozen pale-green-skinned beings threatened the preteen boy, an even younger girl, and a woman who looked just old enough to be their mom. Goblins. Four of them held spears, the other two swords in their gnarled hands.

I let my eyes unfocus, but the humans remained human. I shrank back into the bathroom and touched my sword. I remembered the human slaves I'd seen in the Underworld. Eliaster had said the Seelie tried to control it, but that fae who wanted slaves found ways to get them. Were these goblins slavers?

I peeked out the door. David, Eliaster, and Larae were still talking by the Porsche, totally unaware of what was going down inside.

A scream from the little girl jerked my attention back to the goblins' prisoners. They were trying to subdue the mother and the boy.

I had to act now.

I was probably going to get hurt. Eliaster was definitely going to kill me for this.

chapter 19

I drew my sword and charged out toward the goblins, screaming at the top of my lungs. I felt like I was running through molasses. My feet slowed and my vision tunneled. Two of the goblins turned back and ran toward me, one carrying a spear, one a sword. This close, I could see the blue veins spidering under their papery-thin skin and the lumps and warts freckling their face and hands.

I lunged sideways as the spear jabbed forward. I swung my sword in a two-handed grip like a baseball bat. The shaft snapped under my blow. The goblin slashed at me with his free hand, the yellowed nails sharp and thick, like knives attached to the ends of his fingers. I dodged backward.

I whirled around to the swordbearer in time to use a one-handed block on his swing. The goblin's surprising strength knocked me back a step. The goblin's sword grated down my blade, and he twisted, trying to get his hilt between the sword grip and my hand. I pulled away and clutched the grip tighter.

Something whipped across my shoulders, pitching me forward. The spearman laughed and struck me again, cracking the broken spear against my head.

Stars exploded and my vision faded. I tumbled to my

side, bringing my hand to my head. My sword clanged as it struck the floor. I shook my head, blinked hard.

I heard the doors crack open, and Larae ran in, carrying her shotgun. David and Eliaster were right behind her.

A dry, scaly arm wrapped around my throat and jerked me to my feet.

"Let him go!" Larae ordered.

The goblin pressed his sword into my throat.

"I told you to let him go, goblin," Larae snapped, ratcheting her shotgun.

I resisted the urge to squeeze my eyes shut. If by some miracle she was able to get me out of this, I'd need quick reflexes.

The sword edge tightened a bit on my neck. "Sorry, fae. Insurance and a nice addition to our collection. Sounds like a good deal to me."

Larae's finger squeezed the trigger.

The gun exploded. I jumped, felt the sword slice my neck at the same time the goblin's scream pierced my ears. I stumbled forward. Blood trickled down my neck, and I pressed one hand against the cut.

As the smoke from Larae's gun drifted toward the ceiling, the goblins stared as their leader clutched his splintered leg. The rush of the highway filtered in through the open door.

The goblins snarled and charged forward, forgetting about the family huddled in the corner.

"Look out, Josh!" Eliaster shouted.

I rolled. A sword crashed down on the tile beside me. I grabbed my sword. The goblin gave me no time to get on my feet—he slashed and hacked, his sword clanging against the floor. I scrambled backward, crab-crawling, until my back thudded into the wall.

I jerked my sword up, knocking his aside. He snarled. That gave me enough time to get to my feet. Right. Note to self, don't pause to snarl at the enemy.

From the sounds of the battle, the other five goblins were giving the others enough to think about. Fine by me. This goblin was mine.

He limped around, snarling, spitting, his forked tongue licking his fleshy lips. "I may be wounded, but no tan-flesh is gonna skewer me!"

I lunged. He dodged, remarkably fast even with shreds of gray-green flesh hanging from his bony leg. As his sword connected with mine, my foot slipped on a smear of blood.

I staggered, twisted to dodge another jab, and sprawled on the ground. The goblin slammed his hand to my neck and his sword swept over his head.

Out of the corner of my eye, I saw Eliaster lunge toward me, a split second of fear frozen on his face.

I was not getting rescued again! I kicked the goblin's bad leg. His swing faltered, slicing into my arm instead of my throat. With a howl, fire racing up my arm, I swung my sword as hard as I could into the goblin's side.

The blade met little resistance and swept halfway through him. The goblin's eyes bulged and he folded over to the ground. I got up, slipping in the green blood pouring over the floor.

The goblin hacked a wad of blood at me. "Stupid…human…"

His eyes dimmed, as if I'd flicked off a light switch. A trickle of blood snaked from the corner of his mouth.

My stomach heaved. The blood of my first kill was smeared everywhere—the floor, my shoes, my hands, my clothes…

"Josh, you okay?" Eliaster asked.

"I, uh—" I doubled over and threw up.

Eliaster quickly stepped back.

"I think you got your answer." Larae knelt beside me. Her cool hands touched my face, turning my head so she could see the cut on my neck. "Eliaster, David, either of you need attention?"

"Couple cuts on my arms," David said. "Nothing big."

Larae nodded and hurried out to the car.

"I'm good." Eliaster turned to the tiny huddled family.

The mom stared at him, her eyes wide. "You—you're crazy!"

"I'm sorry you had to go through that," Eliaster extended his hand toward her.

She slapped it away and, picking up her daughter, hurried for the door. Her son followed close on her heels. They shoved past Larae in the doorway and ran to their van.

Larae snorted as she set down a small red box on the floor beside me. "When will you learn, Eliaster?"

Eliaster's shoulders stiffened. "Well, you can a hardly blame her when she thinks she just saw some bizarre gang war."

He shoved the door open and walked out, watching the family's van screech out of the parking lot.

After Larae taped bandages to the wounds on my neck and arm, I retreated to the bathroom and tried to scrub the goblin blood off my skin. The stuff had the gummy consistency of dried glue. Eliaster handed in my backpack, and I changed into a new pair of jeans and a new t-shirt, tossing the others into the trash. There was nothing I could do about the stains on my shoes, but I could live with that. I scrubbed the stains on my jacket out and dried it under the bathroom hand-dryer.

When I finally got out of the bathroom, it was ten o'clock. David and Larae were already in the Porsche, and Eliaster leaned against his bike, helmet in his hands.

"Think you can make it a little longer?" he asked.

"I'm good."

A breeze ran through the parking lot, blowing dried grass and leaves along with it. It pushed my hair off my forehead, and I took a deep breath. It felt good. Alive. I'd survived.

Eliaster cleared his throat. "Good job in there, Josh. Piece of advice?"

"Sure." This time I said it like I meant it. I did mean it.

"You're a good fighter. You're fast. You think well. The only thing holding you back is your pride in your own cleverness." He gave me a quick glance. "Don't let your pride become your downfall."

Pride? The only thing holding me back was my lack of technical knowledge. Pride had nothing to do with it.

The energy drink I'd chugged before the fight got me three hours longer, then I made the group stop at a hotel on the outskirts of Chicago. I collapsed on one of the beds in our room and fell asleep in minutes. The last image my brain registered was of Eliaster opening a laptop.

Sometime later, a crashing sound interrupted my sleep. I jerked upright. Larae sat up in the other bed, cursing.

Eliaster shook the smashed laptop free of his boot and sat back down in the desk chair. "Sorry."

"Amadán," Larae muttered, pulling the covers over her head.

I eyed the broken pieces littering the hotel room floor. "That wasn't mine, I hope?"

"Nope. Just another in a long line of technology that I've fried, gotten irritated with, and put out of its misery." Eliaster saw my look and said, "My glamour. Most fae can use technology, even if they're not very good with it, but I tend to randomly fry electronics."

"I don't know why you even bother anymore," Larae said, her voice muffled by the quilt.

David stepped out of the bathroom, toweling his hair. He raised an eyebrow at the broken laptop. "You could've asked me or Josh to do whatever it was that you needed to use technology for."

Larae sat up, huffing in exasperation. "Okay, jabberwockies, if you're not going to let me sleep, we may as well get moving for the day."

We gathered our stuff and tromped downstairs to the lobby. I managed to stuff down two donuts while Eliaster checked out. Within a few minutes, we were pulling onto the interstate.

The suburbs of Chicago zipped past us: houses, stores, and strip malls speeding by in a blur of urbanity. Clouds obscured the sun. As we pulled into downtown Chicago, David and Larae started talking in low voices. I ignored them and watched the skyscrapers slip past. The wind funneled through the towers, sounding like the howls of monsters and the baying of other Underworld denizens that I didn't even want to think about. It sent a shiver up my spine.

Soon we pulled into the lakeshore drive. Skyscrapers rose to the sky on one side, and on the other, the lake stretched out, flat and gray, for miles.

Eliaster led us down the marina and parked at a small lot close by the docks. A concrete wall curved from the end of the parking lot and around the marina docks, creating a small harbor.

"Our vehicles will be fine here, right?" Larae asked, stepping out of the car.

"Yeah, they'll be fine." Eliaster grabbed his backpack. "C'mon, let's move. If someone sees us accessing the Underworld hatch, we're going to be in trouble."

I hitched my backpack over my shoulders and jogged after the fae. "So this is the only entrance to the Underworld in Chicago?"

"No," Larae said. "But fae are protective of their cities. There are the underground entrances, of course, that everyone knows, but only one publicly known entrance above world. Who knows how many privately owned, heavily-guarded entrances exist."

We reached the wall. A rusted metal hatch was set into the wall at head height, with metal rungs leading up to it. Eliaster climbed up, pulled the hatch open, and ducked inside.

Underground again. Wonderful.

I dutifully climbed in, David and Larae following me. Eliaster pulled on the hatch. It creaked shut, enfolding us in darkness.

David snapped on a flashlight. We stood on a lip of

concrete on the side of a concrete tunnel. The tunnel sides shone in the light, slick with condensation. Outside, muffled waves shushed against the wall. Eliaster jumped down into the tunnel, and water splashed up around his boots, soaking the hem of his jeans. He reached down and pulled open what looked like a storm drain. Water swirled down the opening, the stream echoing through the drain.

Eliaster lowered himself down onto the rusted metal ladder and disappeared from view.

I glanced at Larae. "Ladies first."

She snorted, but followed Eliaster without a fuss. I stepped down into the tunnel. Slime squished under my feet. "Beautiful ambience the fae have created, don't you think?" I leaned down and set my slick sneakers on the ladder rungs.

"Just wonderful," David said, following me.

I hadn't gotten far before lights flicked on, illuminating the sides of the slime-greened drain. A damp, thick stench hung in the air. The washing of the waves died, replaced by the ping of water droplets. Orange rust from the ladder smeared my fingers. My tetanus shot was up to date, right? Right. Like that was the biggest threat to my health right now.

Eliaster and Larae waited at the bottom of the drain. As soon as David stepped off the ladder, Eliaster flicked the switch set into the wall, and the drain lights turned off, leaving us in darkness again. David turned on the flashlight.

A metal grate blocked the way in front of us. In the darkness beyond the gate, the beam disappeared into black. Something shuffled at the edge of the beam of light. A pale, clawed hand snaked out and coiled around a couple of the gate's bars.

I jumped as a garbled voice came out of the darkness.

"Who wishes to pass beyond this gate and enter the Underworld?"

"Four we are," David said in an obviously ceremonial answer. "My name is David of Springfield."

A deep, wet sucking sound came from the shadowy

figure just outside of David's flashlight beam. "Please, enter."

The clawed hand pulled, and the rusty gate screeched open. I cringed at the sound.

David stepped forward.

The hand snaked out, the claws curling to slap at his head.

Eliaster grabbed David's arm, shoving him back, and slashed his sword at the hand. A crimson streak opened across the pale skin. With a hiss, the monster withdrew into the gate.

Eliaster stepped closer. "Eliaster Tyrone, son of Seelie councilman Cormac Tyrone, seeks passage."

"You, I recognize," the monster growled. "You should have spoken up first. Enter—no harm will befall you or your party."

Eliaster confidently led us through the gate, though he kept a tight grip on his drawn sword as we passed a pale, mountainous thing. I didn't turn my head to get a good look at it. It made me feel like I was five again, refusing to acknowledge the stuffed grizzly at the Bass

Pro Shop in Springfield, afraid that if I actually looked at it, it would come to life and jump after me. Stupid idea, especially down here. But I still couldn't make myself look at the monster.

The gate clanged behind us, and David jumped. His face was pale, and a trickle of sweat tracked down the side of his face.

"I was told—" he started in a whisper.

"You should have been cleared," Eliaster said. "A long time ago. But monsters like that can't necessarily be trusted."

"Then why was he guarding the gate?" I asked.

"Most likely he's a prisoner bound to do so," Eliaster took the flashlight from David and continued forward. "I'll be sure to report him if we have time to find the proper authorities."

We continued walking along the tunnel, the flashlight beam dancing along as Eliaster played it back and forth in front of us. The longer we walked in the darkness, the more

I could feel the tension in the group rise. Even I recognized that this was a perfect place for an ambush. The cut on my neck throbbed as I twisted my head back and forth, straining my eyes into the shadows.

Finally, we spotted the familiar orange glow of the light globes ahead. Eliaster sighed and clicked off the flashlight.

"So…plan?" David asked.

"Find a friend of my da's," Eliaster said. "We'll come up with the rest of it once I've talked to him."

Larae glanced at me and pursed her lips. I shrugged.

The tunnel took us about five hundred yards inland before stopping at two large metal gates. Four fae stood outside the gates. Two of them looked like ceremonial guards—brightly-colored uniforms, swords, et cetera—but the real guards stood beside them, armed with machine guns.

"Security's obviously a lot tighter here," I muttered to David as Eliaster announced himself.

He nodded. "Springfield's a relatively small town in the Underworld. A lot of the bigwigs live here in Chicago— several councilmen in both the Seelie and Unseelie courts, as well as some powerful businessmen."

"Sounds like Overworld Chicago," I quipped.

David nodded. "A fair assessment. The important from both worlds tend to gather in the same place, whether they realize it or not."

As we stepped through the gate, I stopped in amazement. Spread out below me was a city I couldn't see the end of. A colorful market of tents, booths, and twisting brown ribbons of streets sat below the hill we stood on. At the far edges of the city sat mansions and houses, disappearing into the distance of the cavern.

David prodded me forward. "C'mon, Josh. It's not that amazing."

But it was. Even after seeing Springfield's market, it was.

The fae let me trail a few steps behind them, soaking up the atmosphere. Springfield's market had smelled dusty, but clean. Chicago's market smelled like a weird, head-turning combination of sewer, flowery perfume, spicy curry, the musty cologne of old books, and the moth-eaten smell of canvas. I kept an eye on Eliaster's black leather jacket as we weaved in and out of the crowd.

We stopped outside a peppermint-striped tent. Two human attendants stood outside, both wearing dark suits that bulged with muscle, looking like bouncers at an Overworld club. Eliaster gave his name to one of them.

The man nodded and stepped inside the tent.

While we waited, I scanned the small market square around us. It was a dead end, with our tent at the very end and two long tents flanking it, before shrinking down to a one-lane street with small booths on either side. In the middle of the square, a group of acrobats were somersaulting and leaping their way into a six-person pyramid. A few people stood around them, watching with keen interest. The tent to our right was empty, with a *For Sale* sign dangling from the wall.

The tent at our left was smaller, just an awning with folding tables set underneath it. The tables were bowing under an assortment of knives. Only two customers stood at the front of that. The first, a tall, thin fae with a scruff-covered chin and a sweeping blond mane, picked up a knife, frowning as he weighed it. He wore a red leather coat styled to look like a tailed tuxedo, and black skinny jeans with leather knee patches tucked into half-laced boots.

The other guy was about my height, with broad shoulders and well-muscled arms. Both of his wrists were encircled by wide leather bracelets studded with chunks of bronze. He rattled as he moved, and no wonder—the guy wore more chains than a gangster. Several thick chains looped from his back pockets to his front pockets, with more hanging from his front pockets, and each chain sported several visible pocket watches of varying sizes. Surprisingly, he only wore one chain around his neck, with a small, almost delicate-looking gold pocket watch hanging from it.

Eliaster elbowed me. "Don't stare. Gren will take your

head off likely as not."

"Who?"

"Gren Silver. The pocket watch guy. Everyone knows him—he's from New York and has quite a reputation. He has probably about a dozen grenades concealed in those pocket watches, and who knows what else. He likes explosives. The guy with him is his half-brother, Coriander."

I sidled a few steps to the side. "Okay."

David laughed and threw his arm around my shoulders. "Welcome to the Underworld, as if you haven't noticed yet."

The gesture made me uncomfortable, but I tried to cover it by chuckling. Eliaster gave me a sharp look, but said nothing.

The attendant came back out and bowed to Eliaster. "My master says he will see you. Please, come this way."

chapter 15

We followed the man into the tent. Tables heaped with scrap metal and junky car parts were crammed into the space. We all had to turn sideways and suck in our guts to squeeze through the smallest spaces.

The attendant stopped at the back of the tent and opened a panel, gesturing inside.

This part of the tent was richly furnished. Thick, colorful rugs covered the floor and the walls of the tent. A long, low table dominated the center of the space, with cushions scattered around it. Sitting at the opposite side of the table was a tall, thickset fae who looked completely engrossed in a thick stack of paper in front of him. His white business suit made me think of Sydney Greenstreet in *Casa Blanca*.

The attendant gently cleared his throat, and the fae looked up. A too-white smile appeared on his face, and his bright blue eyes widened. "Eliaster Tyrone!" He stood.

"Councilman Aifric." Eliaster extended his hand.

The fae grabbed him in a bear hug. "It's been too long, my boy, too long."

Eliaster patted Aifric's back and wiggled free, his neck turning the color of a bad sunburn. "Um, yeah. Way too long."

"I think I'd pay to see Eliaster this discomfited every day," Larae whispered in my ear.

I snickered.

Eliaster shot me a glare.

Aifric busied himself by pushing cushions into place with his feet and making expansive gestures for us to sit down. As we chose spots around the table, he darted to the opening in the tent wall and spoke to his attendant in hushed tones.

"No food!" Eliaster protested.

Aifric raised an eyebrow at him. "Since when did you develop such sharp hearing?"

He grinned. "I just know you, Aifric. You'd have us so fat from a feast that we couldn't even roll ourselves out the door."

With a sigh, Aifric waddled back to his cushions and sat down. He picked up a horsetail flyswatter and flicked it at a couple of bluebottles buzzing around Larae.

She flinched away.

Definitely Sydney Greenstreet. That guy had it in for flies too. I bit the inside of my lower lip to restrain a snicker.

"So, down to business. Just like your father." Aifric folded his hands on the table.

"I'm not just like—" Eliaster started.

"So much like him, in fact, that you've focused all your attention on what you're here for and ignored the basic tenets of civility. I haven't been introduced to three-quarters of the people in the room."

Technically, since you already know yourself and Eliaster, it would be three-fifths of the people in the room. I managed to keep my mouth shut.

Eliaster rolled his eyes. "This is David North and Larae Ó Dáleigh. And this—" he jerked his thumb at me. "Josh MacAllister."

Aifric eyebrows rose to nearly meet his thick mop of blond hair. "A newcomer to the Underworld, I see."

"How could you tell?" I asked.

"Your eyes," he said.

For a moment, I thought he meant the d'anam fuinneog. But David, as a human, didn't have that either.

Aifric clarified in a quiet tone. "Everyone has layers in their eyes, even humans. Your layers are not yet hardened and cynical like so many Underworlders. And I can tell—you view our world as something new and exotic, something to be treated as an adventure. Always, it begins in this way."

I stared at Aifric, gap-mouthed. How was I supposed to respond to that?

Eliaster snorted. "Great. Can we cut the mushy stuff and get on with it, Aifric?"

Aifric sighed.

I ventured a quick glance at Eliaster. Every muscle in his body looked drawn and tense, like he wanted nothing more than to run away.

Aifric folded his hands on the table. "What can I do for you, Eliaster?"

"For reasons you don't need to know, we need to get into the Lost Tunnels," Eliaster said shortly.

Aifric's flabby face went pale. He shook his head and his jowls wobbled like a bull-dog's. "No one comes out of there alive. *No one*. People say it's haunted by those who died in the fire."

Larae sent Eliaster an *I told you so* look.

"And you believe that?" Eliaster's tone was skeptical.

Aifric spread his hands in a helpless gesture. "What can I say? People who go in don't come out. Eliaster, please, what harebrained scheme are you up to now? You don't want me to be the one who has to call your father and tell him of your death. Do you know what he would do to me?"

"Regardless," Eliaster said. "We need to get in. It also wouldn't hurt if you could find maps or something."

Aifric's breath whistled out and his chest deflated like a popped balloon. His fingers moved along the table as he thought, running through the condensation of the water glass sitting to the side. Beads of water trailed away from the fae's fingers in a series of twists and turns, a rudimentary Celtic knot.

He shook his head. "There are no maps of the Lost Tunnels. Perhaps, however, there might be a sniffer or two available to be hired as guides."

A what? I kept my mouth shut, not wanting to miss any of the conversation. There'd be time later to ask questions.

Aifric raised his hands in a shrug. "Still, your father—"

"Sent me on this quest," Eliaster said sharply.

Aifric's eyes widened. "Why didn't you tell me this in the first place?"

Eliaster shrugged.

Aifric grunted. "One of these days... Well. Let me see what I can do. This may take some time. In the meantime, again, would you share a meal with me?"

Larae butted in before Eliaster could answer. "I'm hungry."

"As the lady commands, so it shall be!" Aifric winked at her and gestured to his attendant.

Eliaster bowed sarcastically to Larae. "Forgive me for not listening to your wishes before, my lady."

"Oh, stop it. It's got to be past midday, and the only one of us who has eaten anything is Josh. Though I'm not sure donuts count as food."

"Food-like enough for my stomach to digest, though not happily," I said. "What's a sniffer?"

Larae answered. "A fae who has the uncanny ability to find whatever it is that you're looking for, be it a person, place, or thing. Supposedly they can smell the difference between Earth and Otherworld things like a normal person can smell the difference between Indian curry and a greasy-spoon hamburger."

"Hey, was that a Josh-inspired simile?" I asked.

She grinned and playfully nudged my ribs with her elbow.

Marc's girlfriend, I reminded myself as I scooted a few inches away.

David leaned in close to her other side and whispered

something to her, brushing his knuckles against her shoulder as he did so. I watched them, feeling a vague sense of unease settle in my chest.

What was it with those two? The motion was so casual that it looked like he'd done it subconsciously. I'd never seen them touch intimately like that before, and it felt wrong for their relationship. That was a touch a guy would give his girlfriend, not one that casual, platonic friends would use.

Aifric finished giving instructions to the attendant. The man disappeared through the tent's side door. Within two minutes, several servants—men and women—came inside, carrying large metal trays stacked with steaming bowls of food. The meaty, spicy aroma that wafted around us made my nose twitch.

"Speaking of curry," Larae said with another smile as several bowls of vibrant cumin- and chili-colored rice and meat were laid on the table.

The servants loaded our plates with portions of everything and left the tent. Aifric motioned for us to dig in.

Lamb and chicken curry spices exploded in my mouth, leaving my taste buds tingling. The cold cucumber salad cooled my tongue, as did the sweet, pink, watermelon-flavored drink. Something was slightly different in all of the food—nothing nasty—but different. The flavors and smells of the food and the Underworld mingled, creating a pungent scent that flavored all of the food so it tasted not-quite-normal, just a tinge of pleasant strangeness. Roe's food hadn't tasted like this at all.

During the meal, fae came and went from Aifric's side, often staying just long enough to whisper a few sentences before heading back outside. Eliaster kept a careful watch on them all as he ate.

The servants seemed to know instinctively when I was stuffed to the breaking point. As I set my fork onto my plate with a sigh, one of them swooped in and snatched it up.

As soon as the table was cleared, Aifric leaned forward and folded his hands on the table. "It seems I was correct that this would take time. Of the three sniffers I know of residing in Chicago, one is busy and one is an Unseelie. I doubt very much you'd want him included in your plans."

Eliaster nodded.

Aifric continued, "The third, we're still looking for. He's a bit of a loner, but also fairly easy to pay if we can find him. In the meantime, I'd be delighted if you chose to stay at my house."

Eliaster frowned. "This is time-sensitive, Aifric."

Aifric dipped his head in agreement. "I have a dozen people out looking for the sniffer, and that's almost more than I can spare from my own personal affairs. As you're waiting, it only makes sense for you to be in a place where you can rest comfortably and prepare for the Lost Tunnels."

Eliaster glanced at us and shrugged.

I raised my eyebrows. "You're going to let us make a decision?"

"It's not a vital one, so there's no chance you guys can screw it up," he growled.

"We'll take the offer, Aifric," David said quickly. "Thank you."

Aifric bowed his head again, then called, "Efran!"

A fae around my age hurried into the tent. "Sir?"

Aifric waved at us as he turned away. "Please escort my guests to the house. Then join the search for the sniffer Dywor if the guardmaster has no further need of your help."

"Right away, sir." Efran motioned for us to follow him and ducked out of the tent.

We left the dead-end street and wound our way back through the Market, heading, as far as I could tell, back in the direction of the mansions we'd seen when we first entered Chicago. Efran never got too far ahead of us, but kept enough distance that made it plain that he didn't care for conversation.

As we walked through the crowded marketplace, I kept getting bumped and jostled. At first, I put it down to how busy the place was—it seemed the streets were no bigger than the Springfield Underworld, definitely not built for the flow of people crowding them.

Someone rammed into my back. I staggered and bounced off a scaly side. The troll shrugged me away, growling.

"Sorry, sorry," I muttered, finding my balance. I looked around. Yards ahead of me, I caught a glimpse of Larae's turquoise striped hair as she scanned the market. "Larae!" I started to hold up my hand to gesture for her to wait for me.

A hand grabbed my arm and forced it back down to my side.

She must not have heard me, because she turned away.

I turned to face the person who had grabbed me. "What the—"

Llew dug his fingers into the pressure points of my elbow. I cringed away from him. The Unseelie wrapped his other arm around my shoulders, and I felt a small blade come to rest against my ribcage, mostly concealed by his hand.

"Let's move," Llew murmured under his breath. "Carefully, now. Wouldn't want you to trip."

I took a deep breath and obeyed, letting the Unseelie's hand on my arm guide me through the crowd. We cut sideways through several streets. As we navigated the narrow alleys between tents, Llew shifted the knife to press into my back. I stepped carefully over the tent ropes, not wanting to give him the slightest excuse to stick me. My mind raced. How had he found us? No one other than Tyrone and Roe knew we were coming here.

We reached an empty street, and Llew jerked me to a stop. I stayed beside him, not fighting, and scanned the street. It truly was abandoned. The tents and booths were all closed, *For Rent* signs swinging above tattered doorways. Then I spotted the fae leaning in a broken-down doorway. The one who had found me at my parents' house, the one I'd dubbed Goldtooth. That metal-encased incisor flashed as the fae grinned and straightened. He leaned into the shop and said something, his voice too muffled to make out the words, then came toward us.

Three other fae exited the shop, one of them the fair-skinned fae with a brown ponytail. I recognized him as well—he'd been one of the ones who had kidnapped Marc.

Llew dropped his arm from my shoulders.

Goldtooth reached us. "Hey, crow-bait." He planted his hand in the middle of my chest and shoved.

I rocked back one step. Before I could get my arms up, Goldtooth punched me in the gut. I grunted and doubled over, wrapping my arms around my stomach. He grabbed my hair and held me down, punched into my diaphragm. Air whooshed from my lungs and I dropped to my knees. I tried to gasp in a deep breath, but my lungs felt frozen.

"That's enough!"

I glanced up in time to see the ponytailed fae grab Goldtooth's wrist and jerk him back from me.

"Blodheyr doesn't want him harmed."

"Aww, the poor little puppy," Llew said, kneeing me in the side.

I collapsed onto my back. My torso ached, pain radiating from the places Goldtooth had hit, but my lungs were starting to work again, slowly.

"I'm not joking," Ponytail snapped.

Goldtooth snorted. "He's not so delicate that a couple of punches will kill him."

"What's a broken rib or two between friends?" Llew grinned.

The other two fae were still halfway across the street, but they were still coming. If I had any chance of getting out of this, I had to act now, even though I hadn't fully caught my breath yet.

I rolled to my side and kicked upward, driving my heel into Llew's groin. He squealed and dropped. I drew my sword as I stood, already swinging at Goldtooth. He jumped back. Ponytail calmly stepped out of reach and drew his own sword.

Well, at least I had someone scared.

"Back off," I growled.

Ponytail lunged, his sword coming in at a sharp overhand angle. I dropped down and slashed at his legs. He jumped backward just in time, my sword tip tugging the fabric of his pant leg.

He struck again. I rolled, scrambled to my feet, and just managed to catch a third blow. The strike of the swords jarred my arm and shoulder. The fae kept coming, pushing me backward every chance he got. My vision tunneled, focusing so narrowly on him that I barely caught the motion of a sword coming in at my side.

I twisted to avoid it. Ponytail stuck his foot behind mine, and I crashed to the ground. Goldtooth dropped to one knee beside me and pressed his hand to my throat, his sword hovering a few inches away from my face.

I released my sword and held up my hands. "Surrender."

Goldtooth sneered. "Good choi—"

A knife ricocheted off his head, opening a gash in his temple, and his eyes rolled back in his head.

I jerked away. The sword, falling with all the weight of his unconscious body behind it, drove into the dirt beside me, the body slumping over my chest.

A tall, lanky fae in a tailed red leather jacket jumped over me, brandishing two long knives. The ponytailed fae blocked two slashes before getting a deep cut to his arm.

As I got to my feet, I spotted Llew running at me, his sword raised and his lips drawn back in a wild snarl. I grabbed my sword from the ground and squared off, ready to face him. His swings were wild, relying on brute force. I blocked a few, waiting until he swung wide before stabbing at him.

Llew cried out and stepped back, favoring his left leg.

I brushed sweat and hair from my eyes and grinned.

One of the other fae yelled in Gaelic. Llew glanced away, back at me, then turned and ran, following Ponytail and two other Unseelie down the street.

A footstep behind me reminded me of my unwelcome guest. I spun around and raised my sword.

The lanky fae held up his hands, fingers spread and knives balanced between thumb and palm. "Ah, c'mon. I just saved your sorry butt and this is how you thank me?"

"Doesn't mean anything. No one has friends down here."

He grinned, his blue eyes twinkling.

Everything clicked into place. He was the guy Eliaster had pointed out to me at Aifric's place. I recognized the tall, spiked hair and the red leather jacket.

"You're Coriander, right?" I asked. "A friend pointed you out."

"Hard to miss, aren't I." With a flourish of his coat, he sheathed his knives. "Eliaster told you who I was, didn't he?"

"How do you know him?"

"Only by reputation."

"Okay, so how did you just happen to show up when I needed help?"

Coriander shrugged. "I saw Eliaster at Aifric's and wanted to know why he was back in Chicago, so I tailed him. Saw that Unseelie ambush you. Thought maybe my help might be needed. Lucky for you I was right."

I dropped the sword point to the ground. "Thanks."

"I should be thanking you. Having a favor owed to me is always handy."

Agh, he's right. I gritted my teeth. "Great. How will I know when you want to cash in?"

"You'll know." He dipped his head in a sardonic bow, turned, and walked off.

Crap. Owing Eliaster was bad enough, but now a fae I didn't know held a favor. Who knew what he'd call it in for.

Eliaster. I was going to get an earful. I shoved my sword into the sheath and ran back the way Llew had taken me.

When I reached the street where I'd last seen Larae, it wasn't hard to spot them again. Eliaster had clambered onto a rickety bench not far from where Llew had ambushed me and was scanning the crowd. When he caught sight of me, he jumped, momentarily disappearing before bursting between a small group of people with no regard for where his elbows landed.

He grabbed my shoulders. "What happened to you?"

David and Larae followed a few seconds later. Larae wasted no time in throwing her arms around me for a hug. Her body was soft, despite her lean build, and my heart rate spiked in a way that had nothing to do with adrenalin.

I squirmed away as quickly as I could. "What happened—"

David thumped me on the back, nearly sending me into Larae's embrace again. Eliaster shot him an annoyed look. Efran finally showed up, brows drawn together in a frown.

I coughed. David's thump had jarred something loose in my throat. "Llew's here. He's working with Blodheyr's thugs."

Larae stepped back from me and ran her eyes around the street. "What do they want?"

"Me, obviously. They're probably not getting anywhere with Marc." I looked at Eliaster. "I thought Llew and his buddy weren't associated with Blodheyr."

"I didn't think they were any longer either." Eliaster's eye color spiked a muddy green. "The more important question is, how did they know we were here?"

"And I suppose you think it was me, right?" David growled. "Or Larae. Surely not your precious pet project."

"Again, really?" I muttered.

Eliaster smirked. "Your willingness to jump to that conclusion certainly begs the question, doesn't it?"

David took a step toward Eliaster, chin thrusting forward. A smirk curled one corner of Eliaster's mouth, and he angled sideways, fingers curling.

I grabbed his arm. "Let's not do this here." I turned to Efran. "Aifric's house was our destination, I believe."

The thin fae shrugged and started off again. With a last glare at Eliaster, David followed.

"Nice save," Larae said, nudging my shoulder with hers as she stepped past.

I grinned.

As we followed Efran, Larae and David stayed on either side of me, and Eliaster tagged along so closely that he stepped on my heels a few times. I finally threw my elbow back into his ribs. He got the hint and backed off a little.

"Do you really think they wanted you?" Eliaster asked.

I shrugged. "The only other thing I can think was that they were going to kill me. But if they'd sent Llew to do that, why did he drag me off to meet other Unseelie? Why not just cut my throat and let my body drop? It's not as if anyone would be paying attention or care in this crowd."

Eliaster eyed me with approval. "A week ago, the mere thought of dying would have had you whimpering in a corner. This is an improvement."

I frowned. I didn't like the thought that I'd changed so drastically in such a short amount of time.

"How did you escape?" David asked.

I didn't want to tell anyone about Coriander's help, so I just shrugged. "Kicked Llew in the nuts and ran."

The three of them burst out laughing, and David thumped my back again. I smiled, but my thoughts were already drifting back toward Eliaster's last comment.

Maybe I didn't necessarily change. I remembered how quickly I'd been able to shove away my fears and act, as if on autopilot, until danger had passed. I'd done that a couple of times now, in fact. *Maybe I've had the capacity for this all along, but my circumstances just never brought it out until now.*

It wasn't a comforting thought.

We made it to Aifric's house without further incident. From the outside, it looked huge, but we didn't get to see much of the interior, just a side entrance, a staircase, and a couple of hallways. Efran immediately showed us to Aifric's guest rooms, one for each of us, tucked into a quiet corner of the mansion.

"I'm going to enjoy the last long, hot shower and good amount of sleep I'll probably have in days," Larae announced. "See you guys in the morning."

"Smart. She's bugging out before Eliaster starts squawking," David muttered.

Eliaster gave no indication that he'd heard the none-too-quiet complaint. "She's got the right idea. Rest up for tomorrow—we'll be heading out before breakfast."
He shoved his door shut with his foot.

David and I were left standing in the hall.

"You tired?" I asked him.

"Nah. You?"

"No. Wanna hang out?"

He looked surprised, but shrugged. I stepped into my room and gave it a quick glance. It wasn't too much bigger than the room I'd had at Roe's, but an open door led into a tiny bathroom. I dropped my messenger bag on the desk, unzipped it and took out my laptop.

"What're you doing?" David asked, flopping into the recliner set between the bed and the desk.

"Just gonna check...email..." I snorted and threw the power cord back into my bag. Right, no wifi. When was the last time I'd even thought about checking email, or my phone? "Nice to know I haven't changed too much." I pulled my phone from my back pocket and sat down in the desk chair. I had one bar of reception. When I swiped across the screen, five notifications—two texts and three missed calls—popped up. They were all from my parents.

I groaned and dropped the phone in my lap.

David leaned forward in his chair and clasped his hands between his knees. "Are you doing all right?"

Was I doing all right? I had no idea. *At least I'm still thinking about normal, human things like making sure my folks aren't worried. I'm not turning into a robot. Or a fae clone. Or whatever the correct analogy would be here.*

I shrugged. "Are any of us doing all right? Nothing I can do about it, I guess. The Underworld changes people's lives, or so I've been told by just about everyone."

David snorted. "Heh, I suppose it does. For the better, in my case, I'd like to think."

I gnawed on the inside of my lower lip. "Guess we'll just have to see how I end up."

We sat in silence for a minute.

"So..." David leaned back in his chair. "Did you ever think about what I asked?"

It took me a second to mentally switch gears. "You mean about teaming up with you, and leaving the fae to their own devices?"

"Essentially."

"I don't know anything about you."

"You don't know anything about Larae or Eliaster, either."

"They're not the ones asking me to ally with them."

David sighed. "Fine. Born and raised in Springfield. Played high school football for Kickapoo, was your typical selfish, spoiled jock. Thought I was headed somewhere with sports until I got mixed up with the wrong group, half of whom happened to be Unseelie. Larae befriended me, got me straightened out. Couldn't play football anymore, so I started working in the Underworld as a bodyguard. That's where Marc met me. I introduced him to Larae. They started dating about a year ago, and then this spring, he asked me to help him with this mess." He spread his hands out. "So there you go. My life story in a nutshell."

The story sounded fairly typical for a normal Midwestern boy, up until the Unseelie part. I nodded, slowly. "I'll think about it."

David rolled his eyes. I ignored it. I just didn't want to end up in debt any more, not since I already owed favors to two fae. And I had a feeling that no matter how much spin David put on it, this alliance he wanted was more about covering his back than it was mine.

David stood up. "Well, if that's all—"

I cleared my throat. "How come everyone keeps calling

me 'Eliaster's pet project'? Even Llew alluded to it."

David laughed as he turned back to me. "Wondered when you were going to ask about that. You remember at Cormac's place, when he mentioned Iain?"

I nodded.

"Iain was Eliaster's older brother who was raised outside of the Underworld by their mom's dying request. When Eliaster finally met him, Iain had already met Llew and Ghurdan and was, for all intents and purposes, an Unseelie. Eliaster took him under his wing, tried to help him. It didn't end well. Rumor is, Eliaster not only caused his brother's death, but he disobeyed a direct order of the Springfield Seelie lord *and* caused the death of a curator. I've heard it said he killed the curator himself, just because she got in his way."

That actually explained a lot—Eliaster's feud with Llew and Ghurdan, the tension between him and his father, even Eliaster's attitude. "So people see me as another Iain?"

"Basically."

I grimaced. And this was the guy who was trying to be my mentor? He saw me as the little brother he couldn't save. Awesome. Why hadn't he mentioned this before? "Eliaster needs to stop keeping secrets."

"Yeah. Good luck with that." David rubbed his chin, palm rasping across the three-day growth of stubble. "Listen, if you want to bail, I'll still cover for you."

"You already asked me that. Why would my answer change?"

He shrugged. "Just thought I'd offer again." He pulled the door open and stepped out into the hall.

As the door clicked shut behind him, I rubbed my hand over my face. I wanted nothing more than to accept his offer, but I couldn't. *Too far in to quit.* I picked up my cell phone again and stared into the blank, dark screen, wondering what my parents thought was going on.

chapter 16

David and Eliaster's voices in the corridor woke me the next morning. As I rolled out of bed, my shoulders twinged. Why were my muscles so tight?

I opened the door. Eliaster jerked back, his hand raised as if ready to knock on my forehead.

I grinned. "Beat ya to it."

He rolled his eyes. "Don't get used to it, punk."

I grabbed my messenger bag and pulled on my shoes, getting out into the hallway as Larae emerged from her bedroom, looking gorgeous in a turquoise tank top and close-fitting black pants, her leather jacket slung over one shoulder.

She wrinkled her nose at me. "Those clothes look like they could stand on their own."

The sound of her voice turned my stomach. Why? I forced a laugh and shrugged. "Hard to change when your only other pair of clothes was ditched because they were full of goblin blood."

"Oh, right." She pursed her lips. "Sorry."

"Don't worry about it."

"If any creatures attack us on the trip, I'll blame your smell," Eliaster called over his shoulder.

Larae walked past me and gently brushed my arm with

her fingertips. Her touch made me go cold, and my mind flashed back to the dream I couldn't remember until now. Larae, her touch just as icy cold as it had been now, sliding a knife across my throat. I'd bled out on the floor while she kissed a man whose face changed from David to Eliaster to Marc.

I twitched my shoulders, trying to get the image out of my head. It had just been a dream, conjured by my over-tired brain and the stress I'd been under for the past week. *It's not like Larae and I have ever been more than—well, can't even really call her a friend. Stupid dream.*

That explained my sore shoulders, though. I'd probably slept like the bed had been made of rocks rather than a down mattress and feather pillows.

As if on cue, our guide from yesterday, Efran, appeared at the beginning of the corridor. "Aifric would like you to join him in the dining room."

Eliaster groaned. "Does the man ever sleep?"

"That's ironic, coming from you," I said.

He shoved me into the wall and headed after Efran who, as usual, hadn't waited to see if we were following him or not. We walked through a few more halls and an atrium that looked like it was the size of my parents' entire house before entering a small room just off the kitchen. Aifric was there, seated at a table that could hold about ten people.

He smiled and pointed his fork at his plate. "Breakfast?"

"Since you won't let us leave without one, sure." Eliaster hooked a chair with his foot and flopped into it.

I waited until Larae sat down, then headed around the table and chose a seat diagonal to her. As she sat, she made eye contact and smirked at me.

What was that about? A few minutes ago she'd been friendly, now she was making faces because I didn't sit next to her? I rubbed my forehead. This was why I'd never had a steady girlfriend before.

A servant set a plate full of hash, pancakes, and bacon in front of me. It was a relatively mundane breakfast after the dinner that Aifric had treated us to last night, but it felt good to see something mundane again. I dug into the food, and for a while, the only sounds were of forks clinking off plates.

Eliaster finished about half his food before shoving the plate away and eyeing Aifric. "So?"

Aifric raised an eyebrow. "So?"

Eliaster sighed. "Did you find the sniffer?"

Aifric glanced at Efran, who had been leaning against the wall next to the doorway. "Please bring Dywor in."

Efran ducked out of the room and returned a moment later leading a light-skinned fae with bleach-blond hair. The first thing I noticed about the newcomer was the twitch. Though he held his left hand loose and casual, his fingers bounced toward his palm, like he was constantly reminding himself not to ball them into a fist. His left eyelid was more subtle, but after watching for a moment, I could see that it had a continual tiny tic to it.

Eliaster gave Aifric a quick frown.

Aifric waved one hand while heaving himself up using the other for leverage. "Dywor. How good of you to come."

Dywor shrugged. "Needed a job." His voice was raspy. He scanned the group. "Big group to be taking through the tunnels. Too big. Too many Overworlders. Too noisy."

"That's not your concern," Eliaster said.

Dywor grinned. His teeth were stained brown. "Is if I'm to guide you."

Larae sat up, spine stiff and shoulders thrown back. "I don't know that I like the thought of a rager guiding us."

"Of course you don't," Eliaster muttered. "You haven't liked anything on this trip so far."

Aifric glanced between the two, and his eyes narrowed.

"Just give it a rest," David whispered to Larae.

Aifric frowned, his forehead wrinkling until it was all loose skin.

Eliaster stood, slapping his palm against the table. "If it's agreeable to you, Dywor, we'll negotiate on the way there."

Dywor nodded.

As the others headed out, Aifric caught my eye and beckoned me close. "I don't like it."

"What?"

"Much of it. Eliaster and Larae. David and Larae. Too much conflict. I thought perhaps that Dywor being a rager would be a problem, but it has revealed to me more than I ever thought—"

I waited for a moment, hoping he would continue. The image from my dream popped up again, but I pushed it away. "What, Aifric?"

"C'mon, Josh!" Eliaster shouted from the atrium.

Aifric shook his head, his eyes darkening with spikes of midnight blue. "Join your friends. Keep an eye out for yourself and Eliaster." He reached out, clasped both hands around one of mine, and murmured, "*Go dte tu slain I gcomhluadar De.*"

It sounded similar to the Gaelic blessing Cormac Tyrone had said as I'd left his place. Aifric released my hand, and I nodded, acknowledging his words, then joined the others in the atrium.

Efran pushed open the doors for us, and we stepped into the Chicago Underworld. Dywor wound through the streets at a long-legged lope, forcing the rest of us into a jog to keep up. I stuck close to Eliaster. I still felt jittery from my dream, and unnerved by David's revelation last night of why Eliaster protected me. But even with all that, he *was* protecting me. At this point, I didn't think it was wise to abandon that, just based on rumors David had half-heard.

I nodded to Dywor. "A rager?"

"Addict. In the old legends, fae are supposed to be warded off with branches from rowan trees. In reality it makes us go insane while we're in contact with it. Within the last century, some dimwit figured out that it's addictive. I've never seen a rager completely under the stuff, but I've heard that some of the more hardened addicts have to be tied to a bed for the safety of everyone around them."

"It can also be used as a poison," Larae interjected. "Like

deliberately overdosing someone on Overworld drugs."

I glanced up at Dywor. The barrel-chested, lanky-limbed fae slowed as he rounded a corner and came to a section of the tall, wooden wall that fenced in the entire city.

"Up and over," he said, jerking his thumb over his shoulder.

Larae narrowed her eyes. "Why?"

"This side of the city, the gate guards won't let us through unless we have written permission from a council member. I'm guessing you don't have time for that."

"Better to ask forgiveness than permission. Keep a sharp eye out for guards," Eliaster said to David and Larae. He looked at me. "You first."

"Got it." I set down my messenger bag and took off my sword. With my luck it would probably get caught in the fence.

"Watch yourself, then," he said, bracing against the wall and making a stirrup of his hands.

I set my foot in his hands and grabbed for the top of the flat fence. Dywor gave an extra shove on my free foot. I almost went tumbling headlong, but managed to latch on the top of the wooden fence and steady myself. I swung my legs over and dropped to the ground. My sword hit the ground a second later.

I grabbed it as I scanned the area. Boulders and chunks of rusting metal lay scattered around me, spilling from a rocky wall a football field's length away. I watched the area, waiting to see a flicker of movements, but the debris field appeared empty. I just hoped it really *was* empty, and that nothing nasty was just waiting for me to turn my back before it charged.

"Anything?" Eliaster hissed.

"Nope, I think we're good."

"Great. Here comes our gear."

Eliaster and Larae's backpacks came over, then my messenger bag, treated much more carefully than the rest of the gear. Dywor came clambering over next.

Larae came after him, and a few seconds after she hit the ground, David's backpack came sailing over the wall. The fence shuddered, and his head appeared with a grunt. He rolled over the top and landed heavily on our side.

"Well, that wasn't too hard. I'd thought we would have more trouble with a guard patrol," David said, grabbing his backpack.

Eliaster flipped himself over the fence and landed in a crouch beside Larae.

"Hard part starts here," Dywor said, jerking his head at the boulders. "Lots of hiding places. Be alert."

"He's right—we'll have to keep on our toes." Eliaster rubbed his palm on the hilt of a sword.

"Sounds like it'll be a nice jaunt in the park," I muttered.

There was a slight incline of loose gravel leading up to the cavern's edge. The gravel, mostly made up of rocks the size of my palm, turned and slid underfoot as we walked, making me constantly shift and throw my arms out for balance.

As we drew closer to the cavern wall, I realized the lower half of the wall was made up of huge pieces of rock. Jagged edges created fissures and overhangs, making the entire thing look like a pile of blocks ready to tumble down on us. Dywor led us to a deep black rip in the collapse and stepped inside without a word.

Eliaster paused and glanced back. I followed his gaze. The globes over the city shone bright, and from the slight rise we stood on, we could see over the fence into the Chicago Market, golden and glittering with flairs of brilliant color. For a moment, I wished I could go back, sit with Aifric, and forget about this stupid quest. From the tight lines around Eliaster's eyes and mouth, it seemed he was thinking the same thing.

"Are you coming?" Larae asked.

I turned around. She stood just inside the passage, half-turned toward us. In the beam of her flashlight, I could see Dywor and David waiting.

Eliaster sighed. "Yeah. You first, Josh."

We wound single file through the passage, twisting and ducking to avoid the rocks and timbers that protruded in odd spots. The flashlights flickered and made weird shadows on the wall. Gravel crunched underfoot, and our breaths sounded loud in the claustrophobic space. The taste and smell of dust clogged my nose and mouth.

After some time, the passage widened and started becoming more like a maze, with tunnels branching out from ours. At times the roof was supported with single boulders. Here and there, I caught glimpses of painted, sculpted wood or stone, the last shreds of the grandeur before the Chicago Fire.

Eliaster moved to the head of the line beside Dywor. As we walked, snatches of their conversation echoed back to me. Eliaster was explaining everything we knew about the relic and the cipher to the sniffer.

"What's he doing?" I asked Larae.

"Sniffers need clear pictures in their heads of what they're searching for. Don't ask me how they do it."

Her answer reminded me of what Opti and Eliaster had said regarded Opti's sword-smithing. "So, in essence, magic?"

She smiled. "You humans always call what you don't understand 'magic'."

Thanks a lot. "What would you call it?"

"One of the most wonderful things the fae ever discovered."

That was way different than the answers Eliaster and Opti had given. Why would she have that kind of attitude toward it, when the others didn't seem to want to talk about it at all? I shrugged. Maybe it had to do with different kinds of upbringing.

Dywor broke into a jog, his nose angled into the air like a hunting dog. We hurried after him. After a few minutes at that pace, I fell behind, only able to see the others by their bobbing flashlights.

Before long, we ran into an area where the floor was made up of huge boulders, probably several tons each. We had to jump from rock to rock, over gaps either big enough to swallow us or just big enough to break a leg in. In some places smaller rubble filled the gaps, but those stones were an awkward size—not small or big enough to walk on, but just right to wrench an ankle.

Our flashlights danced and bounced on the walls and disappeared ahead of us into the dark tunnels. Occasionally a flashlight beam caught the open end of a tunnel—or worse, something darting across the tunnel opening. Every time a shadow moved, my heart felt like it had been zapped with a defibrillator.

I'm not sure how long we lasted like this. It must have been several hours before we came to a sort of clearing nestled down among the rocks and Eliaster called a halt. I staggered to a stop, dropped my bag on the floor, and rested my hands on my thighs.

"Right, let's get a fire going and set up camp for the night," Eliaster said, dumping his backpack on the ground.

Larae raised her eyebrows. "Do you really think a fire is a good idea?"

"Do you really believe in ghouls?" Eliaster smirked.

Larae looked at Dywor. "You're the sniffer. Back me up."

He shrugged. "Smelled more than rats, but it's old. Could be nothing. No reason to deny ourselves a hot meal at this stage of the trip."

"He's probably right, Larae," David said.

She huffed. "Fine. Just to prove to you that I'm not scared, Eliaster, I'll go gather firewood. And if any misguided male tries to follow me, he's going to get kicked in an unpleasant place."

"Yikes," I muttered.

"Shut up." She slugged me in the arm and stomped away.

David, Eliaster, and Dywor opened their backpacks and started going through them, pulling out silver packages of dehydrated food. I hadn't carried any of the food, so I sat down with my back against a boulder and pulled out my cell phone. No reception down here, of course. There was only one new notification, a text from my sister Lindsay. I opened it.

Hey bro. Haven't talked for a while. Doing ok?

That was it. Short and simple. Typical Lindsay.

I sighed and held the power button down until my phone screen turned black. She was just going to have to wait for an answer until I got aboveground again. I should've called my family before we went to Chicago. My chest panged with a guilty ache at the thought. Would I ever see my family again? How was I going to explain this to them?

"Hey, Josh." David chucked a tiny, rolled sleeping bag at me. "I brought an extra."

"Thanks." I set my phone aside and unrolled the sleeping bag.

Larae came back into the clearing with an armful of splintered wood. "There's plenty of it scattered around here," she said. "I'll go get some more."

David glanced at me and jerked his head after Larae.

"Why me?" I mouthed.

"She won't hurt you because you wouldn't be a fair fight."

I sighed and followed Larae. Our camp was set up in a little valley, cupped between several boulders that towered far over my head. Smaller rocks, still larger than me, filled in the gaps between these boulders.

I slid between a gap in the rocks, expecting to find Larae waiting for me on the other side, but she'd disappeared. She could have taken any of half a dozen little paths that snaked through the boulders, choked with rocks and splinters big enough to impale a troll.

"Larae?" I called, cringing. I half expected her to jump out at me any second with a drawn blade.

No one answered.

A stone skittered along the floor, coming to a stop beside my foot.

"Eliaster?" I called.

"Back here. Whatcha need?"

His voice echoed around the cavern so much that I couldn't tell which direction it was coming from—ahead of me, or behind me at the fire. Was he moving around, looking for me? I hesitated, listening hard for another sound—a scuff of shoe along rock, a gentle breath. Where was Larae?

"Okay, Larae," I said, fitting my hand around my sword hilt. "It's not funny!"

"Josh?" Eliaster called again.

"Never mind!" I yelled back. Where had she gone?

"Why don't you come back to the fire?"

I shook off the advice, squinting into the gloom. That rock could have fallen from the walls—that would have been easy enough, since they were crumbling.

Another pebble skittered by my foot.

Okay, now that was stretching it a little. As much as I was tired of Eliaster trying to keep me on a short leash, I decided that maybe he was right. By the fire would be safer.

I turned back and rounded the chunk of concrete that stood between me and the firelight. Eliaster and David lounged beside the fire, David cleaning his pistol, Eliaster holding a penlight between his teeth as he turned the pages of a book. Dywor wasn't around, presumably out gathering firewood like I was supposed to have been.

"See?" I held out my arms. "I'm fine. All back in one piece, Mom."

Eliaster took the penlight from his mouth. "Forget it. Just stick around here and let Larae fend for herself."

David sighted down the barrel of his pistol. "That's a gentlemanly attitude for sure."

"Here's a thought. How about you go with her next time, David? Give you two time to cuddle in the shadows when you think no one's looking." Eliaster redirected his penlight at his book.

I raised my eyebrows. So he had noticed their weirdly intimate behavior over the last couple of days.

David glanced at me and mimed throttling Eliaster.

I gave a weak smile and flopped down on my sleeping bag. No need to get mixed up in another one of their spats again. The black screen of my phone glinted in the flashlight glow. I grabbed it and started to stuff it in my bag when a flicker on the screen caught my eye.

The screen reflected Eliaster and David's lights, and in the reflection I could make out the outline of the boulders behind me. A lumpy outline, darker than the rock around it, crept forward toward me.

I slowly reached for my sword, keeping both eyes on the reflection. Two eyes glinted from the shadow. "Hey, guys?"

The shape leapt forward. I whirled, my sword at the ready. It slammed into my chest, throwing me onto my back. One hand grabbed my wrist, a clawed finger digging into my knuckles and sending a spike of pain through my hands. I dropped my sword and, at the same time, kicked. The fae-like thing rocked back, but not enough for me to get free. I glanced over at David and saw him go down, buried in a tangle of rag-clad figures.

Eliaster's back was to me, his hands around the throat of the monster that had tried to attack him, pinning it to the rock. Over his head, I could see another figure crouching on the edge of the rock.

"Eliaster!" I shouted.

My attacker clamped a clammy palm to my mouth, digging his fingers into my cheeks, making my eyes water.

Eliaster jumped back, but not fast enough. The monster dropped on his shoulders, knocking him flat. Eliaster squirmed onto his back, throwing up an arm as the thing's teeth flashed at his throat. His cry of pain echoed off the rocks. Even before it had released his arm, the thing's hands were around his throat, thumbs pressing into his esophagus. Eliaster curled, slamming his knees into its back, but it wasn't letting go so easily.

"Stop!" a voice called out.

Eliaster's attacker froze and I got a good look at it.

It was a fae—a pale, hollow shade of a fae, with bulging

eyes and flaccid skin. Rags wound around its pale limbs and made it look eerily like a bad version of *The Mummy*. Another fae stepped into the light. He looked pretty much the same as the one kneeling on Eliaster's chest.

Eliaster gagged and slapped at the hands still choking him.

"Let him speak."

Eliaster jerked his head back and drew in a rasping breath. "Thank the Almighty."

"Is that all?" the tall fae asked.

I glanced over at David. Three fae pinned him down, busily wrapping rope around his wrists and ankles. He stayed still, his eyes darting back and forth around the cavern. Was he looking for Larae? I tucked my chin to my chest, trying to see the other side of the clearing. Dywor was there, pinned down by two other fae, but Larae was nowhere to be seen.

Eliaster tried to sit up, but the fae wasn't moving. "Look, I think this is a mistake. We were just passing through—we didn't know anyone still lived in the Lost Tunnels."

"That knowledge is unknown for a reason." The tall fae clapped his hands. "Bind them. They will make good, fresh meat for our stores."

Fresh *meat*? What the—

Eliaster's eyes widened. "What? Whoa, hold it—"

The fae jammed a wad of cloth into his mouth.

The leader glanced at me, and his eyebrows quirked upward. In long strides, he crossed the clearing and grabbed my hair, jerking me up to look into his eyes. I glared at him. He touched the corner of my left eye, then fingered my ear. His clammy touch turned my stomach. Bile hit the back of my throat and I swallowed hard. His chapped lips split into a grin, dried blood in the corners of his mouth cracking.

He stepped back, twisting my head to the side so my ear was exposed.

"A human!" one of the fae whispered in a soft, awed tone, the same tone an alcoholic might use in talking about his favorite booze.

"A human," the leader confirmed. "We will feast well tonight, my brothers."

The fae holding me reached out and pinched my upper arm, licking his lips.

That was it.

I wrenched my arms free and whirled, slamming my knuckles into the fae's mouth. He staggered back, blood dripping down his face. Pain shot through my hand. I sprinted across the clearing and dove into the fae pinning Eliaster down. We rolled head over heels. Clawed nails raked across my face, one scraping across my eye. I tucked my head down, grunting.

Eliaster's kick sent the fae flying, just as another fae launched onto his back and dragged him to the ground. A hand landed on my shoulder. I didn't even look, just slammed myself backward, crunching the fae between me and a boulder.

"Josh, stop!" David shouted. "Eliaster! Don't make them hurt you!"

Yeah, right. Like I was going to sit still while these guys talked about me like I was a prime rib. I spun around.

A heavy, thudding pain burst in the back of my head. Stars sparked in my eyes. I dropped to my knees, tried to shake away my tunneling vision. Something cracked into my head again, and the last thing I saw was the ground inches from my face.

"Josh."

Someone kicked my leg. My eyelids fluttered, and I caught quick, photographic glimpses of a rocky ceiling, lit by firelight—a face, leaning over me—

"Josh!"

Another kick caught my shin, and the pain sharpened my senses. I shook my head to stop the fluttering eyelids, and a throbbing ache awoke like a monster at the back of my skull.

I barely turned my head, afraid to move any more.

David leaned over me. "You idiot. Just had to show off your new fighting skills, didn't you?"

"What happened?"

"A crow-taken fae clobbered you in the back of the head with your own sword."

I focused past him. Bars formed a grid pattern over our heads. I eased myself upright, wincing as the pounding in my head intensified. We sat in a cage that was pressed against one wall in a huge cavern, big enough to contain several football fields. Eliaster slumped against the bars beside me, head lolling to one side. His face was bruised and dried blood crusted his nose and lips.

I gingerly patted my face. On the back of my neck, a thin trail of dried blood crumbled under my fingertips. My t-shirt collar felt stiff. Other than that, I didn't feel any injuries. "They were much more precise with me than with Eliaster."

"You've still probably got a concussion. Besides, they're not going to beat up the ones who are most valuable," David said. "Here, look at me."

I obeyed him. He clicked on a penlight and shone it into my eyes. I squinted and cringed, but forced my eyes to stay open.

"Eliaster was stupid," David muttered. "Should've just let them take him rather than putting up so much of a fight. The loss of one fae wouldn't hurt them." He clicked off the light. "Okay, you're good. Just be careful."

Something moved in the shadows past Eliaster, and Dywor's drawn face appeared from a corner of the cage. He stared at me, then leaned back and fumbled at the pocket of his army jacket.

As my head slowly stopped pounding, I realized that we weren't the only occupants of the cage. We had our own little bubble of space, but pressed against the other side of the cage sat five or six other fae. Every few seconds, one of them would flick a glance at us, but for the most part we were studiously ignored.

I looked at David and jerked my head at them. "What's up with them?"

"We have humans in our group." Dywor had found what he wanted in his pocket—a limp, stained cloth pouch. He opened it, dug inside, and came up with tiny crumbs which he sprinkled in his mouth. "Not good, not good. Running out," he muttered under his breath. "Not good."

"How about some focus on our situation, rager?" David growled.

I looked around the cage again and realized there was still one face missing. "Where's Larae?" I asked, keeping my voice low.

"Never saw her," David murmured. "They didn't bother looking for more prey, once they found out you and I were human. What's a fellow fae when you have humans?"

"That's the second time you've alluded to something. What aren't you saying?" I said.

Eliaster groaned. I leaned over him. He moved his head from side to side, but his eyes didn't open.

David cleared his throat. "A few years ago, I heard some rumors about fae that believed if they ate humans—specifically, human brains—they would be human-smart."

"Human-smart?"

"You've noticed that the fae hardly touch technology? When they do bother with it, it's always the simplest stuff they can find. Technology tends to go a little haywire around them. I've seen Eliaster blow up a perfectly good laptop just trying to log into email—though, granted, he's worse than any other fae I've seen. Most fae simply can't seem to wrap their minds around how technology works."

"Okay," I said slowly.

"I thought it had just stayed with some of the other Sidhé races, but apparently some fae have subscribed to the view as well." David shuddered.

So some weird group of fae wanted to eat my brain because they thought it would make them good with tech. Awesome. I rubbed my hands on my jeans. The clamminess of the cavern made everything feel sticky.

This is nuts. I had to stop myself from snorting. *Understatement of the year.* I could feel the edges of panic trying to creep in, sweep through my brain, but I shoved it back. *Not gonna break down now. There's a way out. There's always a way out.*

I glanced over at Eliaster. He was moving around, finally looking like he had some life in him. After a moment, he sat up, holding one side of his head like he had to hold in his brain.

"Any bright ideas, genius?" David snapped at him.

"Hey, back off. Give him a break," I said.

Eliaster leaned back, his eyes moving slowly around, taking in the other fae, the cavern. "*Imigh sa diabhal.*" His voice was thick and slow.

David snorted. "This is your fault. Larae was right—we shouldn't have come into these tunnels. We should've left the relic until we knew what we were getting into. Until we'd rescued Marc."

"Are you kidding me?" I asked.

David glared at me, his eyes turning cold. "Are you siding with the fae now, Josh? Against your own race?"

"That's not what—"

"Just stop!" Eliaster yelled.

I jumped and moved away from him. Outside the cage, a few pale fae turned toward the cage, their dark, glittering eyes full of curiosity.

Eliaster noticed their stares and lowered his voice. "We've done nothing but fight, and I'm pretty sure that's the reason we've been plagued with problems."

David grunted and sat with his back to us, staring moodily out into the cavern.

I crouched next to Eliaster.

He rubbed the side of his face. "Before you ask—no, Josh, I have no ideas yet. But I'll figure something out. I always do." His voice had cleared a bit, but his accent was a bit stronger than usual.

"Except with your brother," I muttered.

Eliaster's jaw went tight, and he leaned away from me.

I shrugged and stood up. Fine. Why should I trust him with my fate if he was never going to trust me with anything? It was time I started taking care of myself.

chapter 17

I turned to study the cavern outside our cage. It stretched several stories above our heads, pocked with tunnels and, above those, arches and windows that looked into more passages. One or two light globes hung near tunnel entrances—how were they getting electricity way down here?—but for the most part, flickering torches were jammed into holders along the walls. It created an eerie, shadow-shifting atmosphere. As usual, my stomach was churning like I had a bad case of food poisoning. I tried to ignore it and focused on the area outside our cage.

A few fae hung around the edges of the cavern, but most of the traffic was coming and going from one tunnel in particular. As I watched, a group of fae came in carrying armfuls of split, splintered wood. They tossed it into a pile in the middle of the cavern beside a large, blackened pit.

A voice echoed off the cavern walls, and I searched it out. The pale fae who had led the raiding party stood in a rough stone gallery, watching the fae bring in wood. At his terse words in Gaelic, some of the loitering fae leaped forward and began stacking the wood in the pit. The fae nodded, then turned and disappeared into the well-lit room behind him.

"Hmm," Eliaster muttered. "How nice of their leader to

show us where he hangs out."

"Not that we can use it," I said. "Why didn't you tell me that there were fae zombies out there who wanted to eat my brains?"

"Because I didn't think they really existed until today," he hissed. "Stay quiet and help me think of a way out of this."

I raised an eyebrow. "What, the great and mighty Eliaster has no idea how to worm his way out of this one?"

"Hey, give me some credit. I've gotten you out of a lot of crap so far."

"You've also gotten me *into* a lot of crap."

Eliaster flicked his hands in the air and sat down. "Fine."

"'Fine' what?" David whispered. "There's nothing fine about this. I just hope Larae is all right and that she'll be able to get help—no way am I relying on you, Eliaster."

Eliaster rolled his eyes and pulled his knees up to his chest. "I'll think about it," he mumbled.

"Your 'thinking about it' is likely to get us all killed," David said under his breath.

Eliaster looked away.

David rolled his eyes and leaned against the wall.

Sheesh, we couldn't have more angst going around if we were a teenage soap opera.

I glanced around the cage once again. The bars looked like some kind of metal, but I knew it couldn't be iron, otherwise every fae in here would be sick. I flicked a bar with my fingernails. The dull *thunk* still gave me no clue and made my fingers ache.

Smart, Josh.

A couple of the fae working out in the cavern looked over at me and grinned. The overseer barked and they quickly averted their eyes and kept moving.

I stepped around Eliaster and toward the back of the cage.

The metal structure was all one piece, including a gridwork floor that eliminated the possibility of digging our way out, even if the ground had been soft soil instead of rock. I tilted my head back and looked at the gridwork over our heads. Each square looked too small for me to even fit a shoulder through, and I was the slimmest one in the group.

The back of the cage didn't sit flush with the cavern wall, thanks to the natural unevenness created by a thin, steady trickle of water. I reached between two bars and pressed my hand against the slick rock. This part of the cage was shadowed, and the space between the wall and the bars got no narrower than a forearm's length. If there was a way to get between the cage bars, I, and probably Eliaster, could squeeze our way past the cage and into the open.

But again, the bars were set no more than a hand's width apart, so I doubted we'd be getting between them anytime soon.

Dywor stood up beside me. "Look at this." His shaky fingers went out and touched a thick bar.

I squinted in the gloom. His fae eyes had picked out what I never would have noticed on my own—two bars fastened together by a thick, double-linked chain. His hand traced the chain up the bars, over my head, and down several bars over.

"Looks like it...broke...one time or another." His staccato mutterings covered up the gentle clanks the chain made as he tugged on it. "And, well-well, look." He nudged a padlock hanging close to the ground. "Dumb fae couldn't be bothered to fix it right. Just a wrapped chain and a padlock around the bars."

I eyeballed the space that the broken bars could create. Plenty big enough to slip out. I crouched down and squinted at the padlock. From what I could see, it was a cheap, ordinary double-locking Master padlock.

I grinned at Dywor. "Where did they put my bag?"

He nodded to the corner. All of our possessions except our weapons lay there in a heap, and I could see the corner of my messenger bag poking out from beneath David's backpack. Dywor grabbed it and held it out to me, his hands shaking so much he could barely grip the bag's strap.

"W-what are you planning?" he asked.

His stuttering had gotten worse too. He'd said earlier that

he was almost out of rowan. I wondered how long it would be before he hit full withdrawal.

I pulled open the flap and dug past my computer and clothes. I couldn't use the pick set I'd made from paperclips for this—I needed a couple of shims. Those were not things I carried around regularly, since at college I'd mostly had to deal with forgetting the key to my dorm room. I pulled out a notebook with a plastic cover. It wasn't metal, but it was stiff enough that I might be able to make it work.

Eliaster moved to my side so that he blocked me from anyone's sight. "What are you doing?"

"You'll see." I tore the plastic cover off the notebook.

Now, what to use to shape this? I looked around the cage. There were no sharp corners easily accessible, and the fae hadn't left us with any of our weapons. I dug further into my bag and my finger caught on the edge of something sharp. I winced and pulled the object out. *Huh. So that's where my fingernail clippers went.*

It was going to take a while, but this was better than sitting. I flattened the plastic on the ground and went to work.

Eliaster, David, and Dywor watched in silence as I scraped out two rough M shapes and kept digging at the thin plastic until it finally ripped through. I folded one of the pieces and twisted it thoughtfully. It was a far cry from the pop can shims I'd used in the past, but it was stiff enough. It would work.

Just barely.

I moved to the broken section of the cage and pulled the padlock through to my side so I could see what I was doing. Eliaster hovered over my shoulder as I inserted the shims on either side of the lock where the shackle disappeared into the body. I twisted the shims around, biting my lip.

Please catch, c'mon… If this didn't work, I'd never live it down. If we even lived.

"I hope Larae has a better plan than you," David muttered.

"Shut it," I snapped, resisting the urge to give the shims a vicious twist. Yeah, like I needed one of them to tear apart inside the lock now. That would be just wonderful.

The back side of the shackle gave an almost indiscernible pop. I grinned and started on the other side. "Surprised you didn't know about this, Eliaster."

He grunted. "I usually prefer to enter legally. How do *you* know this?"

"This particular skill came thanks to my sister. We were only eleven months apart, so we were in high school at the same time. She used to think it hilarious to change out the padlock on my locker in between classes. She also liked to trick me into going outside, then lock me out of the house— until I got to where it wasn't a challenge to open most cheap locks anymore." I slid the shim around and this time felt the lock begin to give.

And then a thought struck me.

What if this wasn't a regular old padlock? What if the fae had somehow trapped the padlock to trigger some horrific spell? I wouldn't put it past their twisted sense of humor.

"Are you almost done?" Eliaster looked over his shoulder. "I don't think they're paying attention to us, but I'd rather not risk it."

I took a deep breath and pulled the shim into place. The lock snapped open, and I gingerly undid it from the chains. Eliaster started unwinding the chain from the bars, carefully gathering it in his hands so it wouldn't rattle.

I grinned. Finally.

David clapped me on the shoulder. "Okay, so that worked better than I thought. Good job." He squinted at the gap between the cavern wall and the cage. "I don't think Dywor or I will be able to fit back there."

I nodded. David had too much of a football player's build. Even though Dywor looked like a sack of bones, he was still a thick-set sack of bones.

"That's what I figured," Eliaster said.

"Of course you'd already thought of it." David tapped my arm, then nodded to one of the tunnels across the cavern.

"That's the way we were brought in. I bet Larae went back to the Chicago Market to get help from Aifric, so that's probably the way you should go."

Eliaster chewed his lower lip. "You really think Larae would go all the way back to Chicago? That's gonna waste valuable time."

David grimaced. "It would be more like her to try a rescue attempt on her own, yeah."

"Well…" Eliaster's voice trailed off, and he glanced up at the gallery where the fae leader had disappeared.

Another group of fae came into the cavern, carrying armloads of wood. All of it was ragged and broken, more like enormous splinters than logs. There must have been a ruined building nearby that they were scavenging from.

"We don't have much time to make up our minds," Eliaster said.

"It can't hurt to see if we can find her lurking around. Or, failing that, getting a bargaining chip would be nice. We can leave some sort of sign for her to follow if we can't find her," I said.

Eliaster gave me a cryptic look, the faintest flicker of surprise crossing his stony face.

"Or something," I added.

"I don't think so," David said. "That's too easily sabotaged. We need to go back and look for her."

"And even you know that's too time-consuming," Eliaster said. "So why are you insisting on it when all you've wanted to do is cut corners so far? Larae can take care of herself."

David frowned. "That's gentlemanly."

Eliaster's jaw tensed, but he turned away rather than answer. He swung the broken piece of the cage to one side and slid into the gap between the rock wall and the iron bars. He pressed his hands into the bars and scooted sideways. As soon as I had enough room, I followed. A few of the other fae in the cage stood up, watching our progress. Dywor growled at them in Gaelic, and another fae answered him.

"What's he saying?" I asked.

"He says you're going to get everyone slaughtered," Eliaster said. "Never mind that's what will happen anyway if they don't escape."

I bumped into his shoulder. "Why're you stopping?"

He grunted and leaned to the side as far he could, digging his feet into the ground. We were less than half an arm's length from the edge. The gap between the wall and the cage was narrower than it had been at our entry point. The bars dug into Eliaster's chest.

"I think—" He pushed again and grimaced. "I'm stuck."

"Aw, c'mon!" I resisted the urge to slam my fist into the iron bars. If he blew this escape attempt...

Eliaster blew out a long breath and squirmed, finally slipping past the tight spot and out from behind the cage. He leaned over and pressed a hand to his chest, grimacing.

I slid free and crouched, watching the fae coming and going from the cavern. As soon as I was sure no one had noticed our escape, I snuck around to the front of the cage. The lock keeping the door shut was another simple, modern padlock.

I stuck my hand through the bars and David passed me the plastic shims. I twisted them into the lock.

"Hurry," Eliaster hissed, so close his breath hit the back of my neck.

"Dude, gross." I elbowed him back.

Dywor's clammy hand tapped my shoulder. "Look! That's Larae!"

I twisted around. In the stone gallery where we'd spotted the fae leader earlier, I could see the silhouette of a girl. She turned to look out over the cavern, and the torchlight played on her face. It *was* Larae.

Eliaster raised his hand, catching her attention. Her eyes widened.

"Watch it!" David shouted, backing away from us.

Out of the corner of my eye, I saw Eliaster take off for the cavern entrance. A fae lunged at me. I dodged and ran into another one. The fae grabbed my arms and slammed me against the bars. Air huffed from my lungs. I curled up as much as I could. The only reason I stayed upright was because of the fae holding me in place. He jerked me around, shoved me into the bars again.

Three fae tackled Eliaster. He fought back, but his punches and kicks seemed slower than usual. One of the fae got in a punch to his temple. Eliaster staggered and dropped to his knees, pressing his hands against the sides of his face. The two grabbed his arms and dragged him back to the cage.

The fae gripped my jaw and squeezed hard. "Not smart, little human, trying to escape like that. Not smart at all."

Another fae grabbed my captor's arm. "If you hurt the human, Tuathal will have your hide."

The fae stared past me into the cage, his eyes probing into the shadows. He turned and glared at Eliaster. "Humans should all die, and the fae who fraternize with them should be shunned as Unseelie traitors."

"*Briseadh agus brú do chnámha*," Eliaster replied.

One of his captors slapped him across the back of the head. Eliaster cried out and hunched his shoulders. Tears formed in the corners of his eyes.

Larae's voice rang out across the cavern. "Drop what you're doing!"

She stood at a different gallery opening, beside the leader of the cannibal fae. Her hand held a knife to his throat. I hadn't thought the guy's skin could get any paler, but a bleached sheet couldn't begin to compete with him now. Even from where I stood, I could see the thin trickle of blood sliding down one side of the fae's neck.

"Good girl," David murmured.

None of the fae spoke. They were all staring at Larae in horror. Some of them had their hands stretched out, wordlessly pleading for their leader.

"Release the new prisoners," Larae said, biting out each word. "Let them go, and your precious Tuathal will remain unharmed."

A flurry of whispers ran through the fae. Tuathal raised

his hand and silenced them, then spoke quickly in Gaelic.

"What's he saying?" I asked Eliaster.

Eliaster frowned. "He says he and Larae made a deal, that she must be obeyed immediately."

Sure enough, as soon as the words left the guy's mouth, the fae holding Eliaster and I released us. One of them pushed me aside and unlocked the cage door.

I glanced hesitantly at Eliaster. This was way too easy. They were going to pull some trick or something…right?

Eliaster stepped off to the side and made sure no one was standing behind him. "I think we're good."

"Of course we're good, numbskull! Stand around much longer and I'll leave you to be crow-bait," Larae yelled.

Dywor handed me my messenger bag and the plastic shims as he walked out of the cave. I nodded in thanks and tugged the strap over my head. For a second, we hesitated—then Eliaster stepped forward. David, Dywor, and I followed him closely, weaving around the fae as they stood stock-still, their pale eyes following us. Their silence made me jumpy—at any minute I expected to be clubbed over the head or feel them grabbing at me. Why weren't they protesting more? If David and I were supposed to be some kind of delicacies, why weren't they putting up more fuss? Their silent stares made the hair on my arms and neck prickle.

We stopped at one of the tunnel entrances, and I looked back for Larae. The fae leader, Tuathal, stood alone at his gallery window, staring after us. Even from here I could see the tight, angry lines on his face.

"Well, don't stand there gawping."

I jumped and spun around. Larae stood a little way into the tunnel, grinning and carrying our weapons bundled together under one arm.

"Why isn't he with you?" Eliaster demanded, grabbing his swords.

"We made a deal. He'll uphold his end of it." She smirked, her flat violet eyes staring at Eliaster as if daring him to complain.

Eliaster's eyebrows arched, but all he did was nod. "Thanks."

Larae shrugged, and yelled up to Tuathal, "Remember our deal!"

The fae nodded.

I heard the others break into a jog, and I slowly backed after them watching Tuathal's face as I went. The fae looked right at me, and a nasty smile curled the corners of his mouth. A chill ran down my back. I got the feeling that he wasn't done with us yet. Not by a long shot.

chapter 18

Half an hour's run from the cannibal fae's cavern, Eliaster called a halt. I leaned over, bracing my hands on my knees. My heart pounded. The adrenalin from our escape had burned out in the run, leaving me exhausted and jumpy.

We stood in a small pocket of rock, rubble sealing us in overhead. There was only one entrance and one exit, tunnels someone had dug through the boulders and braced with pieces of salvaged wood.

Larae hooked her thumbs under the straps of her backpack and glanced at Eliaster. "Why'd we stop?"

Under the glows of our flashlights, Eliaster's face was haggard. He scrubbed at the crusted blood under his nose. "Just give me a minute," he said, his voice tight. "I got beaten up pretty bad back there, in case you hadn't noticed."

"Yeah, and I also noticed it was because you thought you had to fight back." Larae crossed her arms. "It's your own fault, just like most of the mishaps on this quest have been."

Eliaster cringed. "Oh, and I was the one who broke into Blodheyr's loan office? That was my fault?"

"It got us here, didn't it?"

I sighed. As much as I wanted answers from Larae too, I knew this wasn't going to get us anywhere. I was about to tell them so when David spoke.

"Guys!"

His shout got Eliaster and Larae's attention. They both looked at him. He spread open his backpack, showing them the empty interior.

I dug into my messenger bag. I hadn't been carrying any food or water, but someone had stuffed the compact sleeping bag David had loaned me into one of the interior pockets, next to my computer. My phone was in the outer pocket where I'd left it.

"Crap," Eliaster said. "My stuff's gone too."

"So now I'm the only one with food and water?" Larae pressed a hand to her forehead and swore. "I had enough for a week for myself. With the three of you sharing my supply, we'll be lucky to last three days for food. Who knows how fast we'll burn through the water."

Eliaster rubbed his nose again. His shoulders slumped, and he stared at the ground, cradling his head in one hand.

"We'll just have to go back," David said, slinging his backpack over his shoulders. "We'll have to get more supplies from Aifric and try again."

"We can't," Eliaster said. "Didn't Llew's attack on Josh in Chicago tell you anything? They're right on our tail. We have one shot at this. Otherwise, Blodheyr gets the relic."

"At this point, who cares?" Larae demanded. "Let them have their stupid relic. We'll figure out some other way to stop the Lucht Leanúna. We should go back to Springfield and try to save Marc, like we should have done in the first place."

"No." Eliaster stood. "We have to keep going."

David and Larae glared at him. I twisted my bag's strap in my hands.

"If we turn tail now, we'll have thrown away days of work. We need to see this through. We have to try to find the relic."

"Two days," David said, holding up the first two fingers of his right hand. "If we don't find this relic in two days, we're going back and resupplying. I don't care if Blodheyr's goons are so close we can touch them, the limit is two days."

"Fine," Eliaster muttered. "Dywor will be able to find it…where is Dywor?"

I looked around. In the intensity of the argument, no one had noticed the sniffer's absence.

"Stupid rager!" David muttered, shining his flashlight down the entrance to the cave.

Dywor stood about ten feet away at a crossroad, staring into a side tunnel. He raised a hand toward us, palm outward. Eliaster motioned for us to be quiet.

Dywor closed his eyes and drew in a long breath through his nose. After a pause, he turned to one of the other tunnels and did the same thing. He shuffled a few steps toward the original tunnel and took another deep breath.

His eyes opened, and he glanced at Eliaster. "Not just rocks and dust and charcoal and fae anymore. There's a new scent. An otherworld scent. I haven't smelled anything like this in ages."

"Think it's our relic?" Eliaster asked, voice tense and eager.

Dywor's eyes flickered from Eliaster to Larae, and he pursed his lips. "Maybe. Haven't caught a whiff of Tir Ni-all in any other place." He went deeper into the tunnel, his flashlight playing on the rocky walls.

"Then this is our best bet." Larae nudged Eliaster's shoulder as she stepped past him. "I'm sorry."

Eliaster grabbed her arm. "Don't lie to me."

She shoved him away, eyes flaring in a blaze of violet. "Don't touch me!"

Eliaster released her arm, glaring at her back as she followed Dywor. He sighed and walked after her.

I stepped down carefully into the tunnel. Eliaster had the flashlight aimed forward, so I could hardly see the rocks under my feet. I took a step forward and my toe caught under the lip of a rock. I crashed into the uneven ground, my bag digging into my gut.

"You okay?" David asked, holding his hand out.

I hiked myself to my feet, and checked my computer again. It was fine. "What's another bruise or two?" I pulled out my phone next. The glass screen had several big cracks across its face. I hit the lock button, but the screen remained dark. I groaned and dropped it back into the front pocket. "Let's get moving."

"Keep your sword close," David said, walking beside me. "I don't trust that rager."

Don't worry. I don't trust anyone.

Eliaster stopped, holding up his hand. The rest of us stopped, though Dywor shuffled forward a few inches and made a funny, whining sound that sounded like an old computer connecting to the internet.

We'd been walking for who knew how long, and my feet were aching even when I just stood in one place. For a moment we were all silent, and I strained my ears for any sound. Had he heard someone following us? Were the cannibals breaking whatever promise their leader had made to Larae?

"What?" Larae asked.

"Ssh." He leaned to one side. "We're being followed."

Larae bent her head, biting her lower lip. After a few seconds, she said, "I don't hear it, Eliaster."

"It's stopped now. But we were being followed."

Here we go again. Barely a week around the guy, and I already recognized that stubborn set to Eliaster's jaw. I leaned against the wall and crossed my arms.

"Maybe," Larae admitted. "But maybe you're being paranoid. Tuathal gave me his word."

Eliaster tilted his head to the side, looking at her out of the corners of his eyes. "Right. Because every cannibal out there has an impeccable sense of honor. Sounds legit."

She sniffed and flicked her ponytail over her shoulder.

"Just what was your deal with him?"

"That's between the two of us."

"We need to know, Larae."

"Why?"

"Because I'm not going to move one more foot until you tell us what your deal with Tuathal was." Eliaster crossed his arms.

She glared. "Could you be more childish?"

"The whole thing was too easy. He didn't even try to bargain, which means you offered him something he couldn't resist. As your partners, I think we have a right to know."

David snorted. "That's rich, coming from you, Eliaster. You haven't let us know much of anything this whole time!"

"Great timing, by the way, guys," I said. "I'm really glad we're doing this now, possibly with a pack of cannibal fae on our tail and barely enough food to make it back out. This is a great time to start fighting."

"If you had an objection, Josh, you should've spoken up back when we discovered our food was missing," Eliaster snapped.

Hello, pot, meet kettle. Kettle, pot. Does he even realize how hypocritical that statement is? I kept my mouth shut, not wanting to make Eliaster even angrier.

The entire conversation, Dywor had been circling around the group, nose in the air. He stopped beside Eliaster. "Don't smell anyone. Can't smell anything but the Otherworld smell now." He darted to the front of the group, started forward, then came back to Eliaster, then started forward again.

Was the guy part hound dog?

Eliaster and Larae ignored the sniffer, their eyes focused on each other. In the dim light, I could see Eliaster's eyes flooding with different shades of green.

"I'm going to lose the scent if we don't get moving," Dywor warned. He stood several feet away, twitching.

"Well, there's your chance," Larae said. "You wanted to find that relic, and we're close now."

Eliaster looked from Larae to him, rubbing his cross necklace. His eyes darted back and forth around the group.

He looked like a cornered animal, and I noticed that his free hand hovered near his sword.

After a moment, he shook his head and walked after Dywor.

Larae stared at his back with flat, steady violet eyes, her hands clenched.

We plodded forward. The dust we raised as we walked made the inside of my mouth and my nose gummy. I glanced over the group. Larae and David's eyes were both red-rimmed, and Eliaster's shoulders slumped forward. What time was it? I started to rummage in my bag, then remembered that my phone was broken anyway.

The rubble underfoot was smaller than the huge boulders we'd been navigating earlier. *Only the possibility of spraining your ankle, not snapping your leg off. Small comforts, I guess.*

Dywor picked up speed, turning into a side tunnel that wound upward. "It's close!" he hissed. "So close—I can almost taste it!"

We scrambled behind him. Eliaster tried to hold the flashlight steady, but it bounced and danced, giving us only glimpses of Dywor and the rest of the tunnel in sharp, jerky movements.

"That's going to make me sick," Larae muttered behind me.

The last bit of the incline was the worst—it was so steep we were scrabbling up with our hands. Rock shards and bits of debris kicked and tumbled down the incline behind us, loosened under our feet, made us slip and slither backward.

Dywor sprang forward, his twitching even more pronounced. He scrambled up the lip of the ledge and straightened, breathing deep. "This is it!"

We scrambled up beside him, keeping our lights on the ground directly in front of us. There was a deep, inky darkness in front of us. It felt—different—somehow. Different than the close darkness of the tunnel. It felt huge. Instead of echoing back to us, Dywor's voice faded away.

"Keep together," Eliaster instructed, putting a hand on one of his swords. "It feels like a big chamber. No telling what's waiting for us in there. Dywor?"

Dywor wandered out of the flashlight beam, his head held high again.

"Dywor, I just said—"

Brilliant lights snapped on, flooding the cavern. I ducked my head, yelping at the sharp stabbing pain to my eyes. The rest of the group ducked with moans of protest.

I squinted my eyes open, my hands flung in front of my face to block the piercing light.

Ten goblins stood not far away, watching us, swords and spears brandished.

Rocks crunched behind us. I looked over my shoulder. Llew, the ponytailed Unseelie, and several other fae stood behind us. And towering over them, the troll, Scyrril. He stepped up into the cavern, so close that I could feel his moist breath hit my face. My gut clenched, and the acidic bite of bile hit the back of my throat. I backed away and noticed the others doing the same.

Eliaster and Larae drew their weapons.

"Drop them!" Scyrril shouted, advancing on Eliaster, his huge scythe-like sword swaying back and forth in front of him. The scales on his forearms rustled as he flexed.

"Why didn't you warn us?" Eliaster yelled at Dywor.

The rager smirked and pointed at Larae.

Larae whirled and sliced her knife across Dywor's throat.

The sniffer's eyes bulged as he grabbed at his neck. Blood gushed between his fingers, and he dropped to the ground, choking.

I stared at him in shock. What was she doing? Why…? In a flash, I recalled her flirting touches and glances with David and me. She'd been lowering our guard, getting us to trust her so Eliaster would stand alone in his dislike of her. So we'd dismiss his caution as paranoia.

I should've known better.

"Get out, Josh!" Eliaster jumped back, narrowly avoiding

a swipe from Scyrril's sword.

I looked up. David stood between me and the other fae, gun and knife drawn. Scyrril and Eliaster were already off to the side, their weapons clanging as they struck and broke apart. Larae stepped in front of me and smirked. I knew she was baiting me, but I drew my sword and planted my feet shoulder-width apart. *No, Eliaster, I am not going to run like a coward.* "So answer me one question, Larae."

She laughed. "Really? You're gonna go with the snarky banter?"

I shrugged. "Why not?"

Her smile was frigid. "You're kind of sweet, so I'll humor you."

"Stop talking and run, you moron!" Eliaster yelled.

Scyrril was backing him toward the wall. He was trying to get to me, but every time he tried to dart past the monster, Scyrril's blade swept out. Eliaster threw his blade up to block another blow, and the troll shoved him hard. Eliaster staggered and fell to one knee, then was up again like a shot.

I pulled my attention back to Larae. She was standing an arm's reach from me, her bloody knife clutched in one hand, that stupid smile still on her face. Her eyes were that flat purple again, and I realized that it was that look that had bothered me when Tuathal let us go. Her emotions should have been running high then, and I should have been able to see it in her eyes, but there had only been that flatness to them.

A sharp, hot spike of rage broke through my calm. "What was your oh-so-convenient 'deal' with Tuathal?"

She laughed. "Oh, that? It was too easy. He pretended to be frightened of me holding a knife to his throat so I could fool you and Eli. In return, I promised him Marc and you, as well as a dozen other humans."

She lunged. For a split second, I thought she was nuts to engage a sword with a knife. As I shifted to catch her strike, I felt a foot hook around my ankle.

I hit the ground hard. The fall slapped the air from my

lungs. My sword jumped out of my numb hand and went skittering away over the rocky ground. David laughed. I rolled, starting up to my feet, looking for him.

Larae's boot connected with the back of my knees. I caught myself with my hands. Another kick in my ribcage sent me rolling. I swept my hands under my body and pushed up. Her knee slammed into my back, driving me down. She pressed her pistol into my temple.

"What are you doing?" Eliaster's voice was as cold and hard and sharp as the pebbles biting into the side of my face.

I squinted open one eye. He stood with his back to the wall, both swords out, glaring at David and Larae. Llew and Scyrril both stood close, hemming him in, but he wasn't even paying attention to them. Llew was still limping a little. I smirked at that as I shifted my left hand, feeling for my sword.

"Drop the swords," Scyrril snarled, edging forward with his blade extended.

Larae's other knee came down on my elbow. "Listen to him, Eliaster."

He laughed. "Right. Good try, vixen."

She pressed the pistol harder into my temple. I grunted as pebbles dug into my skin, a half-dozen little points making jagged cuts.

"Really, Eliaster, did you not expect me to notice your new pet project? It's not everyone who gets a personal recommendation for one of Opti's swords. Let's stop pretending, shall we?"

A *click* sounded next to my ear, rattled through my brain. It put another crack in my mental wall, and fear sent a cold shudder down my body. I clenched my hands, squeezed my eyes shut. *Please don't let me die this way. Please...*

"You have five seconds before your little genius becomes a little vegetable. One..."

Eliaster white-knuckled his swords.

"Two..."

My chest squeezed tight. Why wasn't he dropping them?

"Three..."

I cringed.

"Four..."

Eliaster growled under his breath and threw his swords on the floor. "Happy?"

The pressure on my temple eased a little, and I could breathe again.

"Better," Larae said.

David grabbed Eliaster's arms and shoved him to his knees. Llew grinned and gestured to one of the goblins. It tossed him a length of chain, the links clanking as Llew caught it.

Eliaster clenched his hands, his lips twisting in a grimace. "You're cruel, Larae."

I felt her shrug. "You should know by now that I consider that a compliment."

Llew clamped the shackles around Eliaster's wrists. Eliaster's face turned a sickly pale grey, and he gritted his teeth. He slumped forward, catching himself with shaking arms.

Iron shackles.

"Eliaster!" I yelled, pushing against the ground.

Llew moved away from him, snickering.

Larae shifted her weight off me, but kept the gun pressed against my back. "He'll be fine. Sit up."

I obeyed. David reached down and jerked me to my feet, kissing Larae's cheek as he did so. "Way to go."

"So much for thinking humans have to stick together," I muttered. "Sell out."

David ignored me.

For the first time I got a good look around me. The cavern was large, though not nearly as big as the cannibal faes' main cavern. Several tents and stacks of crates were scattered along the side walls, leaving the center of the cave clear. Now that Eliaster and I were restrained, the goblins lowered their weapons and dispersed, going back to several crates that lay open and half-unpacked near the back of the cavern.

David steered me down the path to the back wall. At the base of the wall, there was a huge well sunk deep into the ground, and above the well, I could see numbers, in familiar groups of five, carved into the stone.

"Another cipher?" I muttered.

"Been camped here for three days now, trying to decipher the dumb thing," Scyrril growled from behind me.

I jumped away from him.

He walked past, dragging Eliaster by one arm. Eliaster shot a glance at me, then looked down. He could barely stand. My heart sank to my gut. If he'd been useless in the cannibal fae's cage, he was doubly so now.

Scyrril shoved Eliaster against the wall next to a tent, and the fae slowly sank down, leaning his head back against the rock surface.

I glanced at Larae. She stood to the side, staring up the numbers with her lips pressed tightly together.

"You told them what the document said, as soon as I decoded it. But you couldn't tell them how to decode it, because—"

"They weren't there when you told Roe and me what the cipher was," Eliaster interrupted. He grinned at her. "So even if you did get a jumpstart on us, you've still been stuck here for three days."

"So that's why you kept arguing that we should look for Marc," I said.

Larae shrugged one shoulder and smiled. "Yeah. Thought I could appeal to your friendship, but I never counted that you'd be such a pansy." She looked at Eliaster. "And you are a *mac cailleach*, you know that?"

Llew sauntered past, nudging her shoulder with his elbow. He waggled his eyebrows at me. "Not that it would've done you a lot of good, pansy-boy, stickin' around Springfield to look for your buddy."

Eliaster groaned. "Oh no—"

Two goblins reached behind a stack of large crates and

dragged out a guy with hands taped behind his back and a hood over his head. My gut clenched. One of the little monsters yanked the hood off, revealing Marc, his eyes wide, mouth covered in duct tape. The goblin yanked the tape off, and Marc hissed in pain.

"Marc!" I said.

His head jerked up. "Josh? Thank the Almighty, I thought..." His voice choked out. He swayed as he stood.

"You okay?" I asked.

He nodded wearily. He was lying. I could see the haunted look in his eyes. Who knew what they'd done to him, trying to force the information of the document from him. The goblins cut the tape around his wrists, and Marc brought his hands forward, massaging his fingers.

David pushed me out of his way. "Get to work. We'll be marching soon."

"You been working on these?" I asked Marc.

"Just a few hours. They moved me out of Springfield right away, but didn't bring me here until late last night." Marc glared at Larae, but I could see other emotions competing with his anger and bitterness. The d'anam fuinneog danced in his eyes.

"I trusted you," he whispered. "I thought ..."

"Please don't, Marc," Larae said.

"How am I supposed to turn away when my heart is still stuck?"

"I'm so sorry." Larae stepped past me and brushed her fingers along Marc's jaw. The motion seemed to soften her, bringing a gentleness to her eyes that I hadn't seen her display before, even when she talked about him.

Marc flinched away from her.

Larae snatched her hand back, doubling it into a protective fist. Her eyes went hard and flat as ice. "I should have been more careful," she whispered, turning away. She walked back to David.

As soon as she reached his side, he leaned toward her, his harsh tone reaching us. I couldn't hear the words, but the look on his face mirrored Marc's—mixed with anger.

Marc snorted. "Looks like she cheated on one too many people."

Scyrril shoved him into the wall. "Work." The monster stomped away.

Marc folded his arms across his chest. "Right. Work. How long will this take you?"

I ran my hands through my hair. My fingers were starting to shake, just a little, but I pushed the adrenalin away and took a deep breath, willing myself to stay calm. I looked over at Eliaster, hoping he had an idea. I looked over my shoulder at Eliaster. He shrugged, his eyes dull.

"What's up with him?" I muttered. "This whole time he's been pushing us through this quest, to the point of plowing over anyone else's concerns. Now he's just giving up?"

Marc groaned. "He didn't tell you?"

Eliaster glanced at me out of the corners of his eyes and just as quickly looked away. He hunched his shoulders, making himself as small as possible.

I turned my back on him and stared at Marc. "What?"

"Idiot. I told him to trust you." Marc shoved his hands in his pockets. "Eliaster and I'd had this deal since the beginning. If I got caught—and we assumed I would eventually—then he wouldn't look for me and would focus on solving the cipher and finding the relic."

I stared at him. "And my involvement was...?"

"Because I didn't expect them to snatch me that night, when we were out together. I knew it would be soon, and I knew Scyrril was coming to talk to me that night, but I thought for sure I could stall for a few more days. You weren't supposed to be involved at all, but it all got out of whack because you were with me when it happened."

My brain stalled. *Sucker-punch.* "What?" That was it?

Eliaster's big secret was that he wasn't supposed to look for Marc and that my involvement had just been an accident? My mind still scrambled to connect the pieces, but all I was getting was a huge red *error* message. Why hadn't Eliaster told me? It would have made everything so much easier if I'd been on his side.

But would I have been? Would I have just gone along with the plan and not tried to find Marc? Probably not.

"I'm sorry, Josh. I never—I wanted to get rid of this problem, just get it over with. Move on." Marc's jaw clenched. "I never wanted to involve anyone else."

"Not your fault," I said, my mind already moving on. How could we get out of this? There had to be a way to use this cipher to our advantage.

I glanced over to Larae and David. They, Scyrril, and Llew stood at the edge of the well, staring down into it and discussing something in low voices.

What if I just didn't decipher the carving? Or maybe I could make a bargain—our freedom for the key to the Fibonacci sequence. Eliaster and Marc wouldn't like the idea of abandoning the relic to the hands of the Lucht Leanúna, but I wasn't about to become a martyr for their cause.

"What are you thinking?" Marc asked, his tone skeptical.

He knew me well. I gnawed the inside of my lip. I couldn't tell him. He'd never agree to it. I stood, keeping an eye on the group by the well.

Llew looked up and noticed that I was watching them. He started around the side of the well, flicking his bangs out of his face.

chapter 19

Llew crowded me close to the wall, his lips curled to reveal his teeth. "Shouldn't you be working rather than just staring off into space?"

I took a deep breath, then reached out and shoved him back.

He staggered a few steps, his eyebrows going up and his chin tucking to his chest in shock.

"I'm not doing this anymore," I said, raising my voice to Larae could hear. "I'm not helping the Lucht Leanúna."

Llew snorted incredulously. He looked over at Larae.

She raised her hand. "Wait, little brother."

They were siblings?

She stepped closer to me, her head tilting to one side. "I thought you were smarter than this, Josh. What do you think being stubborn will accomplish? You know this won't end well for you. The Unseelie, and especially the Lucht, are not at all squeamish about using torture to extract the desired outcome."

Llew grinned, stroking the knife at his belt with his knuckles.

Eliaster clenched his hands.

Marc stepped between Larae and me, holding out his

hands, palms toward Larae. "Give him slack, Larae. He's new...he doesn't understand—"

I shouldered him out of my way. "I understand plenty. I'm not proposing to just leave you hanging, Larae. I want to bargain."

She smiled. "A human bargain with a fae? This should be interesting."

Eliaster groaned and thumped his head against the wall. "Don't be stupid, Josh. Just decipher the *amadán* carving."

I ignored him. "If you let me, Marc, and Eliaster free, I'll give you the key to the cipher. And by free, I mean healthy, whole, with our weapons, and a guarantee of no pursuit." I shrugged, very carefully keeping my face passive. No need to let her see I barely had a handle on my panic. "Better yet, let me sweeten the deal. I'll decipher the carving and give it to you when we leave."

She raised an eyebrow. "How do I know you wouldn't lie to us?"

"How do I know you'd keep up your end of the bargain? The Unseelie have no honor, but apparently as a human, I'm not expected to have any either, so it's a risk for both of us." I held my hand out to her. "C'mon. We can make this deal work."

Larae licked her lips, staring straight into my eyes. I stared back, willing her to shake my hand.

She raised her hand and hesitated.

C'mon. This could work. It had to. It was the only way I saw Marc, Eliaster, and me getting away from these nuts.

Llew darted past me and grabbed Marc's wrist. A knife flashed in his hand. Marc twisted and kicked at him. Llew's strike missed his arm and slashed across his ribcage.

Marc staggered back, pressing a hand to the wound, a deep grunt huffing from his lungs.

"Llew!" Larae shrieked.

I grabbed Marc's shoulders and steadied him.

"I'm okay. Just a scratch." Marc brushed the blood away. His knees buckled and he hit the ground, catching himself with his free hand.

I knelt beside him, pushing his hand away from the wound. He was right—the cut was a shallow graze along a rib, barely enough to bleed. Why had he collapsed? What had Llew done to him?

Llew cackled.

I turned to see him holding up a knife, the blade orange with rust, the edge glazed in Marc's blood.

Larae screeched again and shoved her brother. "Crow-bait! What did you just do?"

"Rust." Marc's voice sounded like he was being strangled. His face was pale.

Eliaster burst into a torrent of Gaelic, scrambling to his feet. His eyes ran a gamut of shades, from muddy-green to a piercing emerald, in a split second. Scyrril grabbed his neck and held him back from charging at Llew.

Llew sheathed the knife without bothering to clean it. "Iron makes full fae sick, and rusted iron is poison to half fae. You have eight hours to get Marc to a cure before the convulsions kill him. I'd get working on that cipher if I were you."

A sick feeling spread through my gut. My face and hands went numb. I pressed a hand against the wall, steadying myself. "Marc?"

"Well done, genius!" Eliaster yelled at me. "Well done!"

I closed my eyes and gritted my teeth. *Breathe slowly. Stop panicking.* My mind spun. Llew laughed again, and I heard him and Larae walk away. She was hissing at him in Gaelic.

"Josh." Marc grabbed my shoulder.

I opened my eyes.

He forced a grin. "I'm not dead yet."

I glanced over at Eliaster. The fae's jaw was tight, his hands and arms tensed like he was ready to hit someone. Probably me.

I was beyond scared, beyond angry. Instead, it felt like I'd flatlined. Every emotion went cold. *I'm gonna get out of this, and I'll make sure Marc does too.*

I stood up and counted the numbers on the wall, then glanced at Marc. "I can have this done in an hour. Two at the most."

He grinned, a spark of blue in his eyes showing that the Unseelie hadn't taken all the fight out of him. "Of course you can. Have at it, genius."

I backed a few steps from the wall so I could see it better. 1832142. *T.* 38493. *N.*

As I worked to decipher the numbers carved into the cavern wall, a cold draft rose from the well behind us, making the dust on the cavern floor swirl in spirals. It sent a cold prickle down my spine. That well was the only exit from this cavern, and I could bet that the instructions I'd find would lead us down it.

"So what are we looking for anyway?" Marc asked, his voice low. "Did you guys ever figure it out?"

I glanced over my shoulder at Larae. "Yeah. Roe thinks it's something called a pathstone."

Marc sucked in a sharp breath. "*Mallaithé.* A pathstone? You're sure?"

I nodded.

He shook his head and closed his eyes. "Almighty help us."

I blew out a deep breath and looked back at the cipher. *C'mon, Josh. Focus.*

It took a little longer since I had to do everything in my head, but finally I finished deciphering the last number. I stepped back from the wall, running the message over in my head.

To any who have come searching for this relic, may I remind you what a dangerous thing it is that you're doing. Taking this stone will change the balance of power in the world, and it won't be for good. Please, reconsider what you are doing, and walk away from this place. Leave the cursed stone to rest where it has been hidden.

"I'm done!" I called to Larae, stepping back from the

wall.

She came over to my side. "What's it say?"

I repeated the message.

"Feel stupid now, Genius Josh?" Llew yelled. "Nothing substantial, and yet you're gonna get your friend killed over it."

"Why don't you find something to do!" Larae snapped at him. She turned back to me and Marc. "I'm so sorry. I didn't even know Llew had that knife." She reached out to touch Marc's arm.

He moved out of her reach. "Pardon me if I don't believe you."

She shrugged and walked away, yelling at the goblins to get moving.

Eliaster got up and came over to us. He had to keep one hand on the wall to stay steady on his feet.

"Any plan?" I asked him.

He shrugged. "I don't know. You seem to be a well of inspiration lately, why don't you have a go at it?"

"Hey, I got us out of the cannibal faes' cage, in case you don't remember."

"Any points you earned just got trashed. Besides, one time out of many? Stop thinking you know it all. You don't know anything, not about the Underworld."

My ears and face grew warm. "Oh yeah, and this is all my fault, right? Maybe if you hadn't gotten me involved in the first place—"

"You got yourself involved."

I talked over him. "And hadn't asked me to solve the cipher, we wouldn't be in this mess now!"

Eliaster flinched. "Yeah," he muttered. "We wouldn't be here at all." He dragged his hands through his hair and clasped them at the back of his neck. "Look, I'm sorry. But if I hadn't gotten to you, Blodheyr would have. You were already in the line of fire, whether you knew it or not. And I didn't know who else to go to. I couldn't trust David and Larae—they just felt off. You were the only person I knew who had a chance at solving that cipher."

The heat in my chest and head started to subside. He was right. He'd probably saved my life. But that just made the sharpness of what I'd just done worse. I'd probably just condemned Marc to death.

Marc cleared his throat. "Well, now that you're done bickering like a couple of schoolgirls, can we get down to business? They're not going to let us go now, so we need to figure out another plan."

I shoved down a flare of panic. Of course they wouldn't. If there was another cipher somewhere in the well, they'd need me. And they weren't going to pass up any chance to use Marc, or even Eliaster—as much as I wanted to kill him myself at the moment—as leverage against me.

"We'll make it," Eliaster said in a low voice. "If I don't keep believing that, then I'm going to cut my wrists right now and be done with it."

Marc nodded. "We have seven hours."

"We'll just see what happens when we find the relic," Eliaster said.

How could they discuss it so calmly? I knew what would happen when that relic was in Larae's hands. They'd kill us. It was a classic bad guy move for a reason: it worked. At least, in theory. In fiction, the good guys always found some way to survive, even if it was the tiniest, chanciest sliver.

As this nightmare was making painfully clear to me, real life wasn't fiction. The good guys didn't always win. But Eliaster was right—if I didn't keep believing that we could, somehow, survive, I'd be tempted to step right off the edge of the well. Except that would be too easy for Larae. If she won, it would be a hard win, because I was going to kick and scream every step of the way.

I didn't want to die down here, buried under tons of rock.

"Eliaster." Larae tossed him a climbing harness and a flashlight. "You first."

Eliaster pulled on the harness and buckled it tightly around his waist. He turned and gripped my shoulder.

"You're right, I should have been honest with you. I should have trusted you. I'm sorry."

I hadn't expected an apology from him. For a second, I stood still in surprise, staring at him. Eliaster dropped his hand and turned away.

I cleared my throat. "Yeah, I should've listened to you too. Sorry."

He nodded grimly and walked to the edge of the well. A goblin started to tie a rappel line into the carabiner on his harness, and Eliaster swatted him away. "I can tie my own lifeline, thanks."

He quickly threaded the line into his harness and tied it off, then spun around and leaned back. Another goblin began paying out the line, and Eliaster disappeared from sight.

Larae tossed Marc and me two more harnesses. I sorted out the tangle of webbing and stepped into it, pulling it over my hips.

"Trusting our lives to a couple of goblins," I muttered under my breath, nodding to the two Sidhé setting up more rappel lines. "It just feels wrong."

"Shows you how limited our options are." Marc winced as he buckled his harness.

"I don't want to die down here, Marc."

"Neither do I. I wanted to escape this place, remember?"

That conversation seemed such a long time ago. Goose bumps washed over my skin. I straightened and crossed my arms, rubbing my hands up and down the sleeves of my jacket.

Marc stepped toward the well and stopped, pressing a hand to his wound.

"You okay?" I asked.

He gritted his teeth and spread the tear in his shirt apart. The graze had stopped bleeding, but the edges of the wound had turned black.

I looked him in the eye. "I swear to you, I'm going to fix this."

"Don't make an oath you can't keep, Josh," he said

quietly, moving away from me.

I clenched my hands and looked over the edge of the well. Eliaster's light bobbed off the walls about fifty feet down. I'd never been scared of heights before, but the darkness made the well seem infinite, and the thought that it could be my tomb sent dry, raspy shivers like insect legs crawling all over me.

I backed away, rubbing my palms together.

Marc tossed me a line and demonstrated the knot to fasten it into my harness. I copied his movements, then jerked on the line as hard as I could. The knot held. At least I wouldn't fall to my death, though that might be preferable to being cannibalized.

A beam of light hit the ceiling of the cavern, and Eliaster's voice echoed up.

"Clear!"

Larae gestured for Marc and me to go next. Several other fae dropped out of sight, bouncing off the walls, some of them laughing like they were having the best time in their life. Marc sat down on the edge of the well, then turned and dropped, gripping whatever handholds he could find in the rough stone. He edged his way down several feet like that, then released his hold and began walking backwards down the wall.

I turned around, braced my feet, and leaned back.

The goblin holding my line slowly let it out. Though every instinct in me screamed not to, I let my weight sink back, then took a step downward, digging my toes into the rock face. The edge of the well rose up past my face. I released my grip on the line, spread my hands to the sides for balance, and twisted my head around. The lights the others were carrying gave just enough light to see the rough edges of the well's sides.

I took another step down and plunged into free fall.

chapter 20

I flailed, a startled scream jerking from my throat.

The line snapped taut. I jerked to a halt, flipping upside down. The harness squeezed my waist and hips tight. I groaned and pressed my hands against my stomach.

I looked up. Llew and Larae stood at the edge of the well, their malicious grins evident even in the dim light.

"Point taken!" I yelled. My voice cracked at the end of the sentence.

The two fae laughed and disappeared from sight.

I started inching downward again. I kicked and twisted myself upright, but my limbs were so rubbery I couldn't support my own weight against the wall. I wrapped my hands around the line and gripped it tight, chest heaving.

Please, please, please don't do that again.

Finally my feet touched the ground. My knees buckled, and I sagged against the wall, breathing hard. For a moment, I just stood there, my hands and forehead pressed against the rough stone face.

One of the fae standing beside me clicked his tongue against his teeth. He unfastened his harness. "Dude, that was a mean trick."

"You're telling me," I muttered, fumbling with the buckles on my harness.

The bottom of the well was a little larger, close to thirty yards across. The floor was unnaturally smooth, especially given how rough the sides of the well had been.

Eliaster and Marc stood on the far side, near the only outlet, a tunnel tall enough that even Scyrril would be able to walk through it without stooping. I joined them.

"You okay?" Marc asked.

"Just as okay as Indiana Jones was when he dropped into a pit of snakes." I peered down the tunnel. The builders of the well had expended all their talent on the smooth floor. The tunnel walls were in worse shape than the well walls. It could have been done in haste, or, more likely, done deliberately to hide any traps.

We stayed out of the way as the rest of the Sidhé rappelled into the well, most carrying large packs of supplies. The last three down were David, Larae, and Llew. Scyrril climbed down the wall, his limbs splayed like a scaly green spider. As soon as Larae got out of her climbing harness, she crossed the room to us.

"You're going first again," she told Eliaster.

"Wouldn't expect otherwise." He extended his hands, palms upward for easy access to the locks on his iron cuffs.

She laughed. "You're getting desperate, aren't you?"

He dropped his hands. "I can't scout with these things sapping my strength and limiting my movement."

"Sure you can," Llew said, grinning. "Didn't she tell you it was entertainment for the rest of us?"

Eliaster rolled his eyes.

Larae glanced at her brother. "Before we continue, there's one more thing to take care of."

David's arm latched around my neck. He shoved me forward to my knees. Llew grabbed my left hand and elbow, twisting my arm so my wrist was exposed. I pulled back, tried to wrench free, but David pressed his weight against my shoulders, keeping me in place.

I heard Marc and Eliaster scuffling and glanced over to them. Goblins clutched their arms, holding knives to their throats.

My heart hammered against my ribs as Larae set the edge of a knife against my wrist. She pressed her fingertips under my chin, forced me to look her in the eye.

"By trying to bargain with me, you volunteered yourself. Remember, Josh, that you do not toy with me." She kissed my forehead.

My stomach turned, but I couldn't look away.

With a sharp jerk, she laid open my wrist. For a second, I felt nothing. Where was the pain? Then I felt it, a white-hot fire that flashed all the way up my arm. My jaw clenched, and I grunted, my hand tightening. Blood pattered on the stone floor.

Larae cupped her hand under my wrist. When her palm was full, she brought her hand to her mouth, then drew it down her throat, painting her skin red. Her eyes burned bright.

Llew and David released me. I wrapped my fingersaround my wrist, the touch sending shooting arcs of pain through my arm. I sucked in one deep breath after another, unable to stop, unable to shove away the fear and panic that crushed into me. Blood soaked into my pant leg.

Larae breathed in deep, then whispered something in Gaelic. My blood soaked into her skin. Her limbs jolted. Larae threw her head back, closed her eyes. Her hands came up to chest level, and she drew in a deep, impossibly long breath. A glow spread over her skin, originating from where she'd spread my blood over her throat, and swept outward, a single wave that turned her into a being of living fire for one split second.

Larae gasped and collapsed to her hands and knees, pressing a hand to her heart.

David crouched by her side, offering a hand up. "Are you all right?"

She nodded, sucking in another deep breath.

I glanced at Marc and Eliaster. They were both staring at Larae, horror frozen on their faces. "What..." My lips felt numb. I couldn't find the energy to form the words.

Larae seized my wrist. Her fingers spasmed tight. I screamed as another flash of pain, this time dark and icy, hit me, spreading through my arm. I jerked free and scrabbled backward, my injured arm tucked close to my chest.

My wrist had stopped bleeding, but I couldn't feel my hand. With trembling fingers, I brushed away the congealed blood covering my arm. A thin, dark line cut across my wrist, marking the sealed cut. I shivered. Magic, drawn from blood.

"What are you?" Marc hissed.

Larae turned toward him. He recoiled as if afraid she would kill him just by looking at him.

"When I befriended you, Marc, I knew that your grandmother would sense any Unseelie magic. I had to purge myself of it. And now, I'm regaining something that I have missed very much."

Marc looked as sick as I felt.

"Blood magic," Eliaster muttered. "The worst of the worst. That's sorcery, Larae! Do you really know what kind of dark powers you're dealing with?"

She snorted. "I should. I've been dealing in these powers since before you were born."

She was quiet for a moment, letting that revelation sink into us. Before we were born... The only thing I could think of was her relationship with Marc. *Ugh. Cougar doesn't cover it.*

Larae smirked. "Now, if you're done pretending to be disgusted by me—"

"There's no pretending about it," Eliaster snapped.

"Maybe so, but even you, Eliaster the believer, would resort to blood magic if it got him what he needed. I know you, Eliaster. I've seen you work. I've heard what you do." She tipped her head to the side a little and smiled. "Don't pull the holier-than-thou act on me, Eliaster. You're no better than the rest of us."

Eliaster's fingers slowly uncurled from his cross necklace, and he turned, heading into the tunnels, his shoulders hunched.

Larae's sharp peal of laughter echoed off the cave walls. She motioned for everyone to follow Eliaster. Llew pulled me to my feet and shoved me forward.

"This day just keeps getting suckier by the minute," I muttered.

We crept through the tunnels at a snail's pace, Eliaster stopping often and taking plenty of time to examine the next few feet of tunnel before walking forward again.

Llew stayed beside me, ready to grab me at a second's notice. A few feet behind us, David and Marc walked beside each other. Larae was behind them, tracing lines that left glowing runes on her palms.

I rubbed my thumb along the dark line on my wrist. It was smooth, not ropey like a scar or lumpy like a scab. I shivered. Was I always going to have this reminder of my brush with dark magic? The sight made me sick. Larae may have called it the same thing, but this felt different than Dywor's sniffing or Opti's swords. It felt heavier, lifeless. I rubbed my fingers together. They were numb, no sensation in anything other than my thumb. I pinched the skin between my first and second fingers. I could feel the pressure of my fingernails, but no pain.

"Hold up." Eliaster stopped and ran his flashlight beam slowly over the walls.

Larae pushed past Llew and me, coming up behind Eliaster. "What?"

"This section of the tunnel is narrower. There's something different about the walls too…can't really tell in this light."

Larae kicked the back of his knees.

Eliaster sprawled forward.

A hail of arrows crisscrossed the area, bouncing and ricocheting everywhere. The rest of us dropped to the ground, curses in Gaelic and English flying as thick as the arrows. I curled in a ball, clutching my arms around my head, and just waited for an arrow to pierce my body.

After a minute, the chatter of the arrows stopped.

I slowly opened one eye.

A dead goblin lay on the floor next to me, an arrow sticking from his eyeball. I scrambled upright and backed away, running into Llew. He grabbed my arm and forced me to stay still. Two more Sidhé—another goblin and one fae— were dead, and several others, including the ponytailed fae, were nursing wounds.

"What were you thinking?" David bellowed at Larae.

Eliaster stood, shaking and pale, one hand clutching the cross around his neck.

"I was thinking that he was taking his sweet time. Now we know that these traps are pressure triggered and what weight will trip them."

"And you almost lost your guinea pig," Eliaster said. He addressed the rest of the group. "Who do you think she'll sacrifice next if I die?"

The circle of goblins around Larae widened a little.

Larae shrugged. "Not your concern. Let's keep moving."

Eliaster's eyes flickered, but without a word, he turned and started forward.

Shortly after the first trap, the tunnel became a series of twists and sharp turns. I'd lost all sense of direction long ago, but now it felt like we were just walking in circles. The goblins huddled close together behind the fae, as if the death of two of their number had made them afraid.

What did they have to fear? I glanced ahead at

Larae, who had stopped playing with her magical abilities and now walked beside David, her shoulders stiff. Eliaster's question must have gotten to them.

Maybe there was a way we could use this, exploit the goblins' newfound wariness of Larae.

In the space of what felt like hours, we'd walked for miles and Eliaster had discovered three more arrow traps. With each trap, everyone would back away to a safe distance before Scyrril threw boulders on the pressure plates until the traps were triggered. After the last trap, the tunnel straightened again.

The longer we walked, the slower Marc became. His face tightened every time his right foot came in contact with the ground, and his right arm hung, limp and nearly useless.

My stomach turned, the bite of acid in the back of my throat. It hadn't really left since we'd been captured. How long did Marc have left? More than anything I'd been through yet, the sight of my friend so helpless made me angry. It hadn't really been my fault—how could I have predicted that Llew would do something so senseless, so stupid? The pride I'd felt at picking the lock on Tuathal's cage had long since evaporated. I'd always thought I was smart enough to talk my way out of anything, to figure out a solution to any problem, but I couldn't see a good end to any of this.

The tunnel suddenly widened, the walls stretching from just feet away to yards. The group spread out a bit, Scyrril shaking his shoulders like he'd been cramped.

"Watch out!" Eliaster shone his flashlight on a wire that ran across the tunnel at its widening point. He followed the wire up along the wall to the ceiling, where it split into a web of silver that held up a cracked, crumbling roof of rock.

I gingerly stepped over the wire, trying not to envision what would have happened if someone had run into it.

In the beam of Eliaster's flashlight, I could see a wall at the back of the tunnel. He swung his flashlight from left to right, searching for a turn, an outlet, a doorway. Nothing.

We were at a dead end.

My brain blanked in panic.

Larae turned around. "Marc, I don't recall a mention of a dead end." Even though he words were directed at Marc, she stared at me through narrowed eyes.

Llew gripped my upper arm, but I jerked away from him. "Where am I gonna run, back through a dozen goblins to a bottlenecked tunnel? Right. That'd be stupid, even more stupid than trying to bargain with you earlier. I'm trying, Larae. I'm only a dumb human, remember?"

"There wasn't a mention of anything specific," Marc said,

his voice calm and soothing. "Just a warning. They didn't even mention the traps."

At the reminder, several flashlight beams flicked upward. The silver wire gleamed, sinister in the cold light.

Larae motioned to the goblins. "Okay, spread out and see if you can find a clue of what's next."

"Anything we're to look for specifically, my lady?" one goblin asked.

She glared. "A door, another cipher—I don't know, do I look omnipotent to you?"

The goblins scattered.

"You four." Larae indicated the ponytailed fae and three others. "Guard the prisoners. Llew, David, I want to talk."

Our guards directed Eliaster, Marc, and me to sit against the wall, then they sat several yards away next to the tunnel exit. Eliaster waited until they were talking among themselves, then scooted away from the wall and crouched next to Marc.

"How're you feeling?" he asked.

Marc raised his t-shirt. Black veins bulged from his skin, radiating from the wound in every direction. Some of them reached nearly halfway across his chest, fingering toward his heart. I cringed.

Eliaster gritted his teeth and gently probed the wound. Marc hissed in pain. Black pus oozed from the scratch. Eliaster avoided touching it. Working from beyond the poisoned veins, he pressed hard against Marc's chest, pushing the poison back toward the wound.

I turned away from the sight, my stomach rolling. "I'm sorry."

"Stop apologizing," Marc growled. "Both of you. We can't turn back time."

"What, you mean the geek hasn't figured that out yet?" Eliaster said, his tone light.

I snorted. "Trust me, I would've pulled out my time machine a lot sooner if I had one."

"Well, *daithairne*, there's my escape plan down the

drain."

Marc laughed, then groaned. "Okay, that's all I can handle."

I looked back. The previously black veins were now just a web of red lines, though black was already starting to discolor the ones closest to the wound again.

"How long did that buy us?" I asked.

Marc lowered his shirt. "Maybe another hour."

"Three have already passed since we came down here. That gives us four, five if what I just did helps at all." Eliaster leaned against the wall and draped his arms over his drawn-up knees.

"How are you doing?" Marc asked, smacking his hand against the iron chain hanging over Eliaster's legs.

"I'll survive. I've handled iron longer than this before."

I'll survive. It was an odd choice of words. Despite his joking of a moment ago, Eliaster looked tense, worry lines crinkled the corners of his eyes and mouth. He looked like he had no hope left. The fae warrior who lost his brother to his own people. His hand crept up and wrapped around his cross necklace again, like he was clinging to a lifeline. Maybe that's what it was to him, a lifeline, a reminder that he had hope, even though at the moment he didn't look like he believed it.

Did *I* believe in hope?

Eliaster had already decided we were going to die.

But I wasn't ready to die yet. And I wasn't ready to give up Marc or Eliaster for dead, either.

"We can do this," I said quietly.

Marc nodded.

"My lady!" One of the goblins waved his flashlight, then pointed it at a section of wall.

As Larae made her way across the cave, several more goblins gathered around the wall, wiping years of dust away. A smooth surface began to appear under the grime, a rectangular shape that was wide enough for me to walk through with my arms outstretched, but so short my hair would have brushed the top.

"Is that a door?" Marc stood.

"Weirdest door I've ever seen," Eliaster muttered.

"Mabon, come look at this," Larae said.

The ponytailed fae stood and ambled over to the door. The goblins backed off as he brushed at the surface, now smooth under just a thin coating of dust. Mabon pulled one sleeve over his hand and wiped the door. The surface was smooth and jet-black. It looked similar to obsidian.

Marc gasped.

"It looks Otherworld to me, Larae." Mabon placed his hand on the door. "I can't think of anything—"

He went stiff.

"What?" Larae demanded.

The goblins scattered, clearing the area directly in front of the door. The obsidian reflected Mabon crouching in front of it, his reflection's hand and his real hand meeting on the glossy surface. In one of the lower corners, I could see the reflection of my sneaker.

Marc kicked my leg so that my shoe was no longer in the reflection.

Mabon's body quivered. His hand fell away, and in the mirror his skin began to melt and boil like acid had been poured over him. The fae screamed and scrambled backward. He dropped onto his back, clawing at his face, writhing, his shrieks echoing in the dead silence of the cave.

The reflection disappeared and he went still.

David grabbed Mabon's arm and dragged him out of the direct line of the door—or whatever it was. He pressed two fingers to the side of Mabon's neck and waited.

Everyone waited, the chamber silent. My ears still rang from Mabon's screams, and a tremor had started in my hands.

David glanced over at Larae. "He's dead."

chapter 21

"What is that thing?" I whispered to Marc.

He was silent for a moment, watching Larae. She paced back and forth on the other side of the chamber, biting her fingernails. They'd pushed Mabon's body to the side, out of the way. He looked pathetic, huddled there, his skin already going waxy.

"It's a soul-mirror," Eliaster answered. "In Tir Ni-all, when fae began learning how to hide their d'anam fuinneog, they began constructing these for places where it was important to know the intent of the people seeking to enter."

"You guys took your security seriously then," I muttered.

Marc shifted and pressed a hand to his side. "Not all of them were designed to kill. I'm surprised there's even one here."

I gnawed my lip. This relic was beginning to live up to all the hype built around it. "So, how do we get in?"

Larae stopped pacing and stared at me. "Excellent question, Josh."

I swallowed. "What are you implying?"

"Did Josh tell you all of the cipher?" Larae asked, looking at Marc.

"He wasn't lying."

"Really? How do you know? Humans don't have d'anam fuinneog. There's no way to tell when one of them decides to lie."

Marc crossed his arms and glared at her. "We've been friends for years, Larae. I know what I'm talking about."

Larae stepped forward but stopped before crossing the mirror's path.

No one was going to come even close to letting their reflection show in that mirror. I glanced at the tunnel. Mabon's three fae buddies were all that stood between us and freedom. Everyone else was on the other side of the chamber, too scared to cross in front of the mirror's path.

"Keep talking," Eliaster murmured under his breath.

Marc said something to Larae, but I barely registered it. Eliaster and I were thinking the same thing. Could we fight past those three? I swallowed again. The fundamental problem with any plan of attack was that it would have to hinge on me, thanks to Marc's wound and Eliaster's iron cuffs. My palms started to sweat.

"Don't even try," Larae said.

I looked at her. Her hands were curled into claws, something dark and cloudy filling her palms. Marc and Eliaster both froze.

Normally, I wouldn't even think about hitting a girl, but at the moment I could very, very easily make an exception for Larae.

"I just had a thought," she said. "The fae who had this relic, who created a hiding place for it. The first cipher, Josh, what was the key number again?"

"Thirty-nine," I answered.

She nodded. "Thirty-nine. The number of Christ's ancestors. Now, who would base a cipher off that, unless they were Christians? Which means that Marc and Eliaster share the beliefs of the people who set the mirror in place. The same values, possibly even the same intentions."

Which meant they might be able to unlock the mirror, to get us moving on the next stage of the quest.

"So. The only question is who should try first." Larae smiled, her lips thin, her eyes sparkling.

She *enjoyed* this. I balled my hands.

"I'll do it," Marc said.

My heart sank. Of course he would volunteer. "Marc..." I stopped, glanced from him to Eliaster. What was I gonna say? That Eliaster should try before my best friend? How could I even think of asking anyone to risk their life like that?

Once more, I glanced at three fae blocking the tunnel entrance. Was it better to die trying to escape, to get stabbed by one of their swords or blasted by Larae's magic?

Eliaster gripped Marc's arm. "You still have a chance."

"I'm gonna be dead in four hours, give or take a few minutes," Marc said, pulling free. "You really think that's enough time to even get me back to Chicago? It makes sense for me to try first."

My eyes burned. I blinked hard.

Eliaster stepped back, shoulders hunched.

Marc took a deep breath and stepped close to the mirror. His image appeared in the glossy surface, small at first, then growing larger as it rushed up to meet him. He reached out one hand to the glossy surface, whispering under his breath. The words echoed off the chamber wall. "Christ be with me, Christ within me..."

I held my breath. Marc had never made much of his faith, but I could feel the depth and belief behind his words.

His fingertips met, and he cringed, turning his head away from the mirror. When nothing happened, Marc eased the rest of his hand flat against the mirror. Again, for a second, nothing happened. Then a ripple of light flashed inward, from the edges of the mirror to Marc's hands. He bowed his head, cringing, as the light worked into his fingers.

"Christ beneath me, Christ above me—" Marc broke off with a growl of pain.

Eliaster took a step forward. I grabbed his arm. *Almighty help us.*

Marc dropped to his knees, mouth open, chest working to

suck in air. Then the light vanished, and Marc gasped. He scrambled away from the mirror, chest heaving, sweat beaded along his hairline.

As his fingers left the surface, a *click* sounded, and the mirror swung outward. David and Llew moved in, crowding Marc away as they swung the mirror outward to reveal a doorway. David shone his flashlight inside, then stepped in, disappearing into the inky black room.

"You all right?" I asked Marc.

He nodded. "I just helped them," he muttered. "The Lucht Leanúna want to open a hidden path, and I just helped them do it. Almighty forgive me."

Eliaster glanced at the wire strung across the tunnel exit, then back up at Marc, his face grim. "We can make sure it never leaves here." He took a step away from us, putting him out of arm's reach.

I'd been right earlier. He had no hope that we were getting out of here. "That's suicide! If you trip that wire, we'll be dead as well as them!"

"I got it!" David appeared in the doorway, holding up a dusty wooden box carved with Celtic knots.

Larae rushed forward and grabbed it from him. With her hands trembling, she opened the box. I, and everyone else in the room, took a step forward. Some kind of white rock, carved with a piece of a trinity knot, lay nestled inside, padded by velvet. A *rock*? That's what we'd risked our lives to get? I clenched my teeth. I wanted to slam it against the wall, to pound the thing into dust.

Eliaster grabbed my arm and swung me around into the tunnel. I bounced off the wall, staggered, and tripped over my own feet. By some miracle, I'd missed the wire. The motion caught Larae's attention, and she opened her mouth to shout at her minions.

Before she could, Eliaster stomped down on the wire.

A pebble bounced off my shoulder, trailing a stream of dust. The silver network over the fae heads shuddered, but didn't fall.

"Eliaster..." Llew reached for a knife.

Larae grabbed his arm, her fingernails digging into his skin. "Eli, what are you doing?"

"If you touch me, who knows how many tons of rock will come down on your head." Eliaster pointed to the box. "Toss it to Josh. Carefully. Marc, get into the tunnel."

"Let me take your place," Marc hissed. "I'm dead anyway."

Eliaster shoved him away and motioned to Larae. "C'mon. I'm tired of playing."

With a snarl, she tossed the box past him. I caught it, the weight smacking into my hands with a satisfying thump. I cracked the lid open and made sure the stone was still there in its velvet cushion.

"Go," Eliaster told us.

I stared at him. "Dude, c'mon. You can run."

"I'm not—" Marc started.

"Get. Going!" Eliaster snapped.

David lunged forward. His shoulder hit Eliaster in the gut and doubled the fae over like he weighed nothing. Eliaster's foot skidded off the wire.

The ceiling in the cave creaked, but held. For a split second, we stood frozen in shock, staring at it. A jagged rock teetered in the net, then slipped out, falling in slow motion to the ground.

"Run!" Eliaster bellowed, shoving David off of him.

I spun and pelted down the tunnel. Rumbling filled the air behind me, along with Larae's shrieks and the screams of goblins. The tunnel shifted and crumbled, the walls breaking apart in front of us. I tucked the box close to my chest with one arm and wrapped the other around my head.

I passed other shorter tunnels that dead-ended or curved around, and it dawned on me—we'd been in a sort of maze the entire time. The tunnel had looped and doubled back on itself, and now it was collapsing in a very precise way, giving us the straightest shot out of here.

Within minutes of running, I burst into the well. Cracks

spidered the floor and walls. I spun around, waiting for the others. Dust billowed from the tunnel. Marc and Eliaster emerged from it, the powdered rock clinging to their skin and clothes.

Marc collapsed, one arm holding himself up, the other wrapped around his gut. He started retching, his frame shuddering with dry heaves.

A roar echoed out of the tunnel.

I ran to Marc's side and pulled his arm over my shoulder, half-dragging him toward the pile of harnesses against the far wall. Eliaster followed, twisting one cuff as hard as he could, trying to force it over his hand.

Marc slumped against the wall, skin gray, his breath coming in harsh gasps.

"What happened?" I demanded, shoving a harness at him. I grabbed another and started knotting a rappel line into the carabiner.

"Pumping blood and adrenalin. Not good for people who have poison in their systems." Eliaster grunted and wrenched at his cuffs again. "Where are my swords?"

Marc coughed. "Scyrril had them, last I saw."

Through the haze, I spotted more people stumbling out of the broken tunnel. Scyrril's bulk and height made him immediately recognizable. Marc groaned and slumped to the ground, eyes and teeth clenched as he pressed both hands to his side.

I dropped the rappel line. Eliaster moved away from me, hands fumbling along the wall in search of anything he could use as a weapon.

"We're dead." I said the words in a flat tone. Funny. Would've thought I'd get a bit more worked up, staring death in the face.

Eliaster glanced at me. "Get Scyrril's attention. I don't care what you do, just make sure his back is toward me."

"Just because I admitted that we're dead doesn't mean I was asking for a suicide mission," I snapped.

"Trust him!" Marc shot back.

Fine. No one had noticed us yet. I dropped the box on the ground next to Marc, stepped away, reached down to the ground, and grabbed a jagged chunk of rock the size of my fist. I clutched it in my right hand.

"Hey, ugly!" I yelled at Scyrril. I was about to hurl another insult, maybe one about his mother, when the monster's head swiveled toward me. He roared and charged. *Okay then. Touchy.*

I squared my feet into a fighter's stance. The rock I held would be no match against the troll. My heart hammered.

As he drew closer, I spotted a bundle of three swords hanging in a quiver-like harness from Scyrril's shoulder. Eliaster had to get a shot at those weapons.

I dodged out of Scyrril's way at the last minute, side-stepping to my left. He swung to follow me, claws reaching out to dig into my neck.

Eliaster sprang forward and hit the troll low, in the back of the knee. Scyrril stumbled, and Eliaster clambered onto his back, swinging the chain around his wrists over Scyrril's neck. The monster bellowed and reached back, clawing at Eliaster's arms, opening deep gashes through the sleeves of his leather jacket.

I smashed the rock into Scyrril's side. He swatted me away. I hit the ground a good five feet away and skidded, scrambling up to my feet before my head even stopped spinning.

The other survivors were moving toward us now, close enough that I could see who they were. Llew, David, Larae, about five goblins, and one other fae. The rest must have been buried in the cave-in.

"Any time, Josh!" Eliaster yelled.

I ran back toward Scyrril. Eliaster was still on his back. The troll's movements had slowed, but he wasn't going to pass out anytime soon. I lunged for the weapons and caught the strap. Scyrril keeled to the side, thrown off by my unexpected weight. My knees dragged the ground.

He shook, and the weapons slid free, clattering on the

ground. I landed with a huff, the bag underneath me. I rolled to the side. Eliaster clung to the chains around Scyrril's neck, one foot dangling and the other dug into Scyrril's shoulder. Scyrril shook again, and Eliaster's foot slipped. He drove his knee into Scyrril's scales, but another shake, and he'd be swinging free, hanging by his arms. I tossed one of Eliaster's swords up to him. He pinned it with his forearm.

I grabbed my sword and swung, feeling a slight drag as I sliced Scyrril's leg. Scyrril howled, buckled to one knee.

Eliaster got his sword around Scyrril's throat and sliced deep. Black blood gushed down the troll's chest. Scyrril crashed to the ground, spasming. Within seconds, he was still. Eliaster pulled free and stood up, grinning.

I grinned back.

A slow clapping echoed in the room. Larae stopped as soon as we both looked at her, though her hands stayed up, palms pressed, fingers pointing toward us.

"Good show, both of you." She smiled. "But just because you've killed a troll doesn't mean you can take nine more opponents."

Marc stepped up beside us, holding Eliaster's other sword. Sweat trickled down the sides of his face, but his feet seemed steady. In his free hand, he held the pathstone. "That's only three each, sweetheart! Not even a challenge."

Larae snarled and motioned the goblins forward. "Kill them!"

The goblins charged, howling.

I stepped forward and caught a goblin's sword on my own blade. The goblins fought with no strategies, their swords forming the same patterns over and over again. My first kill was easy, a cut to the throat. My gut lurched, but then another goblin was swinging at me. I dodged, parried again, and in three strokes had my sword buried up to the hilt in the goblin's chest.

Out of the corner of my eye, I saw David, Llew, and the other Unseelie ganging up on Eliaster. He fought like a whirlwind, never still, his one blade somehow a match for all three of theirs.

No time. I looked for Marc. Two goblins had him backed close to the wall. He was holding them off, but even I could see that his swings were weakening. I started toward them.

A throwing star sparked off the stone next to my foot. Larae. I spun, looking for her. She was running at me, a knife in her hand, violet eyes wide and wild, teeth bared in a snarl. She swung and I parried, driving all my strength behind the move.

Her knife snapped free of her fingers. Before she could recover, I shoved, knocking her to the ground.

As I stepped back, she raised her hand, making a flicking motion at my legs. A thin whip of smoky black matter lashed out from her fingers and snapped around my right leg. She yanked, and I crashed onto my back. My leg burned with cold. I yelled as the magical whip tightened.

Eliaster slammed into Larae, knocking her to the ground again. The magic dissolved, and I scrambled up to my feet.

To the side, Marc hit the ground, the relic bouncing out of his limp hand.

"Marc!" I lunged forward. My limbs felt like they moved through molasses, every motion taking much greater effort than it should.

The goblin reached down to grab the relic.

I reared back and threw my sword as hard as I could. The hilt clocked the goblin in the head, gashing open his cheek. He turned, snarling, blood trickling down his face. I dodged the first strike, scooped up my sword, and parried once, twice, jerked back as his sword slipped past my guard and nearly found my side. The goblin overreached and I stabbed into his gut.

I grabbed the stone just as someone kicked me in the ribs. I rolled and hit the wall. David reached down and punched me in the face. I shoved him away and ran my hand over the ground, feeling for my sword. My ears rang and blood ran into my eyes, blinding me. I wiped my face and kept searching for anything I could use as a weapon. David grabbed my ankle just as I closed my fingers around the pathstone.

I brought it up and around, bashing him in the side of the head.

David dropped beside me. The stone crumbled to pieces in my grasp.

Larae screamed.

I sat up.

Larae grabbed Llew's arm. Wind blew from out of nowhere, whipping the fae's hair and clothes. Eliaster backed away from them, shielding his face as dust billowed around the two.

Then the wind died, and Llew and Larae were gone.

David sprawled on the ground, his glazed eyes staring unseeing at the ceiling, blood puddling under his head. The dead bodies of the goblins were scattered across the cavern, and just a few feet away, Marc lay, a gaping hole in his chest. The metallic scent of blood hit my nose. I leaned over and puked.

"He's still alive!" Eliaster said, crouching beside Marc. He gripped Marc's hand tightly. "Hey, can you hear me?"

Marc squinted his eyes open, then turned his head and looked at me. "The relic?"

I looked at my feet. A few small chunks of carved white stone lay beside David's head, the rest powdered and turning red. I picked up a couple of the chunks and showed Marc.

Marc grinned.

My own smile felt tight and shaky.

"We did it." Eliaster's voice trembled. "We stopped the Lucht from getting the relic."

A spasm tightened Marc's face. Through his teeth, he murmured something in Gaelic. Eliaster nodded. I reached down and grabbed Marc's free hand. My throat tightened, and I couldn't force out the words I wanted to say—how good of a friend he was, how he was gonna be okay, how I was honored to be able to help him. My throat choked on the words. Instead, I squeezed his hand as tightly as I could, hoping he understood.

His eyes flickered, one last shot of bright sky-blue darting through them. His fingers tightened briefly around my hand, then went slack. One last exhale, and he was gone.

My eyes burned. I bent forward, my chest and shoulders caving in from a terrible weight. The smells of blood and dust in the cavern mixed, sending my gut turning again.

Eliaster's shoulders shook as he reached out and closed Marc's eyes.

chapter 22

In movies, in music, in books, we're told that death looks peaceful. That the dead always look calm, quiet, like they've escaped from our noisy, dangerous world. David and Marc hadn't looked like that in death. They had both been in pain. Even though Marc had died for a noble cause, he had still died in pain.

We left Marc's body, one hand holding most of the fragments of the stone relic he'd given his life to find. I took one of the pieces with me. Roe might want to look at it.

We climbed the well and found our gear in the rubble that the goblins had left behind. My phone had been broken into pieces, and though my computer was still operable, the hard drives I'd taken from Blodheyr's pawn shop were gone.

The rager, Dywor, still lay facedown on the cavern floor, blood dried into a tacky pool underneath him.

We trudged into the tunnels, neither of us speaking.

That final fight in the well played over and over in my mind—the goblin's knife pushing into Marc's body, the stone cracking against David's head—a living nightmare that left me dazed. My steps dragged on the floor. I was bone-numbingly exhausted, mind and body.

I don't know how long we walked until Eliaster stopped

and clicked off his flashlight. "Listen," he whispered.

In the echoing tunnels, we could hear footsteps. Dim light illuminated a curve ahead. I shifted my grip on my sword hilt and realized I hadn't sheathed it since I'd retrieved it from Scyrril.

My throat tightened. I didn't want to fight. Didn't know if I could even summon the energy to defend myself. I lifted my sword, and the weapon felt so heavy in my hands that I would have dropped it—except my left hand was locked tight around the grip.

Eliaster groaned and ran his hand through his hair, leaving smears of gore across his forehead.

The lights came around the corner, a dozen or so fae carrying them. In the middle of the group was the one fae I recognized.

"Eliaster! Josh!" Aifric hurried forward.

Eliaster wrapped his arms around the portly fae. "Thank the Almighty. How did you know how to come?"

"I've had scouts watching the Lost Tunnels entrance. This morning they reported seeing Larae and another fae, Unseelie, with a raven tattoo on his arm…I was worried that something may have gone wrong."

Eliaster snorted.

"Llew," I muttered. "Larae betrayed us."

Aifric glanced from Eliaster to me, and his eyes narrowed in concern.

"How long have we been in here?" Eliaster asked.

"Three days."

The knowledge felt like a wall of bricks. Three days in these cursed tunnels, three days since I'd had sleep—beyond getting knocked out by Tuathal's fae—and two and a half days since I'd eaten anything. Strange. I didn't really feel hungry.

I slumped against the wall, rubbing my hands over my face. As if from a long distance, I heard Eliaster and Aifric's voices, but I didn't want to pay any attention to them.

Someplace deep in my mind, someplace that was

somehow still working, told me I'd finally given up and was slipping into shock. I couldn't muster the energy to care.

A dark-skinned face came close to mine, a fae I vaguely recognized. "C'mon, Josh. Let me help you." He tried to pull my sword from my hand.

A surge of panic rose, so rapidly that it took my breath again. I jerked away from him, raised my free hand and tried to punch at him.

Eliaster grabbed my wrist. "Josh! Josh, you're okay. Hey. You're with friends."

The dark-skinned fae's name came to mind, random and clear among the fuzziness that crowded my head. Efran. Our guide from the Chicago Market to Aifric's house.

Eliaster slid his thumb between my hand and the sword grip, easing it from my stiff fingers. He handed it off to Efran, then pulled my arm around his shoulders, just like I'd done so recently for Marc. I glanced at him, the corners of my eyes growing hot.

Eliaster nodded, his own eyes tearing up. "C'mon, let's get out of here."

The next few days were a blur. I remember being given something to eat and drink, and arriving at Aifric's house. I think I slept a full twenty-four hours there, and another fourteen as we drove to Springfield.

At least, I think I did. I have no memory of the trip.

When we arrived at Roe's, I called my parents and told them I'd been out of town with friends and my phone had broken. It was as much of the truth as I could tell them. They accepted the story, as far as I could tell, though Mom did scold me for not borrowing someone else's phone and at least letting them know I was okay.

Then I retreated into the library and sat on the floor in front of the fire.

Eliaster had disappeared as soon as we'd gotten to

Springfield. He didn't tell me why. I didn't care. Even with all the sleep, I still felt tired. I closed my eyes and let the warmth of the flames soak into me. No one had ever told me grief felt like this—an unshakeable chill in my bones, a clenching in my gut.

After a few hours—even keeping track of time felt too difficult at the moment—Roe came in, carrying a tray of sandwiches. She set them down on the coffee table, then joined me in front of the fireplace, leaning her back against the legs of one of the overstuffed chairs.

"How are you?" she asked.

I turned to face her and leaned my elbows onto my knees, supporting my chin with my hands. Before I answered, I studied her face. Roe's clear blue eyes were rimmed in red, and a tear track down the side of her face glimmered in the firelight.

"Marc was the first person close to me that I've lost," I said, my voice low. "I'm lucky, I guess. Even both sets of my grandparents are still alive."

It didn't answer her question, but they were the only words that even came to mind.

Roe nodded and looked into the fire. "I remember when I lost the first. I was thirteen, and my mother was killed by an Unseelie lord. All she'd done was not move out of his way quickly enough. I thought I'd never feel pain like that again…but I did. I've felt it more times than I care to remember. It never gets any easier."

I squeezed my eyes shut. "And here I thought that if I ever found another world, it would be through a wardrobe."

She gave a hoarse laugh.

"Roe…" I bit my tongue. What was I supposed to say now? I opened my eyes.

She leaned forward and hugged me. I wrapped my arms around her, dropped my face to her shoulder, and sobbed until my chest ached.

She patted my back. "You were Marc's brother, you know. He always said that about you."

I nodded and leaned back, rubbing my face dry with the sleeve of my jacket.

She reached into her pocket and withdrew a metal bracelet. Marc's bracelet. For the first time, I realized the two pieces, hammered into a circle and bound together with two pieces of stitched leather, were sword shards.

She fiddled with the bracelet as she spoke. "I spoke to Marc's mother. Aifric's men retrieved his body, did you know that?"

I shook my head.

"We're having his funeral tomorrow. We found a plot of land in the Overworld."

I smiled. "He'd like that."

She nodded. "Marc would want you to have this." She held out the bracelet.

"I can't…"

"Please, Joshua."

I let her drop the bracelet in my palm. It felt lighter than it should have. I held it up, watching the reflection of the flames dance in the smooth metal.

"And as a warning, I think Eliaster wants to speak to you soon. Cormac tells me that he wants you to help us more."

After what I'd been through? I tightened my jaw.

She held up her hands, palms up. "It's not fair to ask of you. After all, you're not accustomed to the Underworld— you didn't grow up here. You don't fully understand us. And really, after Eliaster lied to you as he did, I will not blame you if you leave the Underworld behind forever.

"But please, think about it, Josh. The Lucht Leanúna would have the pathstone, if it wasn't for you. You may not have been born to this life, but I feel as though you belong here."

She stood up and stepped out of the room.

I ran my fingers along the bracelet. Roe had said I could choose, but it wasn't that easy, really. I'd never leave the Underworld behind. I never could. I still had the ability to see through glamour. Maybe it would fade in time, but I doubted it. I would see fae, and they would notice me, for the rest of my life.

I slid the bracelet into my pocket.

Marc's funeral was held that evening. They'd chosen an oak-shaded cemetery behind a white country church some way from town. The funeral was short and simple—just Marc's closest friends and family paying their respects as the setting sun sent orange rays slanting through the tree leaves. I was the only full human in the crowd. Even Cormac Tyrone was there, though Eliaster conspicuously was not.

As the last of the funeral-goers drifted away, I crouched down by Marc's grave. Nearly a hundred little votive candles flickered around the freshly-turned ground, left by the funeral goers as a memorial. The soil was damp, cool, as I put my hand on it. Marc's mom had asked me to say something, but I couldn't, not in front of everyone.

"Marc—" I cleared my throat. My eyesight was blurry as tears slipped down my face.

I couldn't even say anything here, alone. How could I even make sense of the knotted feelings in my gut? In a way, I was responsible for his death. I'd tried to bargain with Larae, and that was why Llew had knifed Marc.

If I'd just listened to Marc that first night—if I had just kept my mouth shut and let Marc and Eliaster handle things, rather than thinking I could solve everything, like life was a math equation…

Cormac had spoken over the grave, had said hollow words about how Marc had died for a great cause. And he had. Marc had chosen to fight and die like a hero.

I pulled away, particles of soil clinging to my palm. "I'll miss you, man."

I stood and pulled the bracelet out of my suit pocket. The sunlight flashed off the blade pieces. Why had he wanted me to have this? If he'd been hoping I would carry on his work, like he'd carried on after his father had died, then I was a poor substitute. I started to lay the bracelet next to a clump of candles.

"Josh?"

I spun around, my hand going to my side, automatically reaching for the sword I'd stowed in the back of my dorm room closet.

Eliaster leaned against a tree close by, arms folded over his chest, legs crossed at the ankles.

I stood, curling my fingers tight around the metal bracelet. "How long have you been there?"

"Didn't want to disturb you." Eliaster stood, walked over to the grave, and pressed his hand into the moist earth. He closed his eyes and murmured in Gaelic under his breath, then stood, leaving a handprint beside mine.

"Did Roe talk to you?" he asked.

"I don't know what I'm going to do yet." I clenched my hand around the bracelet. "Why did Marc have to die?"

"I've asked myself that a thousand times. I don't have an answer."

"I thought you—" I shrugged and gestured to the cross necklace hanging around his neck. "Aren't you supposed to have all the answers to life?"

Eliaster snorted. "No one has all the answers, Josh." He slid his hands into his pockets. "I keep feeling like if I could have done something, maybe…" He scuffed his foot along the grass, not meeting my eyes. "But that thinking will eat at us like acid for the rest of our lives, if we let it. I can't go on thinking that it was my fault. Llew chose to drive in the knife."

I'd never seen him fidget like this. Why was he so uncomfortable?"

He looked me in the eye. "I'm here to apologize again. And to tell you that…Marc spoke to me right before he died. Remember that?"

I nodded.

"He said you were a warrior." Eliaster nodded to the

bracelet. "He told me to tell Roe to give it to you. Said you were a better warrior than he ever was. I wouldn't have agreed with him when I first met you, but your journey with us forged you into someone different. I don't say this as a guilt trip, but to show you that I'm committed to what I said in the Lost Tunnels, that I will trust you. This isn't your born fight, but I'd be honored to fight it alongside you."

I rubbed my neck. I could accept my new role. I could become a Seelie warrior and fight against the darkness pervading my world. I could find Llew and Larae and make them pay for what they'd done to Marc.

Eliaster was right, it wasn't my born fight. But I knew about the threat to my world—my family and friends. If I didn't help, and Fear Doirich broke into my world, I'd never be content knowing that I let it happen while I sat by. I had the knowledge to change things.

I could stop more people from dying.

I slipped the bracelet onto my wrist. The steel was cold and hard, but it somehow conformed to the shape of my arm and flexed as I moved. I looked up at Eliaster.

The fae broke into the first genuine grin that I'd seen on him. "Good choice."

I grinned back. "Let's go kick some monster butt."

Josh and Eliaster's adventures continue! *The Crucible Book 2: Burnt Silver* will release in late 2018! Be sure to read to the end for a peek at *The Crucible Book 1.5: Slag*.

H. A. Titus is usually found with her nose in a book or spinning story-worlds in her head. She first fell in love with speculative fiction when she was twelve and her dad handed her *The Lord of the Rings*. She lives on the shores of Lake Superior with her meteorologist husband and young sons, who do their best to ensure she occasionally emerges into the real world, usually for some kind of adventure. When she's not writing, she can be found rock-climbing, mountain biking, or skiing.

She can be found at hatitus.com and is active on Instagram (instagram.com/hatitus), with an occasional foray into Facebook (/HATitusAuthor).

The Wingard Chronicles

Torfre

Dragonshifter Torfre Wingard is living life on the run, constantly moving from town to town as people unveil his true nature. When he's recalled to his parents' roost, he discovers his family dead and three murderers waiting for him. Enslaved and tortured for information, Torfre is dragged along on their quest to find a powerful, magical amulet that his parents hid years ago.

Torfre is available as a serialized novella in my monthly newsletter. For free fiction, news, and updates, please sign up at hatitus.com!

chapter 1

Four months to the day since my life had been turned upside down.

I rocked back on my heels, staring at the square of dirt that finally had delicate green blades of grass shooting from it. It seemed like the grass should have grown faster. It had been nearly two months ago when Marc had been buried. I'd thought then that I'd never be back, but I hadn't been able to resist the pull back to the grave today.

I rocked back on my heels, staring at the square of dirt that finally had delicate green blades of grass shooting from it. It seemed like the grass should have grown faster. It had been nearly two months ago when Marc had been buried.

I'd thought then that I'd never be back, but I hadn't been

able to resist the pull back to the grave today. They'd put the headstone up. It was simple, a rough-cut block of gray granite with the words *Marc Gillam. Beloved son and brother. Loyal to the last.*

Loyal to the last. He certainly had been that.

Marc had given his life for his people. He'd given his life after I'd messed up the plan he and Eliaster had come up with.

We can't let that eat at us, I'd told Eliaster at Marc's funeral. But I still hadn't let go. And most days, I figured I never would.

I stood up, rubbing the back of my neck. Sweat smeared under my palm. The day was warm, and the clouds overhead were no relief, serving only to make the air more sticky than usual. Summer in Missouri. We'd probably get rain before the afternoon ended.

Two months since my best friend had died, defending the world from a threat most would never know existed.

My phone vibrated, and a moment later, the tinny sound of Survivor's "Eye of the Tiger" blasted through the quiet cemetery. Eliaster. The jerk had changed my ringtone again. I pulled the phone from my back pocket and hit the screen.

"Yeah?" I said, starting for the paved road that wound through the gravestones a few yards away.

"Where are you?" Eliaster barked.

I got to the red-and-white motorcycle parked to the side of the road and leaned against it. "What's up?"

"Got some stuff to show you. Oh, and my dad wanted to talk to you."

I frowned. Eliaster's dad, Cormac, was a bigwig in the fae Underworld, at least in Springfield. He hadn't spoken to me since we'd gotten back from retrieving the pathstone in Chicago. He hadn't even spoken to me at Marc's funeral. I'd gotten the impression that he thought his son had made a mistake in dragging me, a human—an Overworlder—into the Sidhé world. "What about?"

"I don't know, something to do with the hard drives you yanked out of the pawn shop computers. He mentioned it in passing last night. I haven't even seen him today. Where are you?"

"At the cemetery."

A long pause. In the background, I could hear the sound of a shifting motor. Eliaster was probably driving his fancy Danish supercar.

I cleared my throat, took a deep breath to try to shake the weight pressing on my shoulders. "So, where should I meet you? The *rath*?"

Eliaster's voice was a little rough when he answered. "Yeah. It'll take you, what? A half hour?"

"Yeah."

"Should I meet you somewhere?"

"I'm on my bike. I'll drive straight there."

"Okay."

The phone beeped, indicating the call had been disconnected. I put the phone back in my pocket, glanced back at Marc's grave. Overhead, thunder rumbled. The back of my throat felt tight and dry. I grabbed my helmet, pulled it over my head, and started the bike.

The road leading back into Springfield was curvy, with practically no shoulder, not even a gravel strip. Typical of country highways in this area. I hunched close to the body of my bike and took the curves way too fast, forcing myself to concentrate on staying upright, not killing myself, and not thinking about Marc or the relic I'd used to bash in David's head.

Before long I crossed into the city limits, and traffic forced me to slow down. I pulled up to a red light and planted my feet on the pavement. I was being stupid, riding a bike with no protective gear other than a helmet and boots, but I didn't care. I knew if my mom had been home when I'd left, she would've yelled at me, despite the fact that I'm an adult. She had turned into a bit of a helicopter parent the last couple of months. Honestly, I couldn't blame her.

Twenty-four, jobless, and a college drop-out as of a week and a half ago. I'd tried to swing it, to catch up to the classes I'd missed while on the quest with Marc and Eliaster by taking advantage of the summer programs some of the local community colleges offered. But I wasn't comfortable in class any longer, sitting with my back to the door, surrounded by other people. Any loud noise had me jumping half out of my seat, grasping at the sword that wasn't there, that I refused to carry outside of the Underworld despite Eliaster telling me--multiple times--that I was being an idiot.

And then there were the nightmares.

Nightmares of Marc, a rusted iron knife slicing into his flesh, the pain in his eyes as Eliaster worked to squeeze the poison from his veins and give him another hour of life. Nightmares of David's blank eyes, the blood pooling under his skull, caved in where I'd bashed it with the pathstone, the crumbled white rock mixing with the blood.

The ones with Larae were the worst, though. Larae, slicing open my wrist, draining my blood for her dark magic. Larae, her body pressed against mine, her soft lips trailing against my jaw and neck. I'd never even touched her—she'd been my best friend's girlfriend. Off limits, even if she had been coming on to me. But she'd betrayed me, Eliaster, Marc—even David, who had joined her in her treachery, had died because of her.

I hadn't gone to anyone about the dreams. Who could I tell? Eliaster would just scoff at me. My parents would think I'd lost it or started on drugs those two weeks I'd been missing. I wasn't about to draw my brothers or sister into this strange new world I was living.

I could have told Roe, Marc's grandmother. But I hadn't seen her since the funeral, either. And I didn't really know how to approach her now. She seemed to think I was some kind of paragon who would save the fae. Like I needed that kind of pressure.

The only one of the fae I'd had any contact with since was Eliaster, and for one reason—he was teaching me to fight.

When Marc had died, I'd promised him I would keep fighting. In his memory. Roe had told me she believed I was destined to be a part of the Underworld.

I didn't know about that, but I did know that ever since the troll had first come after Marc, that night in April, I had been seeing through the fae glamour. I now could tell who was human and who was pretending without even trying.

So far it hadn't gotten me more than a few dirty looks, and once even a come-on from a gorgeous fae girl with green hair and the perfect hourglass figure, the type of girl most nerds like me never see outside of a video game. I'd turned her down. Ever since Larae, fae girls gave me the creeps.

I turned into a parking garage and guided my bike down to the lowest level. Few cars were parked down here, though I spotted Eliaster's sleek supercar parked near the back.

I pulled up to the back wall and opened the black electrical box that sat on the far side. I put my hand inside, and felt a cold chill as something—I assumed it was more fae magic—washed over it. With the whine of grinding mechanisms, the wall receded, revealing a tunnel strung with wires, pipes, and dim orange light globes.

I pulled my bike through, the wall rumbling closed behind me.

The tunnel echoed back the engine, the sound thrumming loudly even through my helmet. This time of day—mid-morning—the Underworld tunnels were quiet, at least close to the surface. Most Sidhé, I'd discovered, preferred to conduct their business during the night, especially the fae. Sometimes I wondered if fae were the basis for vampire legends humans had eagerly been devouring—no pun intended—for centuries. Eliaster insisted they weren't, but if I knew him, the grumpy, blond fae didn't want to be thought of as a blood-sucking, sparkly fairy. Bad enough that some human cultures saw him as a three-inch pixie with wings.

I spotted a couple of goblins scurrying along the side of the road. Their pale, saggy skin, edged in ragged patches of fur, stood out against the dark walls of the tunnel. All goblins had sharp, claw-like fingernails and slit-pupiled eyes, but these guys had distinctive pointed ears at the sides of their heads were rimmed in fur. *Cat-sidhé.*

I slowed as I went past them, watching them carefully. One of the cat-sidhé actually dropped on all fours and hissed at me through jagged teeth.

I didn't have my sword, but I dropped one hand down to my side, feeling the outline of my nine-mil pistol through my jacket. The goblins backed away, their eyes glowing green in the dim overhead light.

I skirted the outside edge of the Underworld city, passing through a neighborhood that consisted of falling-apart shops and the remnants of a once-grand Victorian home, before hitting the rich section of the town. Mansions dotted the expanse of green grass-like moss, all looking pale and washed out under the orange light. For the life of me, I could never figure out why the rich fae wanted to live down here.

I pulled up at the wrought-iron gate of Cormac Tyrone's rath. From the outside, it looked like your typical Tudor mansion, but when I glanced up at the roof, I spotted the sniper, hunkered down beside the false chimney, rifle trained on me.

I grinned and lifted my fingers from the bike in a half-wave.

The gate buzzed and swung open enough to allow me to pull through. I motored up the gravel drive and stopped at the foot of the front steps.

The front door opened and Lukas, Cormac's head of security, stepped out. No matter how many times I met the fae, my gut still clenched a little. I gritted my teeth.

"Joshua," Lukas said evenly, staring at me.

I returned the stare, all the while willing my breakfast to remain in my stomach. Some fae affected me more than others—Eliaster compared it to a 'fight or flight' instinct that kept most humans away from the *Sidhé* and out of danger. With some fae, like Eliaster, the sensation had faded the more I was around them, until I could barely feel it. Maybe I just hadn't been around Lukas enough.

Or maybe he really did pose a threat to me.

"I didn't know you planned to come today."

I pulled my helmet over my head, hearing a crackle as static pulled my already-crazy hair skyward. "Hadn't planned on it, but Eliaster said Cormac wanted to talk to me." As I spoke, I tucked the helmet under my arm and jogged up the steps, making sure I didn't break eye contact with Lukas.

For a moment, I didn't think he was going to let me in. Then he stepped aside, holding the door open. As I brushed past him, his hand darted to my side, snatching the pistol away.

"Hey!" I spun to face him again, but didn't grab for the gun.

Lukas examined it, thumbing the safety on and off and releasing the clip. He snorted at the caliber. "This wouldn't stop a troll or a rager."

"Well, hopefully I won't run into too many of those." I held my hand out.

He ignored it.

"Give it back to him, Lukas," came Cormac's voice from the side of the foyer.

I raised my head. Eliaster's dad stood at the library door, hands clasped behind his back, his green eyes narrowed at Lukas. Lukas shrugged and extended his hand toward me, the gun clutched loosely in his fist. I grabbed it.

Lukas gave me one last dirty look and walked further into the house.

"Please come in, Josh." Cormac stood to the side of the door, gesturing inside the library.

I walked past him, placing the gun on a side table near the library door. The last time I'd been here, the place had looked neat and precise, like I'd always imagined the Diogenes Club would be. Rather than the neat configuration of chairs and tables this time however, most of the furniture had been shoved to the side, making room for a new desk and several cardboard boxes, each stamped with the logo of a popular computer company.

I raised my eyebrows. "Hope you don't let Eliaster near this."

Cormac chuckled as he dragged two armchairs clear of the mess and settled near the fireplace. As usual, the fireplace was full of crackling flames. Even though it was summer, the warmth was welcome after the chill of the Underworld.

"If Eliaster torches any of those computers, accidentally or not, I might just kick him out on his ear." Cormac strode to the side of the room, where a polished wooden cabinet sat next to the door to his private office.

Funny, I'd thought Cormac had already kicked Eliaster out. Or maybe it was that they just didn't get along. I still hadn't figured out the Tyrone family dynamic.

Cormac came back and sat down, carrying two glasses filled with amber liquid. He motioned to the chair across from him and handed me a glass. As I sat, he sipped from his glass and smiled.

"I suppose Eliaster told you that I wanted to talk to you."

I leaned my elbows on my knees, cradling the glass between my hands. "Yes sir."

"I was impressed by the work you did with those hard drives. It can't be easy to pull hidden information from them in the way you did."

I shrugged. "It's not hard."

"I also hear you have some hacking skills."

I felt my neck and face go warm. How had he found that out? The university I used to attend had handled all of my hacking pranks internally. I'd been careful to not do anything that would have gotten me kicked out or arrested. I cleared my throat. "They're not that good. I got caught each time. I'm better at the whole math angle."

"Still, you have a much different skill set than most people I know."

The understatement of the year. While most fae glamour wasn't as extreme as Eliaster's—which caused him to fry most electronics he came in prolonged contact with—it still interfered enough to make tech difficult for fae to grasp.

"I want you to come work for me."

It was a good thing I hadn't taken a drink yet, otherwise Cormac might have had it all over his face. I stared at him. "Why?"

"Because the fight is far from over."

My stomach churned. I didn't like the idea of backing out on my promise. And I definitely knew too much to bury my head in the sand. But when the nightmares had started coming five days after Marc's funeral, I'd definitely been hoping Eliaster would forget about what I'd said.

"What would I be doing, exactly?" I asked, my voice low.

"Roe needs a research assistant, now that she's actively searching out the pathstones," Cormac said. "And, like I said, you have a unique technological skill set no one else I employ does."

I blew out a deep, gentle breath. "So what you're saying is I'd basically be a glorified IT guy."

Cormac's lips pursed. "I'm not familiar with the term."

I tilted my glass from side to side, watching the liquor swirl. Then I set it on the side table. "So what do you want hacked?" Before Cormac could answer, I held up my hands. "If I come work for you, which I have not agreed to do just yet."

Cormac smiled faintly. "You're beginning to be specific in your wording." I recognized a hint of Eliaster in the tone of his voice.

I allowed myself a small grin. "I do learn, eventually."

"It's not even a guarantee you'll need to hack anything. But I want someone who has the ability to keep track of online activities that might be related to the *Lucht Leanuna*. Before you discovered their forum, I didn't have any idea something like that could have existed." He smiled wryly into the inch of liquor left in his glass. "Maybe I should have listened a little to my son." He glanced up at me, eyebrows raised. "Is that something you'll be able to do?"

I paused, working it out in my head, then nodded. "I should be able to find or write some webcrawler programs that could--"

He held a hand up. "No need to explain it to me. I couldn't understand anyway." He glanced at the door and lowered his voice. "Eliaster tells me that he and you will probably be leaving town tonight."

I stifled my surprise. Eliaster was planning another road trip? To do what? "We'll see. I haven't committed to anything yet."

Cormac stood, draining the last of his glass. He started for the office door that was almost blocked by cardboard boxes. Over his shoulder, almost casually, he said, "Well, try to keep my son from doing anything stupid, would you?" He set his glass on the sideboard and pushed open his office door.

Had that been *worry* in Cormac's voice?

I nearly took Lukas's head off as I swung open the front door. He spun around, scowling at me.

"What were you doing out here?" I asked.

His scowl deepened. "None of your beeswax."

"Where's Eliaster?"

"Why do you ask?"

"What're you, the bouncer? Where is he?"

Lukas sighed. "In the workshop. Should I show you there?"

"Nah, you've got more important things to do than playing butler, I'm sure."

The fae glared at me, but I just gave him my most innocent smile as I started around the house. The workshop was attached to the garage, but mostly hidden around the corner of the house. As I got closer, I heard the faint sounds of some classic rock song playing in the building.

I pushed open the side door.

Eliaster sat at the worktable that ran along the back wall, tightening a bolt on some piece of engine sitting in a puddle of grease on the wooden surface. A pitted, rust-splotched motorcycle frame sat in the middle of the cracked, stained concrete floor, parts scattered around it. The bike's original color might have been red, but I couldn't tell for sure.

As I got closer, I could hear Eliaster singing along under his breath. Something about not feeling something, or not fighting a feeling, whatever. Classic rock wasn't really my thing.

I cleared my throat.

He spun around, wrench half-raised. "Josh. *Adanam*, one of these days I'm gonna split your head open before I realize it's you." He hit pause on the iPod sitting on the table.

"So, whaddya want?" I asked, leaning against the table beside him.

He grabbed a rag and started scrubbing his blackened hands, jerking his head at a dark green file folder that had, somehow, escaped the carnage of grease around it.

I picked it up, flipped it open. The folder had a few bits of paper in it, mostly newspaper clippings. I scanned one. The article had a note scribbled in blue ink at the top in Eliaster's scrawl—*Peoria Journal Star*—and a date, three days ago. The article itself spoke about a rash of kidnappings that had occurred across the state at rest stops, though it seemed to mostly concentrate on areas around Springfield, Illinois. My throat tightened. I flipped through the rest of the articles, including a few printed from websites. All of them were about the alleged kidnappings.

A month ago, on our way to Chicago, we'd disrupted a goblin gang attempting to kidnap a mom and her two kids. At a rest stop near Springfield, Illinois.

I unzipped my backpack, pulled my tablet out of its case, and did a quick internet search about the kidnappings. It brought up not a few articles.

"Not good," I muttered.

"Yeah," Eliaster said. "I thought it was an isolated incident, just those goblins we caught. Should've known better."

"How did you hear about this?" I asked, clicking on

article after article, a pit slowly forming in my gut.

Eliaster's voice sharpened. "Heard it on the news."

I looked up. He leaned against the worktable, still rubbing at the back of his hands with the rag. A rough red spot was forming on his skin under the rag.

He stopped, stared at the reddened area, then clenched his fingers into a fist. "I should've gone back and checked it out. I should've known better."

"You couldn't have guessed this was going on," I said.

"Things like this are never an isolated incident." Eliaster grabbed the iPod. Part of the case clinked to the floor, and he leaned down, grabbing the shiny pink plastic before I could. He fitted it back onto the scuffed iPod.

"You know, it would only cost a few bucks to get a new case," I said. "And I wouldn't have guessed you were a pink kinda guy."

I'd meant the comment as a joke, but Eliaster scowled at me.

"That's above your pay grade." He headed for the door at the side of the workshop and stepped down into the garage.

I tucked the folder under one arm and followed, still scanning articles on my tablet. All the articles talked about the lack of evidence, the way the police were utterly baffled.

One article headline jumped out at me. "Eliaster, check this out." I stepped down into the garage and turned the tablet so he could see the screen.

Eliaster squinted, but kept his distance. "Police discover camera footage of kidnapping in progress." His green eyes shot up to me, widening as flashes of color whirled through the irises. "If they caught something on camera, why..."

I scrolled down. "Because they think the perpetrators were wearing some kind of masks that, as one officer described it, 'looked like those monsters from *The Lord of the Rings* movies'."

"Huh?"

"You've never seen *The Lord of the Rings*?"

Eliaster rolled his eyes and spun around, heading toward

his favorite bike, a blue Suzuki with a dragon's head on the gas tank.

"So you're planning on heading to Illinois?" I asked, trailing him.

"Not alone."

"Yeah, about that... Isn't this more in your line of work?"

He raised an eyebrow. "As I recall, a few weeks ago, you were all gung-ho ready to kick some tails."

I replaced my tablet in my backpack, fiddled with the zipper. I didn't even have my sword with me. I'd shoved the weapon deep into a storage closet at my parents'--where I'd been staying thanks to the whole dropout-slash-jobless thing--and done my best to ignore the trolls and goblins I saw walking around. Yeah, I carried the gun, but I hadn't gone so far as to use it on anything, and I had no plans to, unless something cornered me.

Not that I could tell Eliaster that. The guy had a hero complex, and--combined with the guilt load that made mine look like a rain gutter beside the Grand Canyon--it drove him to try to save everyone he crossed paths with.

"Look." He plunked down on the bike seat. "I know you're regretting that you got mixed up in all this. But the simple fact is, the Underworld has you now. You won't--"

"Won't escape. Yeah, yeah, I've been given the grand tour."

He smirked. "Dude, you've been given the Cliff Notes version."

"You know about Cliff Notes but not *The Lord of the Rings*." I groaned. I'd promised Marc. But this wasn't really part of what I'd signed up for.

Everyone was convinced that the Lucht Leanuna getting their hands on the pathstones was a bad idea all around. After seeing the havoc Lara had wrought just to find one, I tended to agree. Okay, so we'd destroyed one. Roe was trying to track down the others. Once she found them, I'd help destroy or obtain them.

That was what I'd promised Marc.

But for some reason, I couldn't shake the thought of other humans--my kind--being preyed upon by goblins. By things they had no knowledge of, by monsters they couldn't hope to fight. It didn't sit well with me.

Who knew I could be such a bleeding-heart.

"Fine," I muttered.

Eliaster nodded, his smirk twisting into a thin-lipped smile. He stood, grabbing the handlebars of his bike.

I turned and walked back through the workshop. Behind me, the metal garage door squealed open, and the bike roared to life.

Eliaster zipped past me, gravel spitting from his back tire. He parked by the front door and dashed up the steps and inside. Lukas, still standing out near my bike, gave me a frown.

"Where are you two going in such a rush?" He asked.

"Illinois, apparently."

The frown deepened. "Please tell me Eliaster didn't talk you into going after the goblin slaver gang."

Slaver gang. The words made my gut twist. I pulled my helmet over my head, stowed the folder in my backpack next to the change of clothes I now always kept there. Just in case.

Lukas shook his head. "He's trying to turn you into another version of him. You don't belong in the Underworld, Josh. No human does. You should walk away and forget everything you've seen."

"Eliaster says I can't."

He snorted. "And Eliaster is a paragon of virtue and truth, we all know."

I dug my fingers into the rubber handlebar grips. No, he wasn't. Eliaster had lied and manipulated me--but he'd also sworn to never lie to me again. And Marc had trusted him.

If nothing else, I based my trust of Eliaster on my trust of Marc. Marc and I'd been friends since grade school. He'd always had my back. And if he'd trusted Eliaster, that was good enough for me.

For now, it had to be.

Eliaster came back outside, a backpack over his shoulders and wearing his old black and gray leather jacket.

"When should Cormac expect you back?" Lukas asked him, tone dripping disapproval.

"If you don't hear from me in two days, send someone." Eliaster straddled his bike and shot toward the gate, pelting Lukas with gravel.

Lukas rolled his eyes and disappeared into the Tyrone rath.

I gulped a deep breath and followed Eliaster, my brain spinning with possibilities. All of them were grim.